I0764450

Dragon Sparks

Coddiwomple: Book 1

By Lea Carter

ISBN 978-1-951248-01-7

Dragon Sparks is a work of fiction. Any resemblance to actual persons, living or dead, is entirely coincidental.

Learn more about the author at leacarterwrites.wixsite.com/flinch-free-fiction

Chapter 1

Leuna hopefully scanned the edges of the clearing for her prey, but all was still. Suppressing a groan, she leaned back against the berdea tree's smooth trunk. Untxi hunting could be very boring. Needing something to do while she waited, she picked idly at a loose thread on her homespun britches. Since she'd known that she'd be climbing trees today, she'd worn long pack cloth pants and tall boots to protect her legs. Taking a pinch of her collar, she lifted it away from her throat and fanned herself. Thankfully, the thick forest canopy kept the well-risen sun from roasting her. Still…her fingers strayed to the empty game bag at her waist. Larger and better tasting than their 'cousins,' rabbits, which ran wild far to the south, she would only need one, but…was it really worth all of this effort? The village had a perfectly good butcher shop.

She was about to climb down from her perch when a whisper of sound made her freeze in place. Hardly daring to breathe, she waited. And then…

A large, reddish-brown untxi hopped into view at the edge of the clearing. It reared up slightly on its larger hind feet and its wide, flat nose wrinkled, sniffing the air for predators. What was taking it so long? The narioa root she'd planted in the spring as bait was an untxi's favorite meal, but this one seemed in no hurry to feast.

Chuckling silently, Leuna wryly admitted that it hadn't gotten as big as a water bucket by being stupid. She licked her lips, already anticipating roast untxi, untxi stew, or maybe an untxi meat pie. She hadn't decided yet. Inhaling slowly, she checked that the wristband on her dart thrower was secure and lifted her arm into position. Just one more hop into the clearing and it would be in range! Soundlessly, she loaded a slender, metal dart into the spring-loaded weapon.

Drawing back the loaded arm as the untxi came nearer, she took final aim before releasing. She felt a mixture of satisfaction and relief as the untxi collapsed into the grass: satisfaction at her aim and relief that the animal hadn't suffered unnecessarily. Dropping down off the low branch where she'd been waiting since before sunup, she stretched her aching back.

As she did so she became aware, on a deep, instinctual level, of something gliding through the grass near the fallen untxi. She couldn't quite hear it. She could barely see it—or rather, the grass blades bending gracefully around it as it slithered along…for a long, *long* ways back into the trees. Sucking in her breath, she held perfectly still.

A cold sweat broke out on her forehead when a massive bronze narrasti head reared above the knee-high grass and consumed the untxi without even having to unhinge its lower jaw. With any other predator, she might have argued the point, but not a narrasti big enough to eat *her* for its main course.

As the narrasti lowered its head back into the grass, she made a decision. The sun had warmed the small glen. That, plus the snack the narrasti had just consumed, should make the beast sleepy. If she could slip out quietly enough, she might make it back to the village in time to gather a few hunters. Stealth was critical—she knew she couldn't outrun it even with a generous head start.

She took a cautious step backward. Another. Blinked. Had the grass just moved? Arming her dart thrower, she let a dart fly to the far edge of the clearing.

The narrasti's head reared up out of the grass, but instead of going to investigate the disturbance, it looked straight at her. Bizarrely, it appeared silky soft in the sunlight and almost affable as it swayed side to side.

Leuna's heart lodged in her throat, making it difficult to breathe. Her small skinning knife was no longer than her finger and, sharp as it was, wouldn't even penetrate the narrasti's age-hardened scales. It moved toward her and, oddly, her eyes were drawn to the spot where its long tail moved the grass in the distance, the path running back into the trees until she lost sight of it.

Licking dry lips, Leuna determined that she wasn't going to be its next snack. There had to be a way. Slowly, she lowered her right hand to her ammunition pouch, where her darts stood ready in their clasps. She extracted three—the most she could handle without dropping one and losing a shot.

Loading her thrower, she fired. The first dart caught it squarely between the eyes, making it flinch in surprise, but without doing any visible damage. Leuna gritted her teeth. Her thrower spring was low power, suitable for small game. She couldn't stop trying, though. Aiming the next dart at the same spot, she watched in despair as it glanced off the side of the narrasti's head when it swerved. Weaving its way through the grass, the narrasti accelerated toward her. Cursing herself for a fool, she prepared her final shot with trembling fingers.

Just as she let the dart fly, an arrow struck the narrasti at the base of its skull. Her dart bounced off its belly as it writhed in a brief, violent death spasm.

Tearing her gaze away from the scene, she found herself staring into the piercing golden eyes of a stranger. He stood at the far edge of the clearing, longbow in hand, watching. Looking more closely, she again came to the conclusion that she didn't recognize him. He was clearly Marroi, a member of the brown-skinned race known far and wide for their hunting prowess and dragon-riding skills. Not that she wasn't glad to see him, but what was he doing here? Herrixka, her tiny village, was farther into the land of Lurrak than she'd ever known them to travel.

"Wait." She took a half step toward him when he turned as if to walk away. "Don't go."

"So you can speak." He smiled a little to let her know he was teasing, his white teeth standing out against his dark skin like a rift of snow on a straight, young arre tree. His knee-length, robe-like outer garment stirred slightly as a breeze caressed it. The loose britches and thin shirt he wore underneath were the same weak shade of green as his robe…a bata, she thought they called it.

She laughed, his pleasant baritone voice and gentle manner putting her at ease. "Of course I can." She glanced over at the narrasti and shuddered. "Thank you."

He dipped his head in acknowledgement. "I'm glad you're alright."

She watched curiously as he retrieved his arrow, cleaned it on the grass, inspected it, and returned it to his quiver.

"Are you camped nearby?" she asked, her eyes lingering on the dark spot on his shirt. She'd taken it for a patch or a stain at first, but now that he was closer she could see a gap in its center. The clean edges on the cut made her think it was made by something extremely sharp. *Hmmm.* A cut inside a fresh, dark stain on a shirt. That couldn't be good. Automatically, she reviewed what she'd seen of him so far—he was moving pretty well for a man with a side wound.

"More or less." He nudged the narrasti with his boot. "Seems a shame to leave the old boy out here." *A waste.* He would've gladly built a fire and cooked it right then, though he'd just as soon not tell her that. Besides, he had more important things on his mind than hunger, like where she'd come from. Did he come from there, too? He searched her face hopefully, but found no flicker of recognition within himself. Truth be told, her pale complexion and dark hair seemed at odds to him, who knew no more of the world than what he'd seen staring back at him in a calm spot in the stream.

"Then let me help you carry it to Herrixka." Leuna spoke without thinking. His eyes leapt to meet hers, an intensity in his gaze that sent small shivers down her spine. *Who are you?* she wanted to ask. "The butcher there will pay you a fine price for it," she explained a little breathlessly.

"The butcher?" His eyebrows rose in surprise.

"Of course." Her eyebrows lowered in confusion.

"Have you never eaten a narrasti steak?" She grinned and spoke before he could answer. "That settles it. After we sell your prize to the butcher, I'm going to cook you a narrasti steak with roasted potatoes and a pie."

He studied her some more. She'd mistaken his meaning entirely. He'd just spent three days wandering through a forest without seeing a sign of another human being. Now he'd just stumbled across a town large enough to have its own butcher? Would it have a healer of some sort, too? And maybe even someone who could tell him who he was?

"That sounds too good to pass up." He congratulated himself on keeping his voice steady as equal parts relief and trepidation twisted his empty gut.

"I'm Leuna." Smiling up at him, she offered her hand. His fingers wrapped themselves firmly around her wrist, cool and slightly calloused. Remembering belatedly that this was the Marroi version of a handshake, she quickly mimicked his grip.

He stared down at their joined hands, wondering at the strength in her slender white fingers. Wondering how he'd known the correct response to her gesture. Catching her looking up at him expectantly, he realized was expecting him to give her his name in exchange for learning hers.

"A pleasure to meet you." He felt himself frowning as he reclaimed his arm. He didn't want to be rude, but he also wasn't quite ready to tell her how he'd woken up, alone, in a clearing. How he'd followed every track, every broken twig, every clue until the trail faded out completely.

Leuna fought to keep from questioning him when he didn't introduce himself. It was odd, no more. However, it did serve to further pique her already busy curiosity. Strangers were rare in Herrixka, a small town on the edge of nowhere.

He nudged the narrasti again, and she quickly walked to the middle of the body, where she began pulling its length into untidy coils. It wouldn't make it any lighter, but at least they wouldn't trip on it while they walked.

Once he saw what she was doing, he began doing the same with the front end. Together they were—barely—able to heft its entirety off the ground and onto their shoulders. She staggered a little under the added weight, but bit her tongue before a complaint could slip out. He'd already taken the bulk of the weight for himself.

"Ready?" he asked a little gruffly. His wound had gone from a mild ache to a mild burn. Should he tell her about it? He decided against it. Unless she had a doctor in her pocket, what could she do but worry?

"Ready," she agreed. He stepped off immediately and if not for the slight sag in the narrasti between them, she'd have been pulled right off her feet. Irked, she fell in behind him.

Neba, she thought suddenly. It was an old word, so old that she'd almost forgotten it. *Brother.* She'd never had a brother, or a sister for that matter. Oh, she'd never really minded, thanks to the generosity of the village families in adopting her into their lives as if she was blood. Scolding her, spoiling her, teaching her. Mourning with her when her mother died; then again, a few years ago after her father succumbed to a bruma fever. Still, as she took two steps to Neba's one, she admitted that this was a lot like how she'd imagined having a brother of her own might be.

Alarm bells went off in the back of her mind as his stride began to slow and his breathing became discernibly ragged. He went obstinately on, but he was clearly in distress. To keep her mind off her burden, she began running through the probable causes. She didn't know him at all, so she studied his long-legged stride for any sign of joint stiffness. Finding none, she thought back to when he stooped over to pick up the narrasti without hitching or hesitating. So…she was left with the dark, damp stain on his shirt.

Fortunately for both their sakes, the village was close by, easily visible once they emerged from the forest. After blinking a little in the bright sunlight, she couldn't help smiling as the village came into view. Red houses, green houses, blue houses, purple houses, every color of the rainbow was represented in the natural coloring of the local hardwoods. Several houses sported a few planks of each! She'd learned her colors and trees simultaneously just by playing with the other village children.

"Akur, stop that!" she commanded one of the village dogs when it snarled at them. She took a couple of quick, deep breaths before speaking to Neba, as she'd dubbed the stranger in her thoughts. "There's a street just through these houses," she called, shifting the narrasti coil to a new position with an un-ladylike grunt. Sucking in another breath, she said quickly, "Butcher's shop on the left." The butcher was a nice man, but his castoffs quite naturally drew flies, making it practical to have his shop on the outer edge of town.

Stamping down on his worries about what *might* happen, he waved a hand to show he'd heard her and plunged into the unknown. A handful of children had raced over to see what the dogs were barking at and were now lined up beside the colorful houses. Barefoot and rosy-cheeked, the children gaped openly at him. Did they recognize him? Or were they just curious because strangers were rare in this tiny village? Certainly none of them could be his immediate family.

His wound stabbed at him, making him wish he'd stayed deep in the woods a day or two longer. But the cut wasn't healing on its own. And whatever he'd hoped to find when he started out that morning, it wasn't a woman trying to face down a hungry narrasti with a mere dart thrower.

He chuckled softly, the rude children forgotten, as he remembered the picture she'd made, her lovely face set in a determined frown while she let the first dart fly. He'd been so taken with her that, for an instant, he'd expected the narrasti to succumb to her missile. His smile changed to a grimace. Taken with her, indeed. The look of terror on her face when she missed with the second dart had him nocking an arrow and firing before he even realized what he was doing. He still didn't remember aiming.

"Hey." She stopped walking and tugged on the narrasti to get his attention. "We're here."

Blinking, he looked around—he'd been so lost in his thoughts that he'd nearly walked off the worn dirt path and out the other side of town. His cheeks warm with embarrassment, he turned and entered the shop, the one drab-looking building in town. Where the houses and shops they'd passed in the heart of town were a variety of cheerful colors, the gray walls of this shop were made of simple, rough-hewn grisa wood. He was relieved to see that the inner walls had been smoothed and treated, so they hadn't developed the liberal number of splinters that adorned the outer walls. He planned to rest himself against that wall and didn't need to get splinters in his back in the process.

"Rakin!" Leuna called for the butcher, heaving her end of the narrasti onto the empty game table. Lifting her half-empty canteen from her belt, she pretended to take a sip before offering it to Neba. He hesitated, then accepted it. She had a feeling he needed the water more than she did, and not just because of the way he was braced against the wall for support. "Rakin!" She struck the bell on his counter, knowing he would hear that even if he'd taken a load of scraps out to his newest compost hole.

"I'm coming, I'm coming!" shouted a deep voice from a distance.

She chuckled. "Don't let his bluster fool you," she advised, pretending not to notice the fresh blood on Neba's shirt. It explained a lot, though. "He's a good man, he's just got a voice as big as he is." She'd only just finished speaking when Rakin entered, his head barely clearing the back door without ducking.

As always, Leuna gave herself a little shake to overcome the sensation of having shrunk a few inches. "Well, it's about time," she teased her old friend. From the corner of her eye, she saw that the stranger had straightened away from the wall and was standing tall as if worried about showing weakness in front of the newcomer. Hastily, she began introductions.

"This is Rakin," she pointed needlessly at the butcher. "And this," she grinned at Neba, "is the man who kept that narrasti from making me its morning snack."

Rakin whistled as he ran an experienced eye over the reptile's smooth, deceptively soft-looking scales. There was a smattering of dried blood on the throat just below the jaws, but that was it.

"One shot?" Rakin asked, eyeing the stranger with considerable interest. "That must be some bow you've got there."

The stranger took another sip of water. "Shoots straight," he responded nonchalantly. The butcher's answering guffaw rattled the shutters.

"I can see that," Rakin hooted. "Now," he rubbed his immense hands together. "I assume you're here to sell it." The folks in Herrixka butchered their own meat when they had it, so a visit to his shop inevitably involved buying or selling.

"That we are," Leuna grinned.

"And a good thing, too." Rakin walked over to heft the body and get a better idea of the amount of meat he'd be getting. "Jartz' traps were looted again each of these past five days, making the sixth week in a row. All told, it's been a whole lunar."

"A whole lunar," Leuna repeated, shaking her head. Jartz was a good friend, more of an uncle really, and she knew that the summer months were bad for trappers even without trouble like this. "Will he be alright? I mean, he usually goes into Gertuk to trade his pelts for supplies about this time, doesn't he?" There were still a few months until bruma, the cold time. Long enough, she hoped, for Jartz to solve the problem of his trapline robber.

"Hmm? Yes, that's right." Rakin shrugged. "I wouldn't worry. He told me there's enough left in the traps to prove he's doing his bit to keep the vermin down. Ought to be a decent bounty." He muttered something under his breath about the last time a horde of sharp-toothed, ravenous kastore swept through the area, eating everything in reach.

Leuna was distracted from his grumbling by the frown on Neba's face. She raised an inquisitive eyebrow at him, but when he spoke, it was to Rakin.

"What kind of game does this Jartz usually bring you?" he asked casually.

"Jartz?" Rakin scratched at his stubble as he tried to figure how much the tanner would give him for prime reptilian skin. This reptile was large but relatively scar-free, so he estimated it at four, maybe five years old and recently molted. "He goes for the small stuff mostly. Of course, he *catches* anything stupid enough to get caught, and that includes some varmints too big for his gear. This trouble all started almost two lunars back. Claims he's seen some strange paw prints near his line." He added the last tidbit with a shrug. Turning to Leuna he offered, "Eight gold arranos."

"Twenty." She folded her arms across her chest. "You'll get six arranos from the tanner just for the skin." More like eight, but she didn't want to offend him.

Rakin chuckled. "Fourteen," he countered. "Not a pikor more." He mirrored her by folding his arms across his chest.

The pain in the stranger's side had eased enough that he was able to smile at their haggling while he waited for her to respond. She would sell and Rakin would buy, for nothing else would suit them. All that remained was to agree on the price and he happily let her take charge of selling his kill. She clearly knew what she was doing.

"Twenty," she maintained firmly. "If you truly have so little meat coming in, you can make a tidy profit off this."

"Bones and ashes, girl," Rakin muttered darkly. "Would you have me raise my prices just because there's less to be had?"

She ignored the question. They'd both grown up in Herrixka and neither of them would dream of gouging their fellow villagers just because they could.

"Seventeen arranos." He thumped his big fist on the game table, making it shake. "My final offer."

"Seventeen arranos *and* two steaks."

Rakin threw up his hands in surrender and disappeared into the back of his shop, muttering to himself about bargaining with women.

"Well played."

"I told you, he's a fair man." Leuna grinned back at her peculiar new friend and shrugged a little to hide the excitement that she always felt when she got to do any real bargaining.

*"So seventeen," he paused, trying to wrap his tongue around the strange word, "are-ah-nos is a fair price for this monster?"

She tipped her head slightly to one side as she considered him. "For this area, yes."

"Here." Rakin had the grace to offer her the coins instead of slapping them down on the counter as he might've done if someone else had bested him. Wasn't wise to get on the village healer's bad side. Not that she had one, so far as he knew.

"Well?" Leuna cocked her head at Neba. "Take it." She assessed the way he straightened away from the wall a second time, moving more easily than she might've expected. The rest had done him good, but he still hadn't mentioned it. Odd.

Recovering as quickly as he could from his surprise, he reached out his hand and let Rakin pour the arranos into his palm. The sound the gold coins made as they struck each other was almost musical. Having nothing else in the small pouch at his waist—he'd checked, repeatedly—he dropped the coins inside. Not until they were outside with two thick steaks on a line of butcher's string did he speak.

"Why did you do that?"

"Do what?" she asked, measuring the shadows with a practiced eye. It was well past time for the noonday meal and her stomach had been complaining since shortly after her simple breakfast of bread and cheese.

"Give me the money." He tapped his bag, making the coins jingle, to recapture her attention.

"Oh, that. Your kill, your money." Holding up the steaks, she grinned. "I got what I wanted! Now c'mon," she motioned for him to follow her. "I live at the far end of this street."

He grimaced as he tried to keep up, the ache in his side escalating to a searing burn.

"Leuna, wait!" An older woman bustled out of her yellow house, complete with yellow split-shingles of the same horia wood, giving him a chance to catch up when Leuna dutifully paused. "You forgot to come by the other day and get your fresh eggs."

Leuna hesitated, torn between protecting the woman's pride and her livelihood. Old Ama was the only one in the village with enough chickens to sell surplus eggs, and her flock was about ready for the soup pot. She should be hoarding the last lay of eggs for the next round of chicks, not exchanging them for medical services.

"I'm sorry, Ama," she apologized. Motioning for Neba to keep walking, Leuna smiled at Ama. "I got to reading Dad's journals and lost track of the time." That was mostly true, she assured herself.

Ama patted her on the arm. "Just like your father, you are. Forgetting to eat, too, sounds like." Ama grinned as Leuna clenched her stomach muscles against a second embarrassing grumble.

"It has been a long morning," she agreed quickly. "I started out hunting untxi and almost became the prey for a narrasti." Glancing over her shoulder, she saw that Neba was halfway to her house. Holding up the steaks, she added, "I was just on my way home to cook these up, so I really couldn't take any eggs right now."

"Well…" Ama mock-scowled at her. "Alright. You come by tomorrow morning and I'll give you some then. I got my best setter tendin' a batch for the next brood, but a few of the others are still layin'." She shook her head sorrowfully. "Worst part about raisin' chickens, I figger, is eatin' them once they can't lay no more." Her face brightened as she had another thought. Casting a speculative glance toward the stranger's broad back and square shoulders, she giggled like a young maid. "Better give you a full dozen. Looks to me like your man could eat that many on his own!"

"Thank you, Ama." Leuna smiled brightly as if that would make the blush warming her cheeks less noticeable. While the truth always came out eventually in their little town, she saw no reason to let Ama's mistake take root in her mind. "I'm sure my patient will enjoy them."

"Patient?" Ama frowned. "He don't look sick to me."

"You know I can't discuss that with you," she scolded gently. Leaning in to give Ama a quick peck on the cheek, Leuna turned and hurried after him. He was nearly to her house already!

He paused at the end of the street—or at least, at the end of the rows of modest homes on either side of him. Looking back over his shoulder, he saw a handful of simply dressed youth pretending to draw water. Since most of them ducked their heads when he looked back, he had a pretty good idea what was really on their mind. Deciding they meant no harm, he noted Leuna's progress. She wasn't motioning for him to walk back toward her, so he considered where he was.

The path he was on led past the last house. Partway between the village and the woods stood a blue building that was too small for a shop but otherwise too big for the village, comparing it to the cottages he'd just passed. And yet, somehow, he knew without a doubt that was where Leuna lived. Maybe it was the modest garden plot he could see in the back, filled to the bursting with plants he somehow recognized as medicinal. Maybe it was the friendly way the bell on the front door jingled, greeting him as pleasantly as its mistress had.

"You found it!" Smiling, she breezed past him. "Help yourself to a chair while I get lunch on." Kicking off her shoes, she slipped through the house and out the back door to where the summer fire pit was located. She could cook inside in case of bad weather, but that would heat the entire house, making it harder to sleep. So she carefully set the narrasti steaks aside and began laying wood for a fire.

He followed more slowly, giving himself time to take it all in. Directly ahead of him loomed a huge fireplace, flanked by closed doors on either side. He was pleasantly surprised to see a bookshelf built into the wall beside one of the doors. Leather-bound volumes of a uniform size filled most of the shelves. A pair of comfortable-looking chairs faced the fireplace, waiting for someone to accept their invitation to sit down and rest. Resisting the temptation, he continued his visual journey through her home.

To his far left, cupboards lined the wall above a u-shaped counter that ran along at about waist height. If he followed the counter to where it ended, he'd walk out the door she'd just gone through, which he proceeded to do. He caught a whiff of soot as he passed the fireplace, and could easily visualize her curled snugly in one of the chairs while an icy bruma storm raged outside.

A wood box that stood nearly as tall as he did protruded from the outer wall on his left and he realized it must belong to the little door he'd seen on the other side of the wall, held shut with a simple hook-and-eye latch. It certainly explained how she'd gotten wood for the fire so quickly.

Shadows were already stretching out from the plants in her garden, reaching their thin, spindly fingers toward the coarse grass at the edge of the path. The scents of earth, blossoms, herbs, and wood smoke blended into a perfume that he inhaled greedily. The sweet sound of wind chimes greeted him merrily as an afternoon breeze tickled them. The peace of the moment seeped into his weary bones and for the first time since he'd woken up a few days ago, wounded and with no idea of who or where he was, he allowed himself to relax.

Leaning against the doorjamb, he watched her expertly kindle a small, hot fire using flint and steel. He wished he could capture the image of her in just that pose: the wind teasing at a loose wisp of her cocoa brown hair while the heat from the fire brought a comely flush to her smooth, suntanned cheeks. It was a pleasant change after three days of struggling to survive, nearly going mad with unanswered questions.

"There." Grinning triumphantly at the fire, Leuna reached for a cook knife and deftly halved the steaks. "Sorry about this," she apologized to him as she ran each piece through with a metal spit. "I know I promised you steaks, but right now I'm too hungry to…" She glanced up at him and stopped, astonished. He'd fallen asleep where he stood, his bow propped against his side. The side with a fresh damp spot on the stain. Grimacing at the thought of how tired he must be, she hung the spit across the fire pit.

Silently, and with one eye on the spit, she filled a metal pot with clean water and set it next to the fire to heat, then slipped past him to retrieve her travelling medical case.

Chapter 2

Leuna hesitated, her fingers so close to his arm that she could feel the heat coming from his skin. This was the first time she'd really stopped to look at him. And what she saw made her take a long step back. It was more than the well-defined muscles, too.

She was accustomed to the small, lightweight bows that most of the villagers carried, made with wood from the forest. His bow, however, looked like it was made from *three* kinds of wood. That is, three bands of color traversed the bow from top to bottom, the leather grip standing out by its very plainness. Then there was the steel-tipped arrow he'd pulled from the narrasti's body. The high grade leather of his boots, the expert tailoring on his clothes (drab though they were)... Too fancy for an ordinary woodsman, but for a Marroi? She honestly didn't know.

The few Marroi she'd met during her time while attending the university in Ibilia were men and women of science and letters. Their clothes were simple, practical, and they carried no weapons beyond the traditional belt knives. So...who was he? *What* was he? A soldier? Perhaps a mercenary? Where was he from? What was he doing here in Herrixka? And why hadn't he exchanged names with her? She didn't wish to pry, but, taken altogether, it made him seem very mysterious.

Retreating to a safe distance, she picked up an empty tin plate and dropped it on the wooden kitchen floor. Her confusion increased when, instead of assuming some battle position, he simply raised his head, blinked, and looked around until he spotted her.

He smiled sheepishly. "Did I fall asleep standing up?" Boyishly, he rubbed his hand over his face and yawned. "I hope you'll pardon my poor manners."

She couldn't resist returning his sleepy smile. "You must be very tired," she murmured. Indicating the chair she usually sat in of an evening, she suggested, "Sit down and I'll take a look at your wound."

"My wound?" He frowned.

"Yes, the one on your left side." She set her case on the table between the chairs and opened it.

"Why?" He placed one hand protectively over his injury.

"Because I'm a doctor."

He still hesitated. "You went to university?" He half-folded his outer garment and flung it across his knees once he was seated. His luck was changing at least. Not only was he going to eat his first proper meal in days, his hostess turned out to be a doctor!

"Yes, for seven years." She met his gaze coolly despite being amused at the question. She was accustomed to strangers questioning her abilities on the grounds of her age, but how long had it been since anyone asked where she was educated? Of course, everyone in Herrixka already knew the answer to that. He couldn't have known that much about the medical programs, either, or he'd have shown some surprise at her graduating in only seven years instead of the usual ten. Growing up as the village doctor's daughter had certain advantages, like allowing her to test out of several of the preliminary courses.

"Please remove your shirt also." She knelt beside him and caught his hand when he had trouble lifting the fabric away from his skin. "Wait." Examining it briefly, she nodded. "It bled quite a bit at some point, and the dried blood is adhering your shirt to your skin. Let me help." Dipping a cloth in the water she'd left by the fire to heat, she used it to gently soak his shirt so she could peel it away from his skin.

"There," she murmured, leaning back to let him finish removing his shirt. "Ouch," she added once she got a good look at the wound. Her hand spanned eight inches, give or take, and this looked just a shade short of that. "Have you been treating this yourself?"

"Yes, a little." He looked down at the top of her head, intrigued to notice soft, golden highlights in her hair now that the sun was behind her. "I didn't have much to work with, I'm afraid."

She continued studying it, noting that the edges of the cut were as clean and straight as those on his shirt. This was no jagged tear as a rock or broken limb might cause. She flicked a glance at him through her lashes. A few old scars marred the otherwise smooth skin of his chest, but there were no bruises or fresh abrasions; his knuckles were also uninjured. A knife fight? Or was it a sword fight?

"What are you doing out here?" she asked, trying for a casual tone. "You're a long way from Marroi." His head swiveled back in her direction and she almost shrank under the intensity of his gaze.

He let the silence stretch for a few heartbeats before coming to a decision. "Marroi?" he asked. "What is that?" He dropped his shirt across his knees, too.

"You don't know." Despite herself, the words came out as a statement, his question was that astonishing.

"I..." He reached out with one long arm to move the spit through a half turn, his stomach muscles clenching against a hungry rumble. How was he supposed to think straight with the food distracting him? "I don't remember anything from before I woke up a few days ago."

She inhaled sharply, her hazel-green eyes warming with concern. The puzzle pieces began falling into place—his reticence about his wound, his failure to introduce himself... What must it be like to not even know who ones' enemies were?

He looked at her, then away again, focusing on the spit. It wasn't pity in her eyes, he could've dealt with that. It was the sincerity that caught him off-guard. He'd firmly set aside the indecision as to whether or not to stay in the area where he'd awakened. He'd done his best to track down his attackers, as far as he could tell. Eventually, with the trail cold and his flesh betraying him, he was forced to stop—to forage for food and tend his wound. The fear, however, he hadn't been able to conquer so easily. It was with him still, lurking in the shadows of his mind. The fear that he would never heal, that he would never know who he was, or what had happened to him or why or…or… He clenched his fists against the vicious, unrelenting fear.

Restless with the need to know who had abandoned him in the wilderness—for there had been prints aplenty not far from the spot where he'd woken up—he began turning the spit too quickly. Half the reason he'd come to town with Leuna was to find out if anyone from there knew who he was and what had happened to him. Clearly, she knew nothing about it.

Her hand settled lightly on his near wrist. "Slowly," she instructed, nodding at the spit. "Reptile meat is very lean and dense. It won't cook evenly if it's turned too quickly." Squeezing his wrist gently, she asked, "Does your head hurt?"

Calmed by her touch and tone, he relaxed a little. "Not really. I had a lump on my head the size of a turtle egg when I came to, but it's gone now."

"Is it?" She got to her feet, biting back the question about which kind of turtle. Some turtle eggs were as large as Rakin's fists, while others were considerably smaller. Instead she asked, "Can you show me where it was?" A head injury would explain quite a bit.

He reached up to pat the back of his head. "Around here, somewhere. Why?"

"Head injuries can be dangerous, so let me just take a look…" As her tan fingers slipped into his thick, black hair, she was surprised by how soft it was. Several of the villagers had black hair, but it was stiff and coarse, rather like the bristles on her hairbrush. Working her way across the back of his head, she paused to examine a lump.

"Right about here?" she asked, carefully tapping the spot with her finger.

"I guess so?" He really wasn't sure. At the moment, he was half-asleep again.

"Hmm." Smoothing his hair into place, she came back around the chair. "Look up," she instructed, slipping two fingers under his chin and tilting it up, too. If she'd been inside, she would've had to use a candle, but the sunlight was quite strong enough where they were. "Look down." Despite her professional intent, the difference in skin tone between her fingers and his face caught her attention. She didn't realize she was staring until his clear gold eyes raised to meet hers. Dropping her hand, she stepped back.

"Your eyes are clear, no sign of bleeding." She smoothed her shirt and resumed her place beside him. "Your pupils are responding normally to light."

Relieved as he was at her pronouncement, he disciplined a smile at her overly-brisk tone. He might not know the name of his own people, but there was no doubt in his mind that the lovely young doctor was attracted to him. That she was comely and fair of face he had seen at a glance. He could now conclude he was pleasing to look upon as well, given her reaction to him. Which told him absolutely nothing about his identity.

"How were you injured?" she asked, opening her medical case. Even though she believed his story, she felt obligated to test him out a little.

"I don't remember."

"What's your name?" Her face turned toward her case, Leuna watched him discreetly from the corner of her eye.

He shook his head. "I don't know."

"What's your mother's name?" she persisted.

He gripped the spit a little more tightly. "I don't know."

"Why are you here?"

"I have no idea."

She studied him briefly, then nodded. "Tell me about your bow."

He glanced at it. "It's a composite longbow, made using thin laths of three separate kinds of wood to increase its power and durability. I found it on the ground beside me when I woke up three days ago." Having answered her questions, he asked one of his own. "Why are you asking me these questions?"

She waved away the irritation in his voice. "Don't you think it's a little odd that whomever did this to you left you with a weapon?"

He threw up his hands. "I think it's *odd* that they left me alive." His fists came down hard on the arms of the chair. "I only know," he spoke through clenched teeth, "that I woke up alone. *Completely* alone. Neither friends nor enemies greeted me." Not even a slain enemy. He glared at her. "You're the first human I've seen." He wanted to say more, to explain that he'd been trying to figure it out, but he didn't trust the anger boiling inside himself.

Leuna tried not to let him see how his declaration affected her. Clearing her throat of tears, she finally 'located' what she'd been looking for in her case.

"I'm sorry if I upset you." Shaking out the clean cloths, she tried to explain. "Those questions helped me better understand your condition. You see, there are different kinds of memories. I'm not surprised that you knew about the longbow because I was there when you used it. I hoped to coax out some other memories as well."

"Oh." He felt foolish for being so angry now. "I didn't know."

She patted his hand. "If I had explained what I was doing, it would never have worked. However, I'm confident that the rest of your memories will return in time." Nodding at his side, she changed the subject. "Your wound is infected." She assumed he knew that already since the discolored skin and seepage were impossible to overlook. Still, she always tried to start at the beginning. It usually saved time in the long run and made her patients more comfortable.

"Yes." He frowned. "I considered cauterizing it, but it wasn't bleeding too badly at first, so…" He lifted his free hand, palm up. His other hand had resumed turning the spit at what felt like an agonizingly slow pace.

"It's well that you got here when you did," she observed quietly. "The infection is still easily treatable. And, given that you're remarkably healthy otherwise, I would anticipate a full, normal recovery. However." She paused when his shoulders, which had relaxed marginally, resumed their rigid posture. "This treatment is extremely painful."

"So is the wound," he interrupted, shrugging with his uninjured side.

"Of course," she agreed easily. Lifting a bottle out of her case, she pretended to focus on it while she continued, "And yet, as your doctor, I strongly recommend using this." She held up a bottle for him to see. "A drop or two of this on the back of your tongue will render you unconscious."

Frowning, he took it from her. The bottle was made from blue-colored glass, dark enough that all he could really be sure of as he looked at it was that the bottle wasn't quite full. He could see the gap and the liquid sloshing slightly from changing hands. Unconscious. Was that really necessary? He'd been planning to keep an eye on her while she worked.

"Seems a bit extreme," he observed, watching her closely.

She shook her head. "It's impossible for me to guess how far the infection has spread, therefore I can't just try to numb a limited area of your body. And when the hautsa dust begins drawing the infection out, I won't be able to stop it."

He blew out a frustrated breath. "How long would I be out?" As much as he hated the idea of being that vulnerable, he believed she was telling the truth.

"You'll be awake and alert before the food is cooked," she promised without hesitation. Surgeons had been using refined loak oil in their work for generations, and its properties were well known throughout the medical community.

Twisting the cap off, he found that it had a thin, grooved rod attached. He deliberately took a few deep breaths while he watched the clear liquid slide off the rod and drop back into the bottle. When he was ready, he tilted his head back and opened his mouth.

Leuna watched silently as he allowed two drops of the bitter loak oil to land on his tongue.

"Good," she approved, taking the bottle and stopper from him. "Now just lie back and relax." With a light touch, she began arranging clean cloths around his wound until it was surrounded. That would help keep him clean during the treatment.

"You were asking me about the Marroi," she reminded, talking softly to give him something to focus on besides fighting sleep. It was a strangely common reaction. She'd only used the loak oil a handful of times, it was true. They agreed to take it, knowing it was supposed to put them to sleep, and yet each time her patient struggled to stay awake. "They are a race of warriors and scholars, hunters and explorers. Brave adventurers." She smiled as his eyelids drooped. "One of my favorite professors was Marroi."

His body slowly surrendered to the medicine while she talked of nothing. Once she was sure he was unconscious, she took a squat container from her case. Opening it, she shook a liberal amount of hautsa dust into his wound. The odorless dust turned from ash-gray to a sick, yellow-green within seconds of contact. She considered the process for a moment, fascinated as always by the transformation as the dust reacted with the infection, carrying it captive as it foamed up out of the wound. The resulting stiff obtrusion always reminded her of the limestone outcroppings near the river-town of Gertuk.

Rotating the spit while she waited for the foam to harden, Leuna allowed herself to marvel at the healing properties of this and so many other medicines. Without the hautsa dust, she might have had to trim away some of the damaged skin. Then, even with her expert care, his body would've been many days in defeating the infection.

Reluctantly, she picked up a pair of long, flat-nosed pliers and tapped the foam to confirm that it had hardened completely. It was ridiculous to feel squeamish about this step, yet somehow she always did. Taking a deep breath, she positioned the pliers at the base of the foam, careful to avoid catching any of his skin in their jaws. Rocking the foam back and forth to weaken it, she abruptly twisted her wrist, snapping the foam off at the base.

"One down," she whispered to herself, setting the foam aside to be burned later. Taking her time, she flushed his wound thoroughly with water, which dissolved and rinsed away the rest of the foam. Still in no hurry, she rotated the spit a few times before replacing the damp cloths with dry ones. The routine motions soothed her as well as letting his body recover.

"One to go." Coating the wound liberally with the dust again, she rose. The second treatment would take much longer, as the dust sucked the poison from where it had settled deeper in his body. Rinsing her hands with vinegar and rubbing them together briskly to sterilize them, she dried them on a towel.

To fill her time while she waited, she stepped into the kitchen. Pulling out the flour bin, she scooped some onto the clean counter. Adding a little water and cutting in some lard, she mixed it until she had a nice pie dough. Humming softly, she rolled it out, then lifted it into her pie tin, trimming the excess dough off the rim with a dull knife. Dusting the bottom of the crust with sugar, she cut fresh baia fruit into it, followed by a second dusting of sugar and a pinch or two of flour. A dollop of salted butter across the top was covered with strips of the dough and a very thin sprinkle of sugar, just on the dough this time. Carrying it outside, she set it in the tiny stovebox by the fire and latched the top in place so she could cook it later.

Holding her braid out of the way, she bent over him, inspecting the second ridge of hardened foam. This time the infection-green color was broken up by several smaller streaks of the foam's natural gray.

Exhaling in relief that the dust had done its job, she picked up the pliers. Another sharp twist and it snapped off, leaving only the raw, red wound behind. Placing this foam beside the first, she rinsed her pliers with vinegar and hung them to dry in the sun. Flushing the wound with more clean water, she dried around it, then dropped the cloths in an empty bucket and poured in the rest of the vinegar.

She lifted his hand and dropped it back onto his leg. Still deeply asleep. Well, at least he hadn't woken during the procedure. Quietly, she opened a bottle of garbi oil and drizzled it into his wound, taking care to completely cover the exposed layers of subcutaneous tissue.

"Oh my." Setting the bottle aside, she quickly rose and went inside. "I forgot all about the potatoes!" Selecting two large potatoes from a bin under the counter, she pierced them with a clean metal nail, then carried them outside and used the small fire shovel to bury them in the warm ashes to cook.

She heard the rhythm of his breathing change, a slow, deep breath as he began to rouse, then a sharp gasp, probably from him trying to move.

"Not so fast," she warned, turning to face him and nearly landing in the fire as a treacherous rock shifted under her foot. "Here, look at me." She clapped her hands to get his attention and he blinked at her.

"You," he mumbled. He looked around the garden, then down at his side. "I thought…I dreamed all this..." He shook his head to clear it. "Something smells good."

She smiled faintly. "Are you sure?" she asked, making a show of sniffing the air. His disorientation was to be expected and wouldn't last long. "Take a good deep breath, see if you still think so." The fresh air would help clear any remaining fog from his mind.

He complied by taking as deep a breath as he could without pulling his wound. He managed a tight grin despite the pain.

"Delicious."

She smiled back at him, pleased to see sharp alertness in his eyes. "I'm glad, because it's almost done. And so are we."

He looked down at his wound as she came closer. "What's that on it?" he asked.

"Garbi oil. As your body absorbs it, it will give your wound strength to heal more quickly," she explained, showing him the bottle as she screwed the lid on. Resuming their conversation as though there'd been no interruption, she remarked, "I'm told the Marroi Empire reaches as far as the distant shores of Baketsu Waters and stretches south into the wild Izutu plains. It's a young empire, I guess." She laughed at how that sounded even as she held a square of cloth bandage up, checking its size against his wound. "Just about ten generations old."

"We must be fierce warriors," he hazarded a guess. "To have taken so much land so quickly."

"I suppose." She set the cloth down and rummaged in her bag for an old, beat-up tin cup. "I think having dragons helped a bit with that. Marroi explorers can cover immense tracts of land in less than a day." Shaking a little of a different powder into the tin cup, she added a few drops of water and stirred it together with her finger to make a weak glue. "Though much of your lands lay wild and empty of man." Painting the edges of the cloth with the glue, she gently pressed it into place over his wound. "There. Does it feel better?"

He shrugged. "It *looks* better."

She repressed a chuckle. "Good. I'll check it tomorrow, but it should heal quickly now that it's been treated." Deftly she repacked her case and returned it to the hook by the front door.

"I think the meat is done," he observed hopefully when she returned. It was about time, too!

She checked the meat and nodded her agreement. "Here." Lifting the lid on a small box, she brought out two tin plates. She watched the muscles of his arm and chest flex as he easily lifted the spit from the fire, not a flinch in sight. Their eyes met as he used his belt knife to slide the meat onto the plates.

He smiled and passed the metal spit through the flames, allowing the heat to burn away any food residue. Meanwhile she dug up the potatoes, blew the ash off their jackets, and gingerly added them to their plates. The buttery flavor of the lumpy gurin potatoes would round off the meal nicely as well as adding a splash of azure color.

But first she stirred the fire back up and added a few sticks, then set the stovebox on top of the prepared fire pit. The ducts cunningly incorporated into two sides of the fire pit allowed air to flow into it even as the stovebox perched on top. Its insulated sides and top absorbed all of the fire's heat, allowing the pie to cook evenly.

They ate in a comfortable silence, each of them hungrily devoting their whole attention to the meal.

"Are you sure you'll have room for pie?" she asked eventually, eyeing the pile of bones on his plate. Hers was the same size, but she couldn't resist teasing him.

"Me?" He grinned. "No problem! Truth be told, I was so hungry I could've eaten that entire narrasti myself, I think." He sat up in his chair and stretched both arms over his head, yawning. He didn't even wince.

"That's good." She hadn't given a second thought to his continued shirtless state until just then. "Because I make an excellent berry pie." Her voice sounded a little breathless even to her. Meanwhile her heart, which had slowed to match the serene setting and routine, suddenly grew wings and began flipping around in her chest like a startled bird. Her reaction to him was ridiculous. She'd seen many well-built young men during her studies, most of them athletes injured during practice or a competition. Her heart had never betrayed her like this before. To distract herself, she opened a vent on the stovebox and took a sniff. Lifting the stovebox off the fire, she unlatched the lid and propped it open so that the pie could begin to cool.

He leaned back in his chair, surreptitiously enjoying the simple pleasure of watching a beautiful woman. He could already tell he'd be sorry when the time came to leave. He frowned as it occurred to him to wonder if his heart was his to give…or if he'd already pledged it to another? That was one question he hadn't asked while alone and lost in the woods. Granted, it was a moot point, given that he'd be on his way as soon as he was well enough.

"That was a meal to remember," he half-teased, surrendering his plate to her when she reached for it. Discreetly, he observed her graceful movements as she passed the plates over the flames, sterilizing them before rinsing them off. "I think I could fall asleep right here," he suggested. He didn't mind sleeping on the grass when it was the only thing available, but he found the chair much more comfortable.

"I'm sure you could," she grinned, remembering how easily he'd fallen asleep standing up. "It's a marvel you've stayed awake this long." They chuckled together and she made her decision. "However, you'll be more comfortable inside. My father's bed might be a little short for you," she shrugged uncertainly, for he was without a doubt taller than her father, "but you're welcome to it."

He pondered a moment before responding. "I couldn't," he shook his head. "I have three days' worth of trail grime on me, for one thing." Odd it hadn't occurred to him to be self-conscious about that earlier, while she was working on him.

"That's easily fixed." She turned her hazel-green eyes on him, a faint smile tugging at the corners of her mouth. "I'll draw some water for you so you can wash up. You can borrow some of my father's things for now. They're in the chest at the foot of his bed."

"And when he gets back, what will you tell him?" He thought he saw her gaze drop for an instant.

"My father passed five brumas ago," she answered quietly. "I usually use his room for patients who need special attention, but I'll make an exception in your case."

It took a moment for him to follow her meaning. "I'm sorry about your father." He watched her nod and felt as though there should be more he could do than just offer his sympathies. Nothing came to mind, so he looked down at where the bandage covered his cut. The garbi oil she'd used must have a numbing property to it, as well. He'd forgotten he was even injured.

"If we start it now," she got to her feet, "the water will have time to warm before you want it."

He rose as well, catching her by the arm and completely forgetting what he was about to say when their eyes met. Hers were positively captivating. It wasn't the lovely scattering of green flecks surrounded by varying shades of brown, either. After staring into her eyes for a few seconds, he felt as though he knew everything he needed to about her. She was kind, considerate, gentle, yet he sensed a stubborn streak a mile wide. More important was the quiet strength that gave her poise enough to meet his searching gaze without flinching.

"Let me do it." He cleared his throat and released her arm. "I'll draw the water," he said, his voice clear this time. He'd seen the private well when he exited the house and now he hurried over to it. Lowering the bucket by the rope, he felt when it reached the water.

"Fill that tank, will you?" she half-instructed, pointing to a metal cylinder on the near side of the wood box. "During the bruma the fireplace heats it." She shrugged and held up an old, blackened pot with a sturdy handle. "During the summer, we heat water out here." Hanging the pot from the arm above the fire pit, she again stirred up the embers.

He wondered at her as he filled the pot to the brim, then moved on to the cylinder. It was more than generous for her to offer him shelter for the night. She didn't know him. He scowled at himself as he filled the bucket a second time. *He* didn't know him as well as he thought he knew her. Had he much experience with women? Assuming that he had any at all, of course. And he was right back to wondering where his heart belonged.

Still, he felt completely comfortable with her. Of course, he'd taken care to discipline his thoughts since meeting her. He shrugged. Maybe that was all either of them needed to know for now. That neither of them would intentionally hurt the other.

"Here." She smiled as she intercepted him on

one of his trips to the well and handed him a plate with a steaming piece of pie on it. "Baia pie tastes best either piping hot or well-chilled, so we better eat it now." She kept her tone casual, yet she was still reeling on the inside from the effects of his inspection. She hadn't been able to look away from his mesmerizing golden eyes while he seemed to sift through her inner self. She wasn't sure what he thought he'd found, but for an instant, she'd thought he was going to kiss her.

Chuckling, he accepted the plate and fork. "You've convinced me."

Leuna pretended to concentrate on her own piece of pie while he took a taste, then another. His silence spoke volumes as he savored each bite instead of wolfing it down the way he had the narrasti.

"I have never," he said at last, "eaten anything that delicious."

She blushed and teased, "That you remember."

"I remember the last three days vividly," he countered without missing a beat, "and they would have been much, much better if I'd encountered this pie sooner." He narrowly avoided saying, *encountered you.*

She laughed outright at that. "Flatterer." She wrinkled her nose at him, then forked her last piece into her own mouth. "Here, I'll rinse the plates while you finish filling the tank. That is," she hesitated, her eyes dropping to where the white bandage stood out against his dark skin, "if you feel up to it?"

"Providing I can stay awake," he rubbed his eyes,

"I feel up to it." He was about to take up the bucket again when he saw her reaching for the heavy pot of hot water. "However," suddenly he was at her elbow, "I should carry this first. If you will allow me."

"Oh," she said blankly. For five years there hadn't been anyone to object to her carrying it for herself and now she was quite nonplussed. "Yes, why…of course. I mean, thank you."

She briefly showed him the washroom, where an oversized basin sat on a table under a spigot, waiting for him to add the heated water. A bar of soap, a few towels and other essentials hung on the wall.

"Just set your dirty things in the hamper there," she pointed at the woven hamper by the door, "and I'll put them out with mine for the laundress in the morning." She'd brought his shirt and bata in from the garden and now she dropped them into the hamper.

"You're too kind." He set the pot on the counter. "How can I repay you?"

"You saved my life," she reminded him. "Perhaps someday, I can repay you. Until then, let us consider ourselves friends." She gave him a moment to nod his understanding, then said, "I've got a patient or two that I need to check on this evening, but if you'd like to go to bed early, that's quite alright. My father's room is through here."

She opened the door and without thinking stepped inside to pull the blankets back and plump the pillow, as she would for any guest. But as he followed her into the room, she found herself taking a half-step away from him. She needed the space. Giving herself a mental shake, she tried to look at him objectively as he stood, shirtless and barefoot, in her father's room. "If you need a snack, there's bread in the box by the kitchen window." She checked the handle of the clothes cupboard for dust, wondering vaguely if Ama would consider trading light housework instead of eggs. "And I just filled the blue pitcher with fresh water."

"You're too kind," he repeated. He bowed from the waist before he knew what he was doing. It seemed appropriate, but it certainly raised questions in his mind. Who and what was he that bowing came so naturally? The Marroi she'd described earlier were warriors and scholars, not courtesans. He smothered a frustrated groan.

"Nonsense," she tried to laugh, though she, too, was wondering at his mannerisms. Professors didn't bow to students, of course, so she couldn't really be sure…but it struck her as odd to have *any* Marroi bowing to her. "I'll be back in a little while." Somehow she navigated the narrow space between him and the bedroom door, breathing more easily once she was outside the cottage. Lifting the strap of her bag to her shoulder, she laughed at herself for her attraction to this stranger who had come into her life unexpectedly and would no doubt leave the same way.

While she made her rounds, he, refreshed from his washing, tried on the pair of loose-fitting sleep trousers. Ruffling his damp hair, he grinned to himself at how short they were on him. He hesitated briefly over the nightshirt, then decided to leave it on the chair for morning. Pausing for one last look at himself in the half-mirror, he reluctantly acknowledged that there was nothing familiar about the face squinting back at him in the faint light streaming through the window.

The bed protested mildly when he stretched out on it, but the pillow was soft and the sheets smelled clean. No, better than that. He couldn't put a name to the soft, flowery scent that surrounded him as he lay there, yet it stirred up a strange mix of feelings, as if he had never been safer—or more vulnerable. If he hadn't been bone-weary, he probably would've lain awake trying to wrestle the memory from the depths of his mind.

Chapter 3

Leuna took care as she re-entered the cottage later, holding the bell so that it wouldn't ring when she opened and closed the door. She'd considered using the back door, but that was right next to the bedrooms. Lowering her bag to the floor beside the door, she slipped out of her shoes and glanced out the western window. Shadows were already pooling around her feet as the sun sank below the horizon.

Her stop at the Korrak house had taken longer than she'd expected because Gai, her dear friend, was worn to a frazzle by her teething triplets. Tiptoeing further into the cottage, Leuna settled into one of the comfortable chairs and rubbed her right shoulder, which ached from grinding enough erlie seeds to make a soothing paste for the gums of all three of the little ones.

Yawning, she resolved to have her apprentice, Sati, help her grind more seeds the next day. For now, she reached for one of her father's medical journals. He'd worked in tandem with his wife to record the medicinal properties of the local—and often rare—plant life around Herrixka. In fact, she thought there was a medical library named after them somewhere in Lurrak, signifying their country's gratitude for their efforts to domesticate and share the plants they found.

"Where was it?" Leuna wondered aloud before remembering she wasn't alone tonight as she usually was. Muttering under her breath, she flipped through the pages of the journal until she'd found the entry on the erlie plant. "Tall, bright orange stalks, the top third being covered with…no, that's the harvesting page." Turning back a page, she nodded to herself. Softly she read the entry to herself. "Spring to late summer, the erlie plant features bright yellow-orange leaves resembling spikes. Favoring damp climes and full sunlight, it can usually be found along stream banks where there is a sufficient gap in the forest foliage."

Yawning again, she slid a marker into the book and set it on the table. When Sati arrived tomorrow, she could start by copying the entry and drawings into her own medical journal. They'd go out together later in the year to harvest erlie seeds as part of Sati's instruction. She smiled as she thought of the young woman, all of eleven years younger than herself. Leuna had taken over Sati's apprenticeship mostly out of a sense of duty after her father's death. Over the years, though, she'd grown quite fond of the quiet girl. And now it was almost over; as early as this fall Sati could go to Ibilia to take her entrance medical examinations.

Sighing, Leuna heaved herself out of the chair and into the kitchen. Finding the loaf of bread intact, she carved off a small chunk, poured herself a cup of water, and meandered into her room. Maybe her exhaustion was the delayed effect of facing down a narrasti, she reasoned as she took a bite of bread and a sip of water. Changing into her sleep clothes, she perched on the edge of her bed while she loosely braided her hair for night. Or it might be that she was a little extra worn out from helping to haul it to the village. Whatever it was, she was glad to stretch out on her side and relax after finishing her supper.

She was half-asleep when the unmistakable sound of snoring came in through her partially open door. To keep from laughing aloud, she buried her face in her pillow, inhaling the sweet scents of the lavender and lemongrass plants that she always added to her pillow stuffing.

The next morning, the energetic sound of birds twittering and chirping and saluting the sun called her from her bed. Scrubbing her face with her palms, she chastised herself for oversleeping. She was swinging her legs over the edge of the bed when she stopped, puzzled. Something was different.

Abruptly, the memories of yesterday returned, and she looked down at her sleep clothes. Thank goodness her father had taught her to always dress for an emergency—even when sleeping! The short-sleeved shirt that she wore used to be a long-sleeved foresting shirt, but after accidentally burning holes in one sleeve, she'd cut them both back to make a summer sleep shirt. Likewise the britches were light-weight pack cloth, sturdy and quick-drying, perfect for her harvesting excursions. When even Sati began giggling at the number of berry and plant stains, she'd removed the protective double-layer at the bottom and hemmed them up to her knees.

Still…she tugged at the bottom of her sleep pants, feeling shy. Stealthily, she crossed the room to her door and shut it softly. Once she was properly attired for the day, she brushed out her hair, fashioned it into a simple bun, and stepped into the common room. From there, she caught a whiff of wood smoke and food, which she followed into the back.

"Good morning." Neba flashed her his perfect smile from where he sat beside the fire pit, toasting two slices of bread impaled on the stick he was holding over the fire. "Your friend Ama came by a little while ago and left these for you." He motioned toward the cook pan where about six eggs were simmering along with potato chunks, some kind of meat, and spinach leaves. "I was hungry, so…" He watched, his apprehension mounting as she inhaled deeply. What if she had other plans for those eggs? They seemed hard to come by in this town and…

"That smells," she let the breath out slowly, "*so good*!"

"You like it?" He somehow couldn't discipline another smile. "The spices are all from your garden."

She looked from her garden to him and back to the pan. "So…you can cook."

"Well..." He rotated the toasting stick. "I certainly hope so."

She burst out laughing and took the seat beside him, leaning forward to examine the contents of the pan. "What kind of meat is that?"

"That? It's grass hen. It woke me from the most wonderful dream," he shrugged, "so I decided to have it for breakfast."

She laughed again and turned to look him in the eyes. She hadn't realized how close she'd come to him.

"Remind me," she requested breathlessly, "never to wake you."

His eyes held hers for several heartbeats, then he looked down at the toast again. It was either that or confess that she'd been a sweet, if subtle, element in his dream.

Slowly, she sat back. He never responded to her remark and she let it go. She had to remember that he was just there for a few days, recuperating. He might even leave before supper tonight if he felt up to it.

"How's your side this morning?" She took refuge behind their doctor-patient status.

"Much better." He smiled without actually looking at her. "I left the bandage on, but I doubt I'll really need it after today." Stabbing the toasting stick into the grass beside the fire, he stirred the contents of the pan. "I think it's ready."

"Mmm, so am I." She gladly held the plates for him to dish up. "I can't eat that much," she laughingly protested, pulling her plate back when he tried to put a fourth scoop on it. "You'd better have the rest," she admonished, answering the hope in his eyes.

"You're sure?" He needed no urging beyond her nod to load the rest of it onto his plate.

"Oh…my…" Her eyes drifted closed as the first savory bite hit her tongue. "I think my taste buds are going to explode!" She took another bite and held it in her mouth, too caught up in the moment to even think about asking what spices and herbs he'd used.

His throat tightened as he watched her exclaim over the simple breakfast he'd prepared. That such a small service engendered such an awed response surprised him. His gut growled and twisted in displeasure at the delay, so he reluctantly began forking breakfast into his mouth. He soon found that he'd emptied his plate without really tasting the food because he'd been so caught up in her delight.

"I am so glad," she finished her last bite of toast, "that Ama chose this morning to bring her payment by." Groaning, she leaned back in her chair and patted her flat stomach. "I haven't eaten this well in a long time."

Neba chuckled as he took her plate, rinsed it and his off, then held them over the last of the flames.

"Why is that? I know you can cook," he pointed out, setting the plates back in their box.

"Oh yes," she nodded, "of course I *can*. My mother got me off to a good start, and my father followed through by letting the village mothers pay his bill with cooking lessons." She laughed fondly, remembering the hours she'd spent learning how to cook in the warm and often crowded village kitchens. She'd finally realized that she spent most of her time under the tutelage of expectant mothers, who naturally saw the village doctor often, but also needed the most help as they tried to care for their families and themselves at the same time.

"But?" he prompted when she fell silent.

"But," she roused herself to finish responding, "I usually get distracted by other things. If I'm not reading my father's medical journals, I'm studying my mother's field guide to the rare plants in this area. And then, of course, there are my patients."

"Hmm, I see." He dipped water into the heavy frying pan and set it over the fire to boil itself dry. "What will keep you busy today?" She looked over at him and they both stopped breathing.

"Why…" She blinked and the spell was broken. "My apprentice will be here soon. I'll have her help me prepare a soothing paste for Gai's triplets, who're teething."

"An apprentice?" He whistled softly. "Will you send her to the university to complete her training?"

"I'll encourage it." She sighed and rubbed her forehead. Sati's father was a nice enough man, but she hadn't yet been able to convince him of the benefits of attending university. In another city. Filled with eligible young men, naturally. Sati was nineteen springs old and he was a little paranoid about her finding the right man to marry. She was his oldest, after all. Things were always harder the first time. "Strongly."

A knock on the front door brought her sharply into a sitting position. Her hand flew to cover her uncomfortably full stomach and she took a deep breath to settle the food back where it belonged.

"I wonder who…oh!" Coming to her feet, she hurried to the front door. "Good morning, Muti!" She smiled at the boy on her doorstep. The small mule who pulled his cart stamped his hoof impatiently.

"I'm here for your hamper, Miss Doctor," he announced, his tousled blond hair moving with him when he bobbed his head respectfully.

"Yes, of course." She held up a finger. "Just one moment, alright?" She left the front door open a little as she scurried into the washroom for the hamper. "Here you are," she brought it to the door with a smile. "And a little something to tide you over until lunch." She handed him the rest of the loaf of bread plus a chunk of hard cheese.

"Thank you, Miss Doctor!" Muti grinned, showing off his mouthful of healthy teeth.

When she'd found him, starving on the streets of Ibilia, he'd already lost most of his baby teeth to malnutrition. Her father readily agreed to her bringing him back with her after her graduation, and they'd both been delighted to have Neska, Herrixka's laundress, adopt him outright.

"My pleasure, Muti." Impulsively, she hugged him to her, marveling at how he'd filled out from the scrawny, dirty child he'd once been.

"You have a good day, Miss Doctor!" he called over his shoulder as he led his mule toward the next house.

"Who is your friend?" Neba asked from where he leaned against the far wall. Since her visitor was clearly not Sati, who was expected, he'd banked the fire and come in to satisfy his curiosity.

"That," she smiled as she closed the front door and rested against it, "was Muti. His mother used to come around and collect the laundry herself. Now that the village has grown so large…"

"And her son has grown, too," Neba interjected.

"And Muti has grown, too," she agreed. "So now he does the collecting, which lets her focus on the washing."

"Very efficient," he approved.

Her eyes fell to where his left hand was fiddling with the hem of her father's sleep shirt. From there they travelled all the way down to the too-short hem of the pants.

Clearing her throat, she suggested, "If you'd like,

my father's day clothes are on the shelves behind the door in his room." She refrained from pointing out that the pants would still be too short. In his bare feet he stood at least four inches taller than her and she was almost as tall as her father had been.

"Yes, thank you." He started to walk away, then turned back. "Perhaps you could take a look at my cut first?"

"Certainly." *So that was what was bothering him!* she thought-muttered at herself as she armed herself with a bowl of water and a clean cloth.

Neba tugged off her father's shirt and shook it out before laying it across the foot of the bed where he'd slept.

Her eyes went instinctively to the stark white bandage, and from there she couldn't help realizing that his skin was darker on his face, arms, and hands, areas where the sun could easily reach. Somewhere in the back of her mind she wondered at the lack of hair on his face and chest, too. Several of her professors had been Marroi and she knew his anatomy under the skin was identical to her people's, yet no one had ever bothered to mention these details—in her textbooks or otherwise.

"Here," she beckoned for him to take a seat on one of the stools by the counter. "I didn't use a strong adhesive," she murmured as she dipped a corner of the cloth into the water, "so this should only take a moment." Pressing the wet cloth to the bandage, she gently peeled the square away from his skin. Automatically, she dipped a clean spot of her cloth into the water and washed the remnants of adhesive from his skin to prevent irritation. "Yes, that looks fine," she nodded, touching around his cut with her fingertips. "Does this hurt?"

"No, not at all."

She looked up, smiled at the surprise in his tone, and straightened away. "I'd like you to use a salve for another day or two at least, but I think leaving it open to the air will do it more good than a bandage now that it's on its way to healing."

"No more bandage? Whatever you say, Miss Doctor," he agreed, craning his neck to see the cut better.

Stifling a chuckle, she reached for the nearest jar of salve. "Here." Unscrewing the lid, she held the jar out to him. "Use just enough to cover the area."

"Thank you." He took a fingertip of it.

"It's longer than you think," she advised, dipping out a little more with her own finger and transferring it to his.

"Right." He looked from her to the cut, grinned, and headed for her father's room. The salve had a slightly slippery feeling to it as he rubbed it in.

The door bell sounded as Leuna finished tidying up the kitchen and she smiled.

"Miss Doctor?" Sati, a plump, shy lass, opened the door enough to poke her head in. "Am I early?"

"It's never too early in the day to learn," Leuna quoted her father for the thousandth time to the girl. "Did you bring your book?"

Sati bobbed her head yes, already following Leuna toward the table, her head cocked to one side like a curious kaleko.

"Wonderful." Opening the book to the page

she'd marked the night before, Leuna settled the young woman before it. "Copy this section in your book, including the sketches, then come over to the counter and I'll teach you how to make a soothing erlie seed paste for children's gums."

"Oh yes," Sati nodded wisely. "I heard Mamma telling Papa that the triplets were teething."

"That's an excellent medical deduction," Leuna winked. "I suppose you'll go home today and tell them not to worry?"

"No, Miss Doctor!" Sati shook her head. "You said not to discuss patients with others."

"Very good." Leuna brought out the slice of baia pie she'd been saving. "Now eat your pie and copy over that entry. There's learning to be done!"

She hummed an old song while she set up for the paste, pulling out two mortar and pestles, measuring out the erlie seeds and other ingredients, and preparing empty jars to receive the salve. Partway through setting up, she felt someone's eyes on her and looked up in time to see Neba going out the back door. For an instant she toyed with the idea of calling him back, asking where he was going and so forth, but she firmly pushed the urge aside. Something she had no cause to question was that he could take care of himself.

If she had called him back, he would have honestly answered that he didn't know where he was going. He couldn't have explained the need to be outside with the sky as his roof and the wind in his face. He just knew, from somewhere deep inside—beyond memories or thoughts—that he needed to escape the cottage which was sheltering him. So, catching up his bow and arrows, he paused for a look at his lovely benefactress, then slipped away into the forest.

Noticing a black-striped insect, he turned to follow its lazy flight deeper into the forest until he came to a small stream. There he stopped, frowning as something tugged at his senses. Squatting, he studied the edges of the bank on both sides for as far as he could see. Nothing stood out to him, but he knew another human being had been there recently. Several silent minutes passed while he worked to access the thought niggling at the back of his mind. His eyes never ceased roving over the area until suddenly, he spotted it. A metal trap, cunningly concealed in the water.

Rising slowly, he flexed his leg muscles to encourage the blood to flow into his toes and back up to his heart. So this was the stream Jartz used. The trap before him was expertly baited, ready and waiting for a careless muskrat or kastore to blunder into it. Glancing up and down stream, Neba took a few steps away from the bank. It was tempting to investigate the source of Jartz' trouble. He naturally supposed Jartz had already tried to solve the mystery, and yet, the trap line was still being robbed as of yesterday according to the butcher, Rakin. Slowly, deliberately, Neba began making his way upstream as quietly as he could.

Chapter 4

"Here's the last one," Sati announced wearily, sliding the jar over to Leuna, who scooped it up and set it in a small bag.

"Four jars of erlie gum paste." Leuna shoved a damp lock of hair off her forehead, her tidy bun a distant memory, and smiled triumphantly at Sati. "I could never have made this much alone." Sati's shoulders straightened a smidge at the implicit praise.

"Will it be enough?"

"Enough to what?" Leuna asked, her hands already busy collecting the dirty things and wiping down the counter.

"Enough to see the triplets through their teething."

"Mmm, that depends. If she uses it every morning and evening, then no." Leuna lifted her arms over her head to stretch out her back. "However, if she just uses it at night to soothe them and help them sleep, there is probably enough."

Sati awkwardly tried to copy the arm stretches Leuna was doing.

"Here," Leuna corrected Sati's hand position on her triceps. "Now relax your shoulders and lift your hand. Good." She considered proper stretching to be an important part of her apprentice's education, especially since it wasn't going to be covered in university classes.

"I think our time is up for today," she sighed, shaking her hands out at her sides. "Please tell Gai what I said about how often to use the paste."

Sati's eyes widened even more than usual, the only sign she gave at her surprise in being asked to deliver the instructions alone. A simple enough task on the surface, she knew it to also be a test of her self-confidence. Quietly, she took up the sack.

"I'll be back tomorrow, Miss Doctor," she gave her daily promise as she opened the door.

As the front door closed behind Sati, Leuna became aware that she wasn't alone. Neba smiled at her from the back door.

"She seems an apt pupil."

"Yes," Leuna smiled. "She loves to learn."

Noticing that she was favoring her right shoulder, Neba stepped forward. "Allow me," he offered, taking the stack of dishes from her.

"Thank you. They just need to be warmed and wiped out."

"Ah." Neba frowned thoughtfully. "That may have to wait…unless… We can at least try."

Perplexed, Leuna followed him outside. "Ohhhh." The stovebox was perched on the fire pit, blocking their access to the heat.

Neba knelt by the ducts and arranged the mortar and pestles around them. They would take longer to warm that way, but he thought it would work.

"What are you cooking?" she asked, relaxing into her chair. Typically, she would be curled up on one of the chairs inside, opening one of her father's medical journals. This evening, though, she had someone to talk to. And she liked it.

"I came on a quiet spot in a stream in the forest. It was thick with wild rice plants as tall as my waist, and ducks were feasting." He rocked back so that he was sitting on the soft grass by the stovebox. The hems of his pant legs rode up to mid-calf, but he ignored it. "I gathered some eelgrass, wild onions, and water chestnuts, too." He sniffed the air, then shrugged. "It should begin to smell like supper soon."

She smiled and rolled onto her side so she was facing him. "I'll bet your dad taught you to cook." She nodded when he cocked a dubious eyebrow at her. "No, really. It's common practice among the Marroi for the fathers and sons to gather and cook socially. I've never been invited," she held her hands out, palms up, "obviously, but some of the Marroi students at university would tell the most fantastic stories about the food they serve at such gatherings."

He leaned forward slightly, resting his elbows on his knees, and she took that as a sign of interest. Describing each dish in as much detail as she could remember, she told him about the scrumptious fare the Marroi men prepared. Savory meats, succulent seafood, fry breads, sweet breads, roast vegetables, and on and on until she could hardly speak for the drool. Swallowing hard, she inhaled deeply, her eyes drifting closed in fond recollection.

Reaching out, Neba opened the stovebox a crack, letting the fragrance escape. Her eyes popped open.

"I think it's done," he laughed. Resettling the lid, he lifted the stovebox clear. "Shall we wipe these out first?" he suggested, holding up one of the warm mortars.

"Yes!" She sat up abruptly, startled to find she'd

forgotten all about them. Together, they were able to get the last of the cleaning up done in a jiffy. She hastily returned them to their places in the kitchen, then scurried out to rejoin him and claim her plate of wild duck and vegetables.

They ate in companionable silence until the last mouthful of food was treasured and swallowed.

"I think," Leuna murmured drowsily, "that I could get used to this."

"I'd like that." Neba met her gaze without flinching when she turned her now wide-open eyes to him. In that moment of comfort and, yes, magic, that tiny garden contained his whole world—the center of which was seated in a chair directly across from him. But it was magic, an evening's bewitching, and he knew it couldn't last.

Inhaling deeply, Leuna leaned back in the chair and stared up at the rapidly darkening skies. Somewhere across the small town, in another backyard not too different from her own, a dog barked. Children laughed and Ama's hens were clucking to themselves as they paraded into their little coop. From where her cottage sat, on the far edge of town and the near edge of the forest, Leuna could hear the wild songbirds performing a similar nightly ritual. They remained there for some time, each alone with their thoughts until Neba stirred.

Rising, Neba walked quietly into the house. Tomorrow, he would leave. He would go to…whatever the nearest town was and begin making inquiries. Someone had to know who he was. What he was. To whom he belonged besides himself. He narrowly avoided punching the bedroom wall in his frustration at his ignorance. Instead, he dropped to the floor, poised his weight on his hands and toes, then began vigorously raising and lowering his body with just his arms. He didn't bother to count.

Leuna lingered outside until the first stars winked at her. Wearily, she made her way inside, shutting the bedroom door behind her while she changed into her sleep clothes. Crawling into bed, she lay on her right side to ease her full stomach. Realistically, she supposed there was a chance that Neba was a terrible person when he knew who he was, but she had seen no evidence of it. Truth be told, without his memories he was almost too good to be true. Strong, capable, handsome, kind…a fabulous cook. So she tucked their moment away in a corner of her heart to dream about during the cold bruma nights.

She heard movement in her father's room and a smile played across her lips at the familiar squeaks of weight settling onto his bed. Assured that Neba was resting comfortably, she blew out her candle and nestled into her soft pillow.

It seemed she'd barely closed her eyes before she was startled awake by the sound of a dog—no, dogs…every dog in town, it sounded like!—barking and growling and howling. Rolling out of bed, she dashed to the door, automatically snatching up a shawl and throwing it around her shoulders as she stepped into the dimly lit common room. Was it morning already?

Neba, likewise disturbed by the racket, leapt to his feet and bolted out his bedroom door. He came to an abrupt halt when he saw Leuna standing barely an arm's length from him. She'd swept her hair back into a braid for sleeping, but several tendrils had escaped during the night and were caressing her face. He clenched his fists to keep from following their example. Her sleep clothes were almost identical to her father's, soft britches and a pullover shirt. The shawl wrapped around her shoulders did nothing to cover the base of her neck, where milky white skin, untouched by the sun's rays, peeked out at him.

He realized he was staring when her eyes widened and she took a half-step back. Dipping his head and averting his eyes, he searched for words to reassure her. Then, from the corner of his eyes, he saw her shoulders relax.

"Good morrow," she murmured softly. While she'd been taken aback by the frank appreciation in his eyes as he looked at her just now, if she was completely honest, he wasn't the only one looking. He'd left his sleep shirt in the bedroom but had his belt knife in his hand. Interesting.

"Good morrow." His deep, pleasant voice filled the silence, warmed it. "I thought I heard something…"

"Something like the sky falling in?" she interrupted as the dogs suddenly went quiet. Hurrying to the window, Leuna peered out. The sun had barely begun shooting early golden rays into the village, to speed the dark of night on its way. Straining a little, she saw a group gathering in the main street. One of them seemed to be doing all the talking…or shouting.

"It's Jartz," she announced. Wrapping the shawl more tightly about her shoulders, she stepped into her shoes. He'd slipped into his shirt but was still stamping his boots on when she lifted the latch and stepped out into the cool morning air.

"The trapper?" he asked, joining her.

"Yes. Something's wrong."

They reached the group in time to hear, "*Every* trap robbed, sixth week in a row! I say we've got to do something!" Jartz held up a bloody trap, jangling it against its chain.

Zaharre, Herrixka's oldest citizen, harrumphed. "Why must *we* do something?"

Sensing that Neba was about to speak, she touched his arm to forestall him. Zaharre would do the right thing; he always did. Judging by past experience, he was trying to help Jartz, a man of surprisingly quick temper when he was riled, think things through.

"Because," Jartz blustered, "if we don't, why, um, the predator will keep robbing my traps!"

"Which would be bad for us," Rakin interjected, "since we use the meat and hides."

"Exactly!" Jartz huffed. Under Zaharre's unblinking gaze he shuffled his feet and some of his anger escaped in a growl of frustration. Looking at the familiar faces gathering about him, he calmed further. "And if it gets tired of my trap line, it will begin searching elsewhere for easy prey." He gestured broadly. "Our chickens, our goats."

Zaharre nodded, a pleased expression on his face.

"Have you seen it?" one of the men asked around

a yawn. He had chores to do if there wasn't a house afire or some other emergency.

"Not hardly." Jartz snorted. "A few paw prints is all."

"We'll get our weapons," eagerly offered Beroa, a broad-shouldered youth who stood a head taller than most of those present. "Help you hunt it down."

Neba cleared his throat.

"Best speak carefully," Leuna whispered. All eyes turned to her, then looked past her at her guest.

Neba drew himself to his full height and found that of all the men in the group, only Rakin was taller.

"How will you find it?" Neba asked. He felt the older men's keen gaze on him. "What will you do when you do find it?"

"We'll track it, of course," blurted the young man who'd spoken before. "And kill it."

"Are you better trackers than Jartz?" Neba asked, carefully keeping his tone neutral.

Jartz frowned at the interloper. "Who're you? I've never seen you before."

Leuna interjected quickly, "He's called Neba." She avoided looking at him. She hoped that he didn't mind her naming him, much as she hoped he'd wait until they were alone to question her about it.

"I arrived just yesterday," he said after a few moments of staring down at her. He had a dozen questions for her, but this crowd wouldn't likely wait patiently while he voiced them.

"He killed the narrasti I've been selling," added

Rakin, his tone thoughtful. "One shot."

Neba sensed a change in the crowd, the hostility lessening slightly in deference to a measure of respect.

"I'll help you find this beast," he offered. He didn't like the idea of an unknown predator stalking the woods around Leuna's house.

Jartz' frown eased considerably. Adding a muscular Marroi to the hunting party suited him just fine.

"We'll get our things!" The young men exploded out of the group like startled quail from the tall grass.

Neba caught Jartz' gaze, held it. "I'll get my bow. Then I'd like for you to show me where you start your trap line." He hadn't found it yesterday, but given that trap lines usually ran for miles, that wasn't too surprising. Hopefully, with a starting point to work from, he would be able to locate the animal's tracks quickly.

Leuna slipped away while the men were still nodding at each other. Snatching up a small shoulder bag, she inspected its contents at a glance. A wrapper of jerked meat, a tin of dried fruit, a flint, and a bit of thin leather holding a metal fish hook and line. Setting the bag on the table, she caught up a water skin and went to fill it at the well.

Neba entered the cottage quietly, noted the bag open on the table, and frowned. He didn't want her coming along. There were too many unknowns here. He couldn't remember when or how he'd learned to treat the unknown with extreme caution. That didn't make it any less true, though.

Leuna came back into the kitchen just then, her forehead scrunched in thought as she dabbed at the water dripping from the freshly-filled water skin.

"Oh!" She stopped abruptly, surprised to find him standing in the middle of the room, arms folded across his chest. "You'd better hurry," she warned him. "Beroa and the others are young and hasty. They won't be happy if you keep them waiting." Mentally, she was still reviewing her preparations. Would the hunt keep them out overnight? Probably. Should she offer him her travelling medical case, too? Would he know how to use it?

"You're not coming," he said bluntly.

"Hmm? Well, of course not," she laughed as his words registered. "I doubt a wrist catapult would be much help against this beast," she continued, setting the water skin beside the bag. She was competent with a bow and arrows, but that hardly qualified her for a hunt like this. "Not only am I too busy to go, I have no desire to! Jartz says it has sharp claws!" She grimaced. "You should probably take my travelling medical case with you. Jartz knows how to use most of it, so you don't have to carry it yourself," she added hastily, when he seemed about to object. "I'm just afraid it might come in handy."

Neba heard excited, boyish voices in the street and closed his eyes. Deep inside of him, a sadness stirred. At some time, perhaps in a hunt such as this, he had doubtless known loss. Forcing his eyes open, he smiled at her.

"You're very wise." Striding past her into the room where he'd slept, he swiftly changed into her father's day clothes and strapped his quiver in place.

He paused, hand on the bags, and cocked an eyebrow at her. "Neba?"

She blushed. "It means 'brother' in the old tongue." She felt her cheeks grow even warmer as his eyes dipped to her mouth while his other eyebrow slowly crept toward his hairline.

Then he nodded, scooped up the bags from the table, and strode out the door.

The sound of it clicking shut behind him made Leuna take a step back. This was not how she'd imagined him leaving. He wasn't even going in search of his identity. Bemused, she'd no idea how long she sat there before Sati walked through her door. She stopped upon spying Leuna.

Beckoning for the girl to finish coming inside, Leuna tugged at her sleep braid, thinking quickly. "While I am getting dressed for the day," she rose, grateful for the second time recently that she always dressed for sleep as if she expected an emergency, "I would like you to begin assembling a travel case." She could always hope that the pack she'd loaned Neba would return intact, but it was better to be prepared.

Sati obediently slipped off her shoes and padded over to the supply cabinets. Leuna watched a moment as the girl began counting out rolls of bandages, then whisked herself off to change. She arrived back in the kitchen just as Sati finished.

"All ready, Miss Doctor," Sati announced as she closed the flap on the case with a satisfied pat.

"So I see." Leuna smiled and pinned her hair back out of her face. "I noticed you packed the tin of menda leaves on top. Why is that?"

Sati's cheeks pinked. "They make a soothing steep and go in many of the remedies you've taught me, Miss Doctor. I thought they should be where you can reach them easily."

"I see." Leuna cut herself a thick slice of bread, dug out a small pocket, and loaded it with mixed nut butter. "How did it go at Gai's last night?" She took a big bite of her breakfast sandwich.

"She was grateful for the paste," Sati answered quickly.

"Did you explain about only using it at night?" Leuna prodded.

"Yes…" Sati sighed. "She is *very* tired."

"And will be for the next few years." Leuna chewed thoughtfully. There was no 'cure' for what was coming for Gai; still, she didn't have to go through it alone. The village would help, starting with Zaharre's wife. "Arrange with Emaztea to have some of the children start helping her. It will be good practice for them."

"Help with the babies?" Sati squeaked.

"Yes, some of them can help with the babies. They aren't crawling in earnest yet, so the children and the babies can get used to that at the same time." Leuna poured herself a glass of water to help wash down the thick nut butter. "The other children can help fetch and carry, chop wood, and so on while Pelo works at the sawmill." At least there was no fear of destitution for the family. The local hardwoods fetched a pretty price when harvested and cut correctly.

"Yes, Miss Doctor."

"Don't leave yet," Leuna laughed, coming over to

squeeze her apprentice's shoulders. She'd tried to be fair but not too friendly during Sati's first few years of instruction, remembering well how her professors kept their distance. A little reassurance wouldn't do any harm, though. "Come over to the table so we can practice your stitching."

Sati shuddered. She didn't mind practicing with the leather scraps Miss Doctor gave her to work on, but a few lunars ago she'd seen Miss Doctor sew up a five-inch gash—in a real person! Her job had been to dab away the blood seeping from the wound while Miss Doctor used small, neat stitches to hold the edges together. Ever since that experience, Sati had struggled with the thought that one day she would have to sew someone up.

Leuna noticed the slight lag in Sati's usually quick step and knew that she'd made the right choice. She could've chosen to take Sati into the forest and gather herbs, or even set the task of copying another entry from her father's journals. But the signs were there that Sati was afraid of sewing up a cut and that was something she needed to overcome.

"Sew these pieces together," Leuna instructed once Sati finally joined her. "Try to space your stitches as evenly as you can."

Leaving Sati to her work, Leuna reached into a storage bin for a handful of garbi seed pods. While the oil she would eventually press from the seeds only kept for a few lunars, it was good to have some on hand. Especially since she'd used some on Neba... Her hands moved automatically, tearing open the thin, rough seed pods and extracting the seeds from the inner fluff, her mind free to wander into the forest, following the small band of hunters.

Meanwhile, the hunters were well under the forest's canopy by then, kept cool by its shade. Beroa, however, was boiling over with impatience as Neba paused to study every paw print they found, every irregular scratch in the trees, *every everything*!

"I'm going on ahead," he announced abruptly. "I'll let you guys carry the carcass back."

"I wouldn't let him do that." Neba didn't look up from the tree he was inspecting.

"More likely we'll carry your carcass back," Jartz snapped, scowling. He wasn't the boy's father and he didn't appreciate having to tend him. "Or haven't you noticed the depth of those claw marks?"

Beroa scowled right back at him.

"Patience is often the most important weapon in your quiver," Neba said calmly, straightening away from the tree. "There is more to this story than just how deep these fresh claw marks are." He deliberately paused to take a sip from the water skin. "Whatever has been raiding the trap lines is either not alone or has grown from that height," he used his bow to point at the older, lower claw marks, then to the knee-high ones, "to that height in a few short weeks."

Jartz scratched his chin and glanced around the woods. "He's right. And I only see one set of prints." Heading away from his trapline, he was happy to note. Maybe towing along a crowd of clumsy, noisy boys hadn't been such a bad idea after all. Leastwise, it looked like they'd scared whatever it was into running for now.

"Agreed," Neba nodded.

"One set?" Beroa interjected, confused. "What about the ones without claw marks? There are two animals, at least." Hearing himself confirm that there might be a second animal, he, too, scanned the forest uneasily.

"All of the tracks were made by the same animal," Neba corrected. "The right front foot has a scar on the pad, small but distinctive. That scar has been on every right front foot print, with claws or without."

"This could explain why it's been robbing my traps," Jartz mused. "A real young animal might not know how to hunt."

"So it's been separated from its parents somehow," Neba guessed. He might not know his real name, but he was discovering that he knew plenty about tracking. Yet he wasn't quite as at home in the forest as Jartz, which told him…what? That he had more experience in a different terrain?

"If the tracks keep heading in this direction," Jartz squinted into the trees as if he could see through them, "we'll wind up at the crags. Tomorrow, next day at the latest."

The crags… Neba felt a shiver of recognition that evaporated the instant he tried to define it.

"Tell me about these crags," Neba suggested as he and Jartz resumed following the trail.

"I've never seen them," Jartz admitted. "No one from Herrixka has traveled that far in generations. My grandfather used to tell tales of them, though. Said they stretched up to the sky, sheer in some spots and pockmarked with caves in others."

Caves… Again Neba experienced a rush of familiarity. Again, it was like trying to grab a fistful of smoke.

"Has anyone ever climbed them?"

Jartz barked a laugh. "Not that I ever heard. Have to sprout wings to reach the sky, wouldn'tcha?"

"Yeah, guess so." Neba shrugged, as much in response to Jartz as in an effort to shake off yet another elusive rush.

Chapter 5

"What do you think?" Chin resting on the top of his bow, Neba deferred to Jartz.

"Ought to do." Jartz looked around the clearing with knowing, appreciative eyes. "Beroa, fill the water skins. The rest of you spread out and look for firewood."

Beroa grumbled something under his breath—he thought.

"No, it ain't wasting daylight," Jartz responded coldly. "We've been walking all day, and most of us ain't used to it. Might be we'll walk all day tomorrow, too. Supposing we find the critter tomorrow, we got to be in shape to handle it. And that ain't even talking about walking back to Herrixka." He didn't bother keeping the irritation out of his voice. Sure, he could've kept going all night with a fistful of dried meat and an occasional breather, but that didn't mean these city lads could.

"Assuming all of us will be able to walk on our own when it's time to return." Neba's helpfulness was rewarded with a narrowing of the boy's eyes and hardening of his face. Clearly that possibility hadn't occurred to him before.

"Taking time tonight to eat a decent meal and get some sleep is just good sense," Jartz finished, his tone softening a little. "Now let's get at it."

"What're you gonna do?" Beroa asked.

"I'm goin' to catch supper." Jartz was losing his patience. "Mind you keep your eyes open for narrasti and harrapari. We ain't in the fringe of woods near Herrixka that you're used to playing in."

"I'll get the fire going," offered Neba, handing his water skin to Beroa. The others did likewise and dispersed into the woods.

Beroa lingered a moment longer, watching in wide-eyed surprise as Neba crossed the clearing, drew his belt knife, and plunged it into the earth up to the hilt. "Funny way to build a fire."

"Different," Jartz agreed. "Strangest bit is that even he don't know what he's doing." He shrugged in answer to Beroa's shocked look. "Told me as we were leaving Herrixka that he don't know who or even what he is."

"But..." Beroa sputtered, "all day long you've been letting him tell you what to do!"

Jartz scowled and gripped the boy's shoulder. "I've listened to him because he's got good eyes and good instincts. I don't know why he's digging that hole instead of just making a fire, but I can tell you he's picked a good spot." He jerked Beroa around so they were looking directly at where Neba was working. "Evening winds come from over there," he pointed to their left, "which means the smoke from our campfire will be pushed toward those trees behind him. Notice anything in particular about those trees?"

Beroa frantically searched his limited store of knowledge before shaking his head in defeat.

"They lean in over the clearing. As the smoke rises, it'll hit their leaves and separate. Be near invisible by the time it gets above the canopy." He gave Beroa a small shove in the direction of the stream. "Don't get lost." Pivoting, Jartz disappeared into the forest.

Neba, who'd heard most of their conversation, watched Beroa from the corner of his eye while pretending to be absorbed in removing the square of sod. Beroa finally trudged off and was soon out of sight, but Neba winced every time the boy kicked a rock or broke a branch. When at last even that sound had faded, Neba cleaned his knife and sat back to enjoy the silence.

He was whittling a sharp end on a broken branch as thick as his wrist when the first wood gatherer returned.

"What's that?" Zoli asked, setting his armload of wood within easy reach of what he assumed was a fire pit.

"This?" Neba looked at the wood in his hands. "I don't know." Frowning, he glanced at the haphazard mound of shavings in the fire pit. Was that why he'd begun whittling, to make lighting a fire easier? That was a reasonable guess, but instead of dropping the branch and reaching for his flint, he sheathed his knife and rose. Upending the branch, he forced the sharp end into the ground at an angle.

Zoli watched in astonishment as the stranger twisted and shifted the branch, driving it further and further along until the sharpened end protruded from the wall of the fire pit, making an air hole.

"There." Neba jerked the branch clear, tossed it aside. "That's what that is for." Sorting through the wood Zoli had brought, he selected several thin, dry branches and arranged them around the mound of shavings in the pit, taking care to ensure the branch ends overlapped. After he'd built a few layers, he stopped and reached for his flint.

"That looks like a small house," Zoli grinned, dropping a loosely-packed ball of dry grass in the center.

Neba chuckled. "It is. For the fire." Striking the back of his knife blade on his flint, Neba expertly directed sparks into the ball of grass. Several of the sparks struck the dense branches around the grass and vanished, but those that breached the grass fed on it greedily. First a small tendril of smoke curled up. Then with the aid of a soft, encouraging breath from Neba, a flicker of flame sprang up that quickly engulfed the grass before starting on the shavings.

Zoli stripped loose bark shards from a few of the remaining branches and dropped them into the pit, then broke the branches into foot-length sections. Working quickly to keep his fingers from getting singed, he added them to the setup, bracing the tops against each other with the bottoms splayed out like a hastily-constructed tent.

"Not bad," Neba approved. The branches were already smoking.

"That's how my dad taught me to do it," Zoli explained.

"Why don't you watch the fire while I get some more wood?" Neba suggested, rising from where he'd been crouched. "Those flames won't be satisfied with this small stuff for long."

He returned to find two large untxi turning on a spit over the fire and most of the young men engaged in debating the size of the animal they were tracking.

"I say it's smallish," Beroa sneered derisively,

speaking over Zoli. "We all saw the size of the tracks. Barely as big as an untxi paw!" He jerked his thumb in the direction of the cook fire.

"I say it's bigger," shrugged Zoli. "Some of the tracks had claws. And don't forget the slash marks on the trees."

Beroa scowled. He had forgotten the slash marks.

"Do they always bicker like that?" Neba asked Jartz, joining him where the trapper was scraping the untxi hides.

Jartz grunted. "Too often for my taste. Makes a body weary listening to all that good energy going to waste." He cocked an eyebrow at Neba. "It's not a bad question, though. How big do you think it'll be?"

Neba sighed and settled back on his haunches, bracing his elbows on his knees and resting his chin on his fists.

"I've been asking myself that question from the moment we started on the cold trail," he admitted. "I thought…I hoped it would come to me, the way so many other things have today."

"You might not know for sure," Jartz squinted at him, "but that ain't all that's bothering you."

Neba chuckled despite his frustration. "It's been raiding your traps for almost a full lunar. We have no way of knowing how long it took for it to venture that far from wherever it began, so..." He shook his head. "My gut says it should be pretty big. The evidence, though…"

"Spit it out," encouraged Jartz after Neba's words fizzled out.

"I don't think it's as big as it should be."

Jartz propped the makeshift pelt frames against a nearby tree and rose. Neba rose with him.

"You know what it is."

"I hardly know what *I* am," Neba snorted.

Jartz swung a fist at him without warning. Reflexively, Neba stepped inside the looping right and slammed the heel of his leading palm into Jartz' chest. Jartz flew backward a bow's length and landed ungracefully on his back.

Neba tensed as the rest of the camp turned to stare at them. Jartz groaned and hauled himself into a seated position.

"Why did you do that?" Neba snapped, barely able to keep his fingers from wrapping themselves around his knife's hilt.

"You…" Jartz held up a hand apologetically and wheezed a few times before he got his breath back. "You don't have to know who you are to trust what you *do* know."

Slowly, Neba allowed himself to relax. Reaching out a hand, he pulled Jartz to his feet.

"Next time," he advised, "just tell me straight out."

Jartz laughed, grimaced, and rubbed his chest. "Good idea."

"Tell me more about these crags," Neba requested.

"Not much to tell." Jartz frowned in thought. "Stories say they're made of granite."

"Do the stories also give them a name? Or are they known just as the crags?" Neba prodded.

"Oh, sure." Jartz grinned broadly. "Firedrake

Crags is how they're called. Didn't think of that before because we only have the one sheer, granite wall in easy walking distance," he joked.

"Jartz." Neba took a deep breath. "I know what we're tracking."

"I knew it!" Jartz thumped him on the back. "Spit it out!"

"A dragon."

Jartz discovered he was having difficulty breathing again.

"A dragon!" The boys had drifted close enough to overhear and now began murmuring amongst themselves. Dragons were practically mythical creatures in Lurrak, something they'd never expected to see.

Neba looked from face to face, trying not to laugh as their comparatively pasty complexions lost what little color they had.

"Maybe we should send the boys back to Herrixka," Jartz suggested gravely. "We can follow it back to the crags and try to come up with a plan to trap it."

"You're not sending me back!" Beroa blustered.

"You're the first one I would send back," Neba retorted bluntly. "You claim you're as strong as an ox and that may be, but you're also as clumsy as one and a braggart to boot."

Jartz cleared his throat to interrupt before Neba could finish. "I reckon we'll all think better on a full stomach."

Zoli was the first of the boys to take the hint, sniffing the air appreciatively before heading over to where he'd left his small kit. Neba and Jartz did the same, which put them as second and third in line for thick, hot slices of the golden-brown untxi meat.

"This could've done with a sprinkling of spice." Jartz shrugged as he led Neba back over to the tree where the pelt frames rested. "But you have to make sacrifices on the trail."

Neba smiled grimly. "Tell that to Beroa."

"Yeah, about that…" Jartz paused to kick a rock away from the tree then sat down and got comfortable. "He's big for his age, and that's always given him an advantage over the others. What he couldn't figure out for himself, he'd get someone else to do for him."

"Smarter than I thought." Neba separated a piece of meat with his knife and blew on it to cool it while Jartz chuckled darkly.

"Point is, they're growing up. Things are changing and he don't know how to handle it. Personally, I'd like to see him get back to his folks in one piece." Jartz stuffed a chunk of meat in his mouth and chewed. "Best way I can think of to do that is to give him a job that takes him to the village."

"How's that different from just telling him to take his kit and get out?" Neba frowned, puzzled.

Jartz shrugged. "Same difference as knocking a fellow back a few steps instead of breaking his nose for him."

Neba blinked, surprised. "I didn't want to hurt you if I didn't have to," he protested.

"Exactly." Jartz grinned. "Must be a way to get Beroa someplace where he ain't in danger without kicking him in his pride, is all."

Neba thought it over while he chewed and swallowed. "I think a kick in the pride, as you put it, might do him more good in the long run, but I'll let you handle it."

"Maybe it would," Jartz admitted. "Can't see the future from here." He leaned back against the rough bark and gazed around the peaceful clearing. The songbirds had resumed their callings back and forth to each other. A few of the braver sort dared the branches at the edges of the clearing, watching the intruders through beady black eyes.

Neba chuckled and relaxed against the tree also, shoulder to shoulder with the trapper. "Nor can I," he confessed.

"Alright, then. We'll set the watch and get some sleep. I'll tell him in the morning."

"Hi, lads!" Zoli's cheerful voice broke the silence. "Look what I found while I was hunting firewood!" He held up a handful of white rods, none smaller than his thumb.

"Gozoa root." Jartz smacked his lips in anticipation. Gesturing toward where Zoli and the others were hovering over the fire pit, he explained, "Bury those in the coals for half an hour or so and they sweeten up real good."

Neba still needed a little persuading to eat the peculiar looking roots. Milky-white before being roasted, the heat turned their outsides a discouraging mottled black and grey. He eventually surrendered to his curiosity after the third member of the group offered to eat his for him.

"That's right," Zoli coaxed. "Peel the outer layer back and take a bite."

Neba heard a satisfying *crunch* as he bit into the root, followed by an explosion of sweetness in his mouth. It was so intense that his tongue started to burn! "Ugh!" Turning, he spat his mouthful into the fire and tossed the rest of the root to Zoli. "That's terrible!"

"Never mind, never mind," Jartz called over the shocked chatter from the boys. "I reckon we all just learned something about the Marroi. They don't like sweets."

Neba tried to cover his embarrassment at his apparent rudeness by volunteering to take the first watch. Jartz paired the boys and admonished them to be alert, then announced he'd take the final watch before dawn.

Neba moved toward the forest while the boys began to spread out to sleep. The light was fading fast and he wanted to take a look at the trail ahead. Among other questions was the puzzling fact that the dragon had apparently left behind a food source—namely Jartz' trapline. At least, the trail was still heading away from it. Jartz would be thrilled, of course, but it didn't really make sense. Unless they'd managed to scare the dragon off.

He half-knelt to study a paw print. The once sharply-defined edges had eroded in toward the center, telling him it was at least a few days old. Not far from it, he spotted a much fresher, and slightly larger, print. Glancing over his shoulder at the camp, Neba frowned. Where did dragons sleep? How often did they sleep? Perhaps the dragon made the trek from Firedrake Crags to the edge of Herrixka in less than a day instead of the two it would take them.

He continued pondering these and other questions while he kept silent watch over the camp for the next two hours. They stayed with him after he'd woken the next watch and stretched himself on the grass to try to sleep. In the last few moments before drifting off to sleep, his thoughts strayed to Leuna and he smiled.

"Wake up!" barked a harsh voice.

Neba was on his feet instantly. His hand fumbled at his waist for a sword but came away with a belt knife. He blinked rapidly, wondering what was going on. Jartz stood in the center of camp, glaring at nobody in particular and everyone at the same time.

"Get yourselves up!" he roared to the befuddled youths staring at him. They all but levitated in their haste to obey. "Back to Herrixka, the lot of you. And don't get lost!"

Neba's eyebrows rose as far as they comfortably could while he waited for Jartz to explain. He realized he hadn't fully dispelled slumber's fog, yet this was hardly the subtle assignment for Beroa they'd discussed over supper.

"Where's Beroa?" one of the boys asked.

Shocked fully awake by that question, Neba did a quick head count.

"Move!" Jartz snapped and made his way over to where Neba was already gathering his gear. "Beroa and Arren shared the last watch," he told Neba in a low tone. "Arren woke me early because he couldn't find him."

"Think he's gone back to the village?" Neba asked

hopefully as he strung his bow.

"I found his footprints on the dragon's trail over that way." Jartz' face tightened. "I think he somehow knew what we were planning and decided to prove us wrong."

"Well, we better find him before he proves us right." Neba slung his bags over his shoulder. "You see the boys off, I'll start tracking him. Maybe I can catch up to him before he catches up to it."

Jartz started to protest, then stopped. "Best guess, he's been gone a little under two hours. That's not nearly far enough to have reached the crags."

"The dragon may have circled back," Neba pointed out. "I was thinking about it last night, and we're driving him from his hunting grounds. He's not going to be in a good mood." He glanced at the lads. "Better warn them."

"Right." Jartz grimaced. "Just don't be too hard on Beroa if you find him before I do."

Neba almost laughed in his face. The boy might be in mortal danger and Jartz was still worried about his pride?

"I won't," he managed to say and took off at a trot into the woods. Thankfully, Beroa's big feet left tracks he could've followed blindfolded. The prints were close together at first, toe-heel, as he'd snuck away from camp. A few hundred feet away, they lengthened out as the boy swung into his usual confident swagger.

Neba's stomach started twisting with morning hunger and he dug in Leuna's case until he found the jerked meat. As he popped a piece into his mouth to chew on while he ran, he thought he remembered seeing Beroa's kit still in the clearing. Didn't the boy have any sense?

He held his bow close to his body to keep it from getting tangled in the foliage, his eyes and ears open for anything amiss. The cut which had troubled him so badly just a few days ago didn't bother him in the least as he leapt fallen trees and ducked under low-hanging branches, sticking to the dragon's trail. Beroa's tracks wandered occasionally when the terrain got rough or the tracks seemed to peter out, but he somehow always found his way back to the trail, so now Neba held to it with firm determination.

Wiping sweat from his forehead as he rounded a large rock with fresh scratches on its top, Neba estimated he'd been trotting for about an hour and reasoned he must be getting close. Easing himself back to a fast walk, he raised the water skin, sloshing the water around in his mouth before swallowing to slow his consumption. Popping another bit of jerked meat into his mouth, he eyed Beroa's tracks. A hundred or so yards back he'd passed a confusion of smudged tracks near a fallen log and deduced that the boy had stopped to rest, so he'd closed the gap considerably.

That was when he noticed a faint odor. Not sweet or sour or anything he could easily put a name to, but elusively familiar. Stepping off the trail, he ducked behind a large tree to his left and slowly edged around it so that he could see what lay ahead. Tree to tree he moved, doing his best to make no noise as he cautiously continued along the trail.

Ahead of him, calmly standing in the middle of a small clearing, Beroa was munching on something. The sound of his chewing was all that broke the unnatural silence. Even the birds seemed to be holding their breath. Neba opened his mouth to call for the boy, but he was too late.

The bushes rustled on the far side of the clearing, drawing Beroa's attention. Still hidden from view, something hissed, making the hair on the back of Neba's neck rise. To his astonishment, Beroa tossed the food aside and pulled an arrow from his quiver. He had just taken his first step toward the rustle when the animal exploded out of the forest.

Rearing up on his hind legs, the dragon spread his wings and roared a challenge. He almost seemed to shimmer as the sun struck his opalescent blue scales. Rib bones were clearly visible when he foolishly raised his head in an effort to prolong the roar.

Beroa's head went back and he roared with laughter at the goat-sized dragon. Then he began to lift his bow. Neba gripped his own bow tightly and raced toward the boy while Beroa sited along his arrow.

Plucking an arrow from his own quiver, Neba scanned the edge of the forest. Finally spotting what he was looking for way up in a tree, he stopped dead, aimed, and fired. The dragon roared a second challenge when it sighted Neba, who ignored it and launched himself at Beroa.

His shoulder struck Beroa in the upper arm, sending his arrow wild and knocking his bow out of his hands as they slammed into the ground. He heard several loud snapping sounds as they wrestled. Beroa writhed underneath him, bucked him off and shoved himself into a sitting position.

Neba saw that the dragon was completely involved in scarfing down the stalk of fruit he'd just knocked out of the tree. Apparently he'd been right about the dragon's hunger. Relieved, Neba settled back to watch Beroa as he pulled arrow after arrow from his quiver only to find that they'd all broken when he fell. A good thing, too, since all he had was bone-tipped arrows. They were alright for hunting untxi or other small game, but would've shattered uselessly on impact with the armor of a moxal, or baby dragon.

Chapter 6

Growling in frustration, Beroa threw aside his broken arrow halves and grabbed one out of Neba's quiver. Springing lithely to his feet, he raised his bow.

Ignoring the ache in his shoulder, Neba retrieved his own bow and literally plucked the arrow from the air as Beroa released it.

"You fool!" Neba snapped in a low tone, his nose all-but brushing the boy's. "What do you think you're doing?"

"I'm trying to kill that beast!" Beroa shoved Neba away. Neba got a grip on Beroa's shirt as he fell and managed to use that as an anchor point, twisting himself back into a stable position while jerking Beroa off-balance at the same time.

Leaving Beroa lying stunned in the grass, Neba stomped on the boy's bow, breaking it. Nocking his arrow to his own bow, he turned to face the young dragon. It crouched warily at the far side of the clearing and he took a slow step toward it. It pranced in place, clearly worried and unsure. Carefully raising his bow, Neba knocked down another stalk of ripe fruit for it.

"That's it, fella," he said softly as it pounced on the stalk, gulping down the fruit. He chuckled as blue juice trickled down the soft, blue skin of its neck. "Alright if I come a little closer?" He felt a ripple of pleasant surprise when the dragon ignored his approach. "I guess you're not afraid I'll try to steal your snack, eh?"

Slipping his bow over his shoulders, he raised

cupped hands to his mouth and took a deep breath. Without thinking, he exhaled sharply, using his hands as an echo chamber.

The dragon abandoned his snack as the cry of a mother dragon sounded. Desperately, it tried to flap its immature wings. When that failed, the poor little moxal tried scrabbling up the nearest tree, issuing his own plaintive cries.

"What is it doing?" Beroa asked, wide-eyed. "Did you shoot it?"

"Of course not." Neba shook his head. Having at least an idea of what he was doing now, he called again and the dragon stopped abruptly, his head whipping around to stare at him. "That's right, it's me."

"Don't do that!" Beroa begged desperately. He'd never felt as vulnerable in his life as he did now and this fool was intentionally drawing the attention of the dragon to them both!

"Be quiet," Neba commanded. Walking easily, he took a few more steps forward, putting himself out of line with Beroa. "Go back along the trail. Jartz is looking for you."

Beroa swallowed hard. He looked at his broken bow and arrows. He'd come ahead to be a hero, to save the day and take his place among the men in the village. Instead, he ducked his head like a little boy and obeyed.

Neba cried again, the same mother dragon sound he'd been making. This time, the dragon took a few, slow steps toward him, nose raised and sniffing.

"Sorry, fella. I'm not your mother."

Beroa stopped at the edge of the forest to

watch. Neba stood stock still while the dragon eyed him. As the moxal edged closer, Neba raised his arm from the shoulder and held out his palm at chest level. The dragon stopped, cocking its head curiously to the side. Slowly, hesitantly, it dropped to its belly.

Feeling an unknown something closing around his arm, Beroa screamed.

"Shut up!" Jartz hissed, but it was too late.

Startled, the dragon reared up onto its hind legs, issue a scream of its own, and bounded away into the forest.

Neba shot an angry glance in their direction, then almost laughed as he saw Jartz and realized what must've happened. Shrugging, he tramped over to the fallen fruit stalks, hunting for his arrows.

Jartz shook his head at Beroa in mild disgust.

"You won't tell anyone that I screamed," Beroa begged. "Will you?"

Jartz rolled his eyes and jogged over to where Neba was standing, arrows in hand. "You've been busy," he noted.

Neba grinned. "It's a gailen," he announced. He didn't remember the word until he said it, but he knew he was right. "One of the best breeds of dragon."

"Good to see you've overcome your self-doubt," Jartz responded drily. "It could've killed you."

Neba squinted in the direction the dragon had gone. "I don't think so."

Jartz heard the faint note of uncertainty in Neba's voice but decided not to comment. "You could've killed it." He held up his hands, palms forward, when Neba scowled at him. "Just an observation."

"It wasn't necessary," Neba insisted. "If not for our hero over there," he flicked a hand in Beroa's direction, "I'm sure I could've connected with it."

Jartz kicked one of the unconsumed fruits at their feet rather than responding. "I don't get it. If it likes fruit so much, why'd it come after my traps?"

"It ate all the low-hanging and fallen fruit," Neba pointed out, gesturing at the fruit-free ground around the rest of the clearing. "When it couldn't reach any more, it had to find another food source. And at that age it would have a ravenous appetite."

"Ravenous?" Jartz repeated, thinking of his traps.

"Exactly. Another few weeks and it would've started attacking the livestock, just as you suggested."

"Neba." Jartz frowned. "I know you don't want to hear this, but I don't see how we can avoid…"

"I do," Neba interrupted firmly. "I'll stay out here with it. I'll teach it to hunt the wild animals and keep it away from Herrixka."

Jartz scratched his chin. "Might work," he conceded at last. "How come it doesn't go hunting on its own?"

"My best guess," Neba nocked an arrow and aimed at another fruit stalk, "is that it has had more experience as prey than predator. It's hard to believe it's survived this long on its own, in fact." He shook his head. "It's small for its age, too. Did you see how skinny it was? How dull its scales were?"

"Which brings us back to our earlier thinking."

Jartz fired an arrow of his own. "Something happened to its parents."

"Exactly," Neba nodded. "Wait," he stopped Jartz from firing again. "Too much of this fruit will give him a sick stomach."

Jartz chuckled. "You musta been some sorta dragon expert before you lost your memories."

"Yes." Neba did his best to smile despite the way his heart was twisting. How could he stay here, tending the dragon, while he was in another town, searching for answers? He had so many questions and no one to answer them here in the forest.

"Hey." Jartz touched him on the arm as he started to walk away. "Zaharre is going to ask me why it won't grow up and *then* attack Herrixka."

"Oh, that's simple." Neba shrugged. "I'll fly it up onto the crags and turn it loose."

"You think it'll stay there?" Jartz hastened to catch up as Neba headed toward the fruit they'd just knocked down. "How can you be sure?"

"Because it came from there. It makes sense, don't you see?" Neba handed him his arrow. "Dragons lay eggs, just like birds." He resumed walking. "They just don't lay their eggs in trees. The crags are the perfect location because they can nest too high for predators from below and too low for predators from above. Not to mention the close proximity to this forest with the musker trees." He gestured at the fruit stalks.

Jartz rubbed his forehead. "I don't think I'll be able to convince him. You better come back and explain."

"Why?" Neba wiped the stalk juice off on the

grass before storing his arrows in his quiver. "I said I would take care of it."

"Right, but if I can't convince them, they'll send a hunting party." Jartz watched uneasily as Neba turned to face him, hot anger in his eyes. "To them, that's what'll make sense. If they stand back and let this dragon get bigger, it becomes a bigger problem. It won't be five minutes before someone suggests that it'll come after people once it's finished off our livestock."

Neba controlled his anger with great difficulty. It would've helped a lot to know *why* the continued—and yes, even quite logical—insistence on killing the dragon made him so angry.

"That would be a very bad idea," he said coldly. "The dragon's hide is already thick enough that a bone-tipped arrow will shatter harmlessly on it."

"I believe you!" Jartz assured him. "I just didn't know it until you told me. Come back with me for one day, two at the most. Convince the council and we can all go our ways in peace."

Neba exhaled slowly, then nodded. "Alright."

"Good!" Jartz thumped him on the back. "It's the best way." Cheerily, he scooped up one of the downed pieces of fruit and took a bite. And spat it out. "That tastes horrible!" Dropping the fruit, he rinsed his mouth out with a squirt from his water skin.

"I'm not surprised." Neba patted him on the back. "There's a reason why musker fruit is only eaten by dragons. Come on, let's get back to Herrixka.

Jartz looked around for Beroa and decided the

boy must've ducked along without them. They jogged along in silence until they caught up with him.

"C'mon," Jartz called to the boy as they passed him.

"What's the hurry?" Beroa looked over his shoulder quickly. "Is it chasing us?"

Neba disciplined a laugh at the idea of being afraid of the moxal and shook his head instead. "If we keep up a good pace, we should be able to get back to Herrixka before nightfall."

"But it took us all day yesterday to get to the clearing," Beroa objected.

"Yesterday," Jartz interrupted dryly, "we had to hunt for sign and study the trail. Now we know where we're going."

"About the clearing." Neba had remembered something. "Did the others take his kit back with them?"

"Nah. Figured he might want it."

Neba grinned a little at the realization that Jartz hadn't fetched it along, either. They alternately walked and jogged back to the clearing, where they stopped to rest.

"Hold up, boy." Jartz jerked Beroa's water skin out of his hands before he could finish guzzling it all down. "You sip it, hear me? I know you're thirsty, but if you just pour it all down your throat and into your empty stomach, you're gonna make yourself sick." Not until Beroa nodded did he return it.

"We've made good time." Neba popped another bit of jerked meat in his mouth. Compared to last night's fresh, succulent untxi it was like chewing flavored leather, but it was better than nothing. "If we walk for the next hour, we should be able to jog again after that."

"We can stop for fresh water where we found the first marked tree," Jartz nodded, his own teeth worrying a piece of the biltong he carried. Thicker than regular jerked meat, it took more time to dry, 'twas true. He enjoyed the tang of the vinegar used in curing it, though, so he didn't mind the extra effort.

Squinting at Neba, he asked, "D'you still think it's small for its age?"

Neba nodded. "He should be half a span larger if I've calculated his age correctly."

"Half a span? You mean half a wing-span?" Jartz whistled and took another sip of his water. "He'll get too big for the forest soon. That ought to make the council feel better."

"Hardly." Neba chuckled. "Once those wings of his finish growing, he'll be able to make the flight from the crags to Herrixka *over* the forest in less than a day."

Jartz gave him a dirty look. "You're not making saving your dragon any easier."

Neba laughed aloud. In fact, he kept chuckling about that all the way back to Herrixka, much to Jartz' annoyance.

"Well, we're not too late." Neba detached himself from Beroa, who'd been leaning on him for the last mile or so. "Lights are still on in the big house over there."

Jartz grunted. "That's Zaharre's home. When it's lit up this late, it means trouble."

Beroa collapsed onto a bench. "I'm out of water."

"Here." Jartz dropped his water skin in the boy's lap. "Catch your breath, then go to bed. You look exhausted."

Beroa rolled his eyes at the two 'older' men as they walked away.

"I see a great future for that boy," Jartz confided to Neba. "Yep, I can see it now. He's going to work for a famous blacksmith somewhere," he let the thought simmer a moment before finishing, "as their bellows worker." He laughed so hard at his own joke, at the idea of Beroa's arrogance safely restricted to the job of stoking the fire and pumping massive bellows, that windows and doors around town began opening.

"What's the joke?" called an irritated voice. "Better be good, waking me up at this hour!"

"Ask me in the morning," Jartz called back without even looking in their direction. "It'll be funnier then."

"It's about time you two got back." Leuna stepped out from the shadows between two houses. "The way those lads came running back earlier today, I expected to see you on their heels."

Jartz snorted, rubbed his nose, and picked up his pace.

Neba watched him go, choosing to stop and talk with Leuna a moment instead of continuing to push himself.

"What did you mean, you expected to see us 'on their heels'?" he asked.

"That's just an expression," she chuckled. "Although

once, a few years ago, Jartz caught some of these very same boys playing trapper—meaning that they were checking and tripping his whole baited line—and chased them clear back to town. He was so close behind them that we tease him he almost ran right up on their heels."

"Ah, I see."

"Come on!" Jartz squinted back into the darkened street, his night vision ruined by the bright light that spilled out when Zaharre's son had opened the door.

Neba sighed and took her gently by the elbow, enjoying the warmth coursing from her to him. "Would you mind coming along?" he invited. "I'm sorry to keep you up, but I might need your help explaining some things."

Leuna smiled and fell into step with him, their arms brushing together as they walked. She supposed she must be hiding her disconcertion well. At least, when they entered Zaharre's home, no one remarked to the contrary. Her heart hadn't pounded this hard since the time she'd encountered a miarma while reorganizing her shelves after her father died. Blasted ten-legged creepy little things… She shivered and accepted the cup of warm, tangy salda that Zaharre's wife, Emaztea offered her.

Across the room from where she'd seated herself, Jartz and Neba stood before Zaharre. Rumor was that Zaharre had more laugh lines than frown lines on his aged face, though Leuna'd never stopped to count. Right now only the frown lines were showing.

"I see you have pelts, young trapper," he addressed Jartz. "But surely it was not an untxi that robbed your lines?"

Jartz shifted awkwardly. "No, Zaharre. It was a dragon." The quiet conversing going on among the assembled villagers halted, leaving an uncomfortable silence behind.

"A young one," Neba specified. "A gailen."

Zaharre cocked his head at them, his gaze lingering on the powerful bow in Neba's hands. "A gailen? The favored mount of the Marroi." He stroked his chin thoughtfully. "We have not seen a gailen dragon in this region since before my father's time."

"He must've brought it here," growled one of the other men, indicating Neba.

Neba thought briefly that the growler reminded him of Beroa, all shoulders and arms.

Jartz snorted. "The dragon's been here most of a lunar and Neba just turned up."

"It's the Marroi alright," asserted a thin, pale fellow. His hands twitched anxiously in his lap. "They're going to raid us."

"Why?" Neba met their gazes without flinching. "In case any of you haven't heard," he grinned slightly, "I've lost my memory. I seem to be able to walk, talk, and hunt all right. I just can't remember who or what I am."

"A likely story," sniffed the pale one. "You're a spy, come here to…"

"To what?" interrupted Leuna. "To sabotage Herrixka's fearsome defenses? To assess our battle readiness?" She smiled at the ludicrous thought. "A

Marroi army mounted on dragons wouldn't even bother with a village this small."

"Then he's planning to move deeper into Lurrak," snapped the same fellow. "Find strategic landing points and places to store supplies and…"

"Excuse me." Neba raised his eyebrows at him. "Who are you, exactly?"

"I am Jakin, the town scholar." He puffed up like a pastry. A relatively small, puny pastry, oblivious to the exasperated looks and frowns aimed at him by the others as he continued abrasively, "You came here expecting to find only poor, ignorant provincials tending their flocks and crops, didn't you? Well. I'll have you know that I have newssheets shipped here from all over Lurrak and I know exactly what's going on."

Neba coughed and avoided making direct eye contact with Leuna, whose cheek looked suspiciously like she was biting it to keep the laugh sparkling in her eyes from getting loose. He couldn't claim to know the first thing about either country, but he got the feeling folks in Herrixka were tired of their town scholar.

"Jakin, how often are your wild accusations correct?" Neba flashed a friendly smile at the pompous twit, then turned his attention back to Zaharre, ignoring the snickers and cackles from the others. "I can't say I didn't bring the dragon here, because I don't remember. I'm offering right now, though, to go and stay with it in the woods. To make sure it doesn't come back to Herrixka or cause you any more trouble."

Zaharre stroked his chin again. "A most welcome

offer, should you be able to bring it about."

"I can," Neba answered, relieved to sense no qualms in himself.

"And when it is grown?" Zaharre narrowed his wise old eyes. "What is to keep it from plundering our herds and flocks? From attacking even our citizens?"

"It is here only because it is trapped here," Neba stated firmly. "Grown dragons can fly and I believe, given the choice, it will return to its home, to be with its own kind."

"You will guarantee that as well?" Zaharre tsked in mild disapproval. "You take too much upon yourself, young Marroi."

Neba held his peace, returning the elder's gaze without blinking. The whispers, which had started again after Zaharre's pronouncement, quieted as the two men continued studying each other.

"And yet, I find I am almost persuaded to believe you." Zaharre smiled for the first time that evening.

Chapter 7

The next morning Leuna lay awake, staring at the ceiling of her small room. She could hear Neba stirring in her father's room, but wasn't quite ready to face him. She hadn't spoken much on the way back to her house; just enough to let him know she was expecting him to stay there again. And now…now she was wondering how she was going to say goodbye.

If he'd been headed for Gertuk or some other towns to find his memories, she could at least have taken comfort in the hope that he'd succeed. This, on the other hand, well, it baffled her. How long would it take for the dragon to be old enough to hunt on its own? To fly up to the crags, where Neba maintained he would remain? Why was the dragon more important to Neba than his lost memories? *Why was all this so important to her?* Squirming away from that thought, she huffed at the memory of Zaharre giving his consent to this plan. She still couldn't believe it.

Pushing the blanket back, she reluctantly sat up. "I'll speak to Ama about having her stay with me this bruma," she decided aloud. "This house is warmer than her shack, and I'm sure we could both use the company." The sound of her voice in the stillness just made her lonelier. Would he come back before he began searching for his answers? Or was this the last time she would see him?

I've been lonely before, she reasoned with herself as she slipped into her day clothes. Tightening the strings on her side-cut shirt, she smoothed the modest gap-backing and tugged it down straight. *That first bruma after Dad died was…painful.*

"Neba?" she called, realizing he was no longer in the house. She had just put the last pin in her bun when she got a whiff of something delicious. It smelled familiar, sort of. Shaking her head, she laughed at herself. She should've known. Following her nose, she found Neba bending over the fire pit. "Neba?"

He looked up, grinned, and offered her the plate he'd just filled. "Hungry?"

"I am now," she agreed, basking in the scents wafting up from the pot. "Not that hungry, though," she laughed, eyeing the amount of food on the plate he was offering her.

Still smiling, he bowed graciously, stepping back to give her access to the pot. He started to seat himself in her father's chair.

"Careful!" Her hands flew out as if she could reach him and hold him in place rather than letting the chair dump him off its side.

"I fixed it." Sure enough, he seated himself, hands out from his body so she could see for herself that the chair was behaving. He even leaned back on the sloped back support.

"Oh." She blinked. It was too late now to explain to him that she hadn't had it repaired yet because she wasn't ready to do so. That she'd been putting it off the same way her father had before he died. Quickly turning her attention back to the pot, she put a few scoops onto a second plate. "Hmmm." Examining it while she settled into her own chair, she began listing off the ingredients. "Onions, duck, potatoes, chopped narioa…"

His attention fully focused on her when she sampled it, her eyes closing in delight, shoulders rising and falling in heartfelt enjoyment, Neba forgot to chew.

"How…" her eyes opened, opened wide, "do you make such ordinary ingredients taste so good?" Her eyes narrowed. "I don't suppose you have been hiding a packet of Marroi spices on you all this time?" she teased, reloading her fork.

He chuckled. "No, I'm afraid not." He dug his own fork into the hearty dish. "Everything in here came from your kitchen." He paused, the fork halfway to his mouth. "And…from a few of the plants in the garden again. I should've asked your permission."

"I'm glad you used the garden. It was my mother's and she was always sharing it."

"Ah, so she was the gardener in your family?" He felt a twinge of sadness for her. This was the second time she'd spoken to him of her mother, and there was no sign of another woman in the house. He deduced that to mean both of her parents were deceased. She was old enough to be on her own, to be sure, and yet so young to be without her parents.

"Absolutely. Dad was a decent gardener," she tucked her feet up under her in the chair, "and I'm not bad, but Mom could grow anything. In fact, that's how we came to move here."

"Really? So you weren't born here?" he asked to give her time to chew the bite she'd just taken.

"I was," she nodded. "What I meant was that

they could've gone anywhere. Any town in Lurrak would've been glad to have my dad as their doctor. It was my mother's interest in botany, um, plants that brought them here." She gestured toward the woods. "She was always bringing home a new specimen or writing her friends in the city about what she'd found."

"And this," Neba looked around the small garden. The fence surrounding it was stone up to about knee height, and covered in creepers or flowering ivy in several separate spots. Above that a deer-high, untxi-tight row of sturdy branches allowed the sun and wind and admiring gazes access to the prim rows of medicinal herbs and vegetables. "She designed this?"

"Yes." Leuna smiled at the serene expression on his face. In the Marroi culture, a well-kept garden was a small patch of paradise. Apparently whatever had happened to his memories hadn't been able to take that away from him.

"A difficult place to leave," he said softly. "I mean," he cleared his throat, "for you. When you went to university."

"Yes," she agreed, ignoring the thought that he'd meant something else. "I missed it terribly."

"Was there a garden, at least?"

"Only the tiniest little thing in the back of the house where I stayed with my grandparents. Some herbs and spices, a few tomato plants, and other things they might use in the kitchen." She wrinkled her nose at the memory. "I used to go there whenever I was homesick or upset. It helped to do something useful, something where I could see the result when I was done. Do you know what I mean?"

"Yes, I think so," he nodded.

"The staff didn't, not at first. They used to try to chase me out of there, like I was a stray kaleko or something." She shook her head, laughing at the memory. "It took me most of a semester to realize that they couldn't order me around just because I was a guest in my grandparents' home." Taking another nibble of the food, she grinned. "Now I know a bit better how they felt. I don't usually expect guests to cook, but in your case," her eyes twinkled, "the kitchen is yours any time you want it."

"An invitation I shall accept gladly." He couldn't seem to take his eyes off her. Perhaps he should've. "Of all the rotten…" He looked down at the forkful of food he'd just dropped on his pant leg, then back up at the sound of her giggle. It was such a contagious sound that he felt his own lips twitching even as he protested, "It's not funny."

"Yes, it is!" she retorted. Suddenly, her smile faded and she couldn't look at him.

"Leuna." She'd gone suddenly still and stopped responding to him. Setting his plate aside, he turned so that he was facing her, the food sliding off his britches and splatting on the ground beside the chair in the process. Doing his best to ignore his less-than-dignified state, he reached out to touch her hand. "Are you worried about something?"

"Of course. The dragon could have killed you without even trying. Any of you." She tacked on that last because it made her sound less infatuated.

He held back a chuckle rather than hurt her feelings. "He didn't and he won't. He's just a moxal, a baby, and he needs me." Smoothing her hair, he got distracted by the dozens of wispy curls that framed her face. They were so soft under his hands and when he smoothed them down, they sprang right back up. "I don't know how I know I can do this, but I promise," he looked her in the eyes, "he won't hurt me."

"You promise?" Shyly, Leuna looked up at him through the fringe of her lashes.

"I promise."

"Well," she said thoughtfully, "if you're going to be out there for a while, you're going to need some things. My father's things seem to fit you alright…"

"I thank you for the loan, but the pant legs are a little short," he corrected. "So far I've been able to tuck them into the tops of my boots, but that won't help if I have to go through a bramble bush or something."

"Oh, that's no problem," she assured him, setting her unfinished breakfast aside. "He'd had those tailored by Hori, our local seamstress. I still have a whole box of unfinished clothes that arrived after he got sick. I've been meaning to send it over to Hori, but I sort of…couldn't."

"Let's take a look," he suggested, coming lithely to his feet and offering her his hand.

Under her direction, he retrieved the box from the storage room and set it on the table, where they pried it open to find that there were indeed several useful items.

"Here," she shook out a pair of pants. "See how the pant legs are reinforced below the knee? That's for when he went into the forest to harvest medicinal plants."

"Hmm." He held them against his waist for size. "Yes, these are long enough."

"What else do you think you'll need? Some food, I suppose?"

"Oh, Jartz is taking care of that," he reminded her. For a single gold arrano, Jartz had agreed to negotiate supplies and help pack them out to the clearing where they'd last seen the dragon. "In fact." He took out the rest of his coin. "I'd appreciate it if you'd hold onto these for me." She hesitated and he insisted, "I won't need them out there. Also, if Jartz needs more money for supplies, he won't have to come clear out to where I am to get it."

"I'll take care of them for you." She gave in with a small smile of her own. "How long will you be gone?" She felt the heat rising in her cheeks again. At least now she could be reasonably certain the he would come back to Herrixka before going elsewhere, to retrieve the rest of his money.

"Unfortunately," he lifted an empty bag off a hook in the closet and shook it out, "I won't know the answer to that question until it's time to come back. I seem to remember things as soon as I need to and not before." To keep his hands busy, he rolled up three pairs of the britches and three shirts, stowing them deftly.

"Right." She jingled the coins. "I'll go put these away while you finish getting ready."

After he'd changed, he sought her out in the garden. She was sitting in her chair and pushing what was left of her breakfast around on the plate.

"I'll miss you." She didn't look up when she spoke.

"I'd ask you to come with me," he grinned, "but you'd just be in the way."

"I'd probably come," she admitted after mock-scowling at him. "I've never seen a dragon." She set the plate aside again. "Do be careful. Even if the dragon was as tame as a house pet, there are lots of animals out there that aren't."

"I promise." Neba looked once more around the garden, enjoying the orderly chaos of it all. The tomato plants and celery stood straight where they were planted while the squash plants sent creepers wherever they wished. Mint, dill, and other herbs flourished in one corner. Marjoram plants crowded around the base of the garden wall, their soft citrusy scent teasing his nostrils.

Neither of them heard the bell as the front door opened and closed.

"Harrumph." Jartz glared at them from just inside the back door. "You comin'? We got a lotta ground to cover."

"I'll be right out."

"Might as well come along now," Jartz insisted. It was just his opinion, but the stranger looked a might too comfortable in Jaun's old chair. When had she gotten that fixed, anyway? He'd offered more than once and she'd turned him down.

"He's right." Leuna got to her feet. "Shall I check your trapline while you're gone?" she offered.

"Nah." Jartz smiled. "I talked to Zoli about that this morning and he's willing."

She nodded her approval. "He's a smart, level-headed young man. Providing he doesn't catch himself in one of your traps, that should be alright."

Jartz snorted. "Boy's been hanging around me for the last year at least, knows half again as much about trapping as I did at his age."

She laughed and came up on her toes to kiss his scruffy cheek. "Glad to hear it, because if there's anything I hate, it's an injury requiring me to set broken bones and stitch up gashes at the same time!" She tucked her hand in the crook of Jartz' elbow and walked him to her front door, Neba following a bit behind.

"I didn't realize you were a trapper, too," Neba observed as he paused to gather the bags.

"Oh, I'm not really," she chuckled. "It's just that Jartz sort of adopted me after my dad got sick and he's a natural-born teacher." She smiled at Jartz' answering harrumph.

"Adopted you?" Neba looked up from the bags.

"Well, yeah." Jartz shrugged. "A pretty woman needs a hand sometimes in beatin' off the fellas." He eyed Neba meaningfully.

"Fellas…you mean suitors?" Neba's eyebrows drew together in a frown. Of course. She was smart, kind, and he'd already admitted his own attraction to her. He'd just been stupid enough to think he was the only one who'd noticed.

"The city folks came in droves after her dad passed," Jartz recounted. "A few of 'em figured to stick around, maybe comfort her." He looked pointedly at Neba. "And maybe more."

"Now Jartz, really," Leuna scoffed. "There you go dragging up ancient speculation as though it was fact."

"What made these suitors so unacceptable?" Neba asked, feigning a deep interest in situating the bags just so on his shoulder.

"One thing or another." Jartz looked fondly at the top of Leuna's head. "Mostly they just wasn't good enough."

"Alright, time to change the subject." Leuna let go of Jartz' arm and walked over to her father's desk, glad to be away from Neba's curious gaze for a few moments. "I have an idea. We moved here because my mother wanted to catalogue the plants and trees in this area, but her work sometimes took her into the larger cities. Whenever she was gone," she straightened, smiling triumphantly as she showed them a book of blank paper and the roll of pencils she'd found, "she would keep a journal of all the things she saw and did. We would read through it when she got back and it almost felt like I was there with her." She held the items out to Neba. "In your case, I think it will help you coax your memories back if you write down things that you see and think and hear that seem important to you."

Neba hesitated. Taking one of the pencils from her, he studied it. It seemed to fit naturally enough in his hand. But could he write in Lurrakian? Or any language, for that matter? He had no trouble speaking or understanding it, so it stood to reason that...

Reaching for a sheet of paper someone had left on the table, he turned it toward him.

"Apples, one peck," he read aloud, frowning at the unfamiliar word. "What's a peck?"

Jartz cleared his throat and answered just as Leuna was about to. "It's a measurement. A peck of apples, that's maybe thirty of them." He shrugged. "However many it takes to weigh ten pounds."

Neba nodded and resumed reading. "Three wheels of cheese." That he understood. Apparently he could read. Setting the pencil tip to the page, he tried to think of something to write.

Leuna, embarrassed to realize she just assumed he'd be able to read and write, waited silently while he stood there, motionless. At last the pencil moved and she relaxed.

"Two narrasti steaks," Jartz read over his shoulder. "One pie." He scratched his head and looked sideways at Neba, who was setting the pencil down. "What kind of pie?" he demanded.

"Delicious." Neba grinned and winked at Leuna.

That taken care of, they set out, the book and roll of pencils carefully tucked in amongst the food stuffs. The mule wasn't much bigger than Muti's, but Jartz insisted it was stronger than it looked. Neba slung his bow over his shoulder and slapped Jartz on the back as they entered the forest.

"My friend," he began, "you must explain to me the customs of men and women among your people."

Jartz looked at him sharply. "Like what?"

"Oh," Neba shrugged. "Anything that will help me when it's time for me to ask people who I am. Are these 'city folks' so different from the villagers here?"

Jartz continued tramping along, choosing the easiest path for the animal and ignoring the slight squelch of water as his boots picked up the last of the morning dew.

"No," he said at last. "Busier, mostly. Always goin' someplace they ain't. Like as not to see someone they don't like so's they can brag about the last thing they got that they didn't need." He shook his head in disgust.

Neba kept walking, each agonizing step taking him further from answers. He'd learned last night that there were simply no other towns between Herrixka and the crags; or for days in any direction. The nearest was Gertuk, a river port he was literally setting his back to. He'd reasoned a delay wouldn't be too bad. He could work with the dragon and hunt by day and plan his strategy at night. Now it seemed he would be alone with his doubts instead.

"I don't know who I am." He hadn't been sure he'd spoken aloud until Jartz replied.

"Neither does the dragon. I don't think he'd much care if he did." Jartz permitted himself a small chuckle, then patted Neba's shoulder. "Don't let it get you down. I've got to go into Gertuk soon, to cash in the bounty on kastore pelts and pick up supplies for the bruma trapping season. Hard to believe anything as little as a kastore fetches a bounty of half an arrano, but they're mean little suckers that eat just about anything what ain't metal or completely spoilt. Sharp teeth, too. Had a wet summer a couple years back and they just about overrun Herrixka. We're finally whittling them back down to size, I reckon." He shrugged off his own cares and returned to what he'd been saying. "Gertuk's not far from here, but since she's a port on the Ibai River, she's twice as big and gets plenty of traffic. Anybody's looking for you, someone in Gertuck will have heard about it."

"Thank you, Jartz. That means a lot to me." Why hadn't he thought of that himself? Sending Jartz was even better than going himself, for the people in Gertuk knew him and would answer his questions. Neba touched his side where he'd been wounded. "Take care whom you ask, though. I'm no child who wandered away from the caravan during a rest stop. Someone deliberately wounded me and left me alone in the deep forest."

"See, now, that would bother me something fierce." Jartz squinted at him, remembering the way the boy had looked at Leuna when he thought nobody was watching. "At least enough that I'd want to figure it out a'fore I got ideas about playin' house."

Neba's mood lightened somewhat. "Playing house? What is that supposed to mean?"

Chapter 8

The next morning, Jartz rose and stretched. The smile on his face was the natural result of waking up to the smell of frying bacon, hot biscuits, and boiling musker fruit. Once boiled with a few crushed phyla leaves, it was downright tasty.

"Thought you was crazy last night," he told Neba cheerfully. "You makin' a fuss over that fruit and all. I never would've believed it could be tolerated if I hadn't tasted the difference myself!" Deftly, he rolled and bound his bedroll. He'd stayed to help Neba cache his supplies under a tarp they'd thrown over a low branch. Then he'd stayed for supper.

Neba laughed and checked the tin of beans. Instead of cutting out one of the round ends, he'd used his belt knife to slit it up the side and spread the gap enough to stir the contents while the tin can heated on the coals.

"Bring a slice of that comb honey over," Neba suggested. "It'll go well with the biscuits."

Jartz gladly opened the protective wax paper wrapping and cut off a chunk of the gelled honey and comb. Setting it in the middle of the tray of biscuits, he watched it melt. Using a clean fork, he spread it over the biscuits until it was a delicious mess.

Halving the bacon and beans onto tin plates, Neba handed one to Jartz and they dug in.

"I been wondering," Jartz poured himself a cup of musker. "What makes you think the dragon's still hereabouts?"

"Remember how I cast for sign yesterday while we were coming this way?" Neba asked, popping a crisp piece of bacon into his mouth. Jartz nodded, his own mouth stuffed with biscuit. "I didn't see any fresh sign leading in that direction, so I'm figuring he hasn't returned to robbing your trapline." He blew on his own musker before taking a sip. "And this is an area where he's relatively safe. Plenty of places to hide from predators, probably enough musker fruit to keep him from starving while he tries to figure out what we are and why we were here two days ago."

Jartz nodded, swallowed the biscuit he'd been savoring, and opened his mouth to speak.

"Besides all of that," Neba allowed himself a slow grin, "the rest of the musker fruit we knocked down yesterday afternoon has vanished, leaving behind only a trail of fresh prints into the woods."

Jartz' jaw hung slack for an instant before he began to laugh. "Had me goin'," he chuckled. Slurping some more of the musker, he smacked his lips. "All these years and I never knew about that stuff. Huh."

With a contented sigh, Jartz used half a biscuit to sop up some of the melted honey that was pooling in a corner of the tray. "Well, I wish you luck. You're gonna need it."

"Luck to you, too." Neba frowned thoughtfully. "Perhaps you should collect a few arranos from Leuna on your way through Herrixka. You might need them in Gertuk."

Jartz chuckled. "It'd be a waste, it would, using

gold to grease an already wagging tongue. Anyway, don't you worry. Those city folk got nothin' better to do than wag their tongues, especially when the news is interestin' or bad. I'll just give them a nudge, then sit back and wait for them to come to me." He'd been thinking about it while they walked yesterday and knew exactly where he was going to start. The Wayfarer's Inn wasn't much to look at, but trappers from all over the region stayed there. As an added bonus, the innkeeper's older brother ran the Crow's Nest, where hordes of sailors gathered to tell tall tales and complain about their captains. He kept his plans to himself, though, for fear of raising Neba's hopes too high.

"I hope you're right." Neba smiled though he wasn't nearly as confident as Jartz.

Jartz inhaled his half of the beans, crunched happily on the bacon, and lingered over the honey-biscuits and musker.

"That was a fine breakfast," he sighed. "Mighty fine. If I thought you'd be around this bruma, I'd hire you as my cook!" Rising, he stretched and patted his stomach. "Biltong's gonna seem like a crime after that." The dried meat was a staple in his life, even occasionally a breakfast food. "Try not to get your eyebrows singed off," he ribbed.

"By the dragon?" Neba laughed heartily. "His fire isn't lit yet, he's too young."

Jartz scratched his head thoughtfully. "But he is a *fire*-breathing dragon, right?"

"Gailen's breathe fire, yes." Neba laughed, slapped him on the back, and saw him on his way.

When it was just him, the birds, and the trees, he planted his fists on his hips and addressed the forest.

"I know you're in there, you moxal. The sooner you stop playing shy, the sooner we can get to work."

Because it was important that the moxal grow accustomed to the sound of his voice, Neba kept up a steady stream of chatter as he worked around the clearing. He also occasionally knocked some of the riper muskers to the ground as he arranged thin ropes in a web between the treetops, and was pleased to find the fruit gone each time he returned to the ground.

"We're going to be good friends, you and I," he promised as he tested the knots on the ropes that held up the tarp tent. "Just as soon as I arrange an introduction." Patting his growling stomach, he grinned. "Sounds like it's high time I set about it, too!"

Retrieving a ball of light twine, he headed toward the stream he'd heard chuckling the night before. As he made his way upstream to where the boulders hung out over the edge of the river, he crafted a small bark container to carry his fishing bait in. He hadn't gone far before he found himself taking up a stick about three fingers thick and roughly as tall as his waist. Deftly, he trimmed the dead offshoots and cut half a dozen notches while he scanned the area for…something.

Drawn to a patch of soft, damp earth with a scattering of old leaves, he hesitated, then drove the stick into the ground. Setting the bark container aside, he took up a second stick. Exhaling, he began rubbing it up and down the notched side of the first stick, doing his best to keep a rhythm. *Up. Down.* To his great astonishment, worms began squirming up out of the ground! Setting aside the rubbing stick, he hastily began scooping the worms into the bark container until he had all he needed.

"See you later," he grinned at the ones he left behind. "That was weird!" he added as he strolled back along the stream to a spot that had caught his eye. It felt better than good to dangle his legs over the boulders, bait a hook, and toss his line into the deep pools with the sun warming him. "I guess it's been a while since I've climbed trees like that," he chuckled.

The naïve fish, unaccustomed to the rude practice of angling, eagerly took the bait and he soon had half a dozen fat yellowfin flopping on the narrow fishhook stick he'd anchored in the water. It was called that because it had a forked branch at the bottom that would keep the fish from escaping when he was ready to retrieve the stick.

Whistling softly, he cleaned two for his own use, tossing the offal into the pool and rinsing his hands before straightening and stretching. It would've been easier to kindle a small fire and roast the fish right there, but his own comfort was secondary. Heading back to camp, he dragged the fishhook branch with the rest of the fish along on the ground behind him to be sure the fish smell was irresistibly spread along his back trail. About halfway there, he leaned the branch against a small tree and walked briskly away, whistling.

He walked a few minutes more before he stopped whistling and doubled back far enough to watch the little moxal devouring the last of the fish. That was quite an appetite. Grinning, Neba resumed whistling and went back to camp, hoping curiosity would bring the dragon along now that there was just one human to deal with.

"The sooner I teach him to hunt for himself, the better for both of us," he chuckled as he built a small, hot fire. "He won't be a baby dragon forever, and his appetite's going to grow with him."

While he waited for the flames to die down to cooking coals, he prepared the fish, sprinkling them with salt and pepper. Dropping diced wild onions and a small pat of lard into the heavy iron pan, he held it over the dwindling flames, tilting it to spread the lard as it melted. Soon the pleasant sizzle and scent of frying fish filled the air, prompting a rumble from the depths of his stomach.

"Something's missing," he muttered to himself. "Ah." Setting the pan on the coals, he reached inside the hut for the small keg of vinegar. A drizzle of the clear, sour liquid on each of the yellowfin steaks satisfied him. "That," he neatly transferred the steaming fish onto his tin plate, "is perfect." A moment later, he had chunked a fist-sized potato into the pan to cook. A low growl from the forest caught his attention as he lifted a forkful of fish to blow on it.

"I know." Neba didn't bother looking for him.

"I'm anxious to begin the training, too. But be patient, alright? You've had your lunch. Now it's my turn." Despite his amused protest, Neba burned himself more than once as he shoveled the fish and potato into his mouth.

"Alright." Pouring water into the pan to steam off the cooking residue, he set it right on the coals. "If you're ready to come out of the shadows, I'm ready to start your training." From the pile of ripe musker fruit beside him, he took three and lobbed them in the general direction of the growl.

Branches snapped as the dragon leapt from the forest, reared onto his hind legs, and gave his most ferocious roar. Neba held perfectly still while the moxal stretched his immature wings in the sunshine, turning the rich green grass beneath him a gorgeous turquoise. Suddenly, scenting the musker fruit at his feet, he forgot his posturing and dropped to all fours to gobble them down.

"Silly moxal," Neba scoffed, tossing another musker fruit into the clearing. Sure enough, after a short, menacing growl at him, the dragon chased the still-rolling fruit across the clearing, going so far as to bat it along with his forepaws. "You've got no sense at all." Taking his time, Neba doled out the rest of the fruit, heaving all of them a respectable distance from himself.

The dragon gulped down the last of the musker fruit and sniffed around for more. After shooting a disgruntled look at Neba, his mouth gaped in an enormous yawn and he sat with a thump. Yawning again, he stretched stiff forelegs out in front of him, raising his shoulders and shuddering all over before slumping to the ground, his spindly fore and hind legs splayed out wherever they would.

Neba chuckled at the first sound of snoring. Right in the middle of the clearing, no cover or defense, and the foolish moxal was fast asleep. Shaking his head, he reached under the tarp and brought out a ball of twine. He'd measured it out last night, tying knots every foot up to twelve feet. Now he rose stealthily and approached the young dragon. Fortunately, one dull blue wing was splayed out to the side, making it easy for him. The stubby wings were a little over three feet long, approximately the same as his height at the withers. The tail was much shorter than Neba expected at just two feet. Overall, his conformation was good. But he needed feeding up. His scales should glisten, his tail should be half again as long as he was, and if he didn't get some meat on him soon, that broad chest was at risk of caving in on itself, severely restricting his lung space.

Frowning, Neba returned to the shelter and noted his observations in the journal. Only after that did he fetch out the round knob of wood he'd found while scouting after supper last night. This late in the season, the once lush blue blossoms were now brown and brittle, but he hadn't gone there for flowers. Forcing his way through the dense cluster of young trunks, he'd made his way to the old father towering in the midst of them. Almost hidden by the brush grown up around the base of the dead tree, he'd found what he'd unwittingly come searching for—this burl about the size of a man's two fists. A few minutes later, he was walking swiftly back to camp, the liberated burl stowed in his game bag.

Now he turned it over, inspecting it. Drawing his belt knife, he bored a hole into the side of the burl until something told him to stop before the blade widened it any further. Lighting one end of a thin stick, he inserted it, letting it burn away the shavings and surrounding wood.

While that smoked and smoldered, he began carefully carving away elsewhere. Soon five holes adorned either side of what he assumed was the top. As the tiny fires burned out, he used another thin stick, rubbing it between his hands, to grind away the charred wood from the sides of the holes. Adding a larger hole for the fipple considerably sped up the work of hollowing it out by fire, and he was glad when the time came to fill it with fine sand so he could clear the rest of the obstructions. The tone finally suiting him, he carefully peeled away the bark, revealing the lustrous blue wood beneath.

"About time you woke up." He cocked an eyebrow at where the dragon had suddenly sprung to its feet and was growling at him. Apparently naps made him forgetful. "I've just finished the deia."

He blinked at the large, round whistle in his hand. So that was what it was called. An overwhelming sense of pride filled him until he feared he'd burst, while at the same time, he suddenly felt very young.

Wide-eyed, he stared at the woods around him. The shadows were dark and full of danger. His head swung from side to side as he tried to locate every creaking branch or snapping twig. Shivering, he curled his arms around his knees. Why was he alone? He wasn't supposed to be alone.

Moxal stopped growling and began looking around as well. His tail curled around his legs as he scuttled over to be closer to the strange creature who'd been sharing its food with him. Whatever was hunting such a formidable creature might hunt dragons, too.

Neba suddenly found himself with a face-full of warm scales. A faint whine came from the depths of a frightened moxal crowding close in to his legs. Reaching out, Neba was surprised at the size of the hand that settled on the scrawny neck. His hand wasn't that big, he was just a boy.

Looking down at his man-sized boots, at the sturdy belt knife in his other hand, he snapped out of the…what was it? A memory? A day terror? His hand still trembled on the moxal's neck.

"Well." He stopped, cleared his throat. The moxal looked up at him, shoving his nose in his face and crowding still closer. "Easy, now." He ran his hand down the dragon's neck, pausing instinctively at a favorite spot and scratching. "It's gone now, moxal. Whatever it was," he looked around the forest, once again green and peaceful-looking, "it's gone for now."

The dragon's ears perked up at the semi-familiar sound of the creature's voice. Had the scary thing gone away? Abruptly, his ears laid back and he bared his teeth. Growling, he began backing away.

Neba picked up the deia he'd dropped, raised it to his lips, and blew softly.

Moxal reared up on his hind legs, scanning the sky. The dragon cry had come from close by. Racing into the clearing, he raised a cry of his own, begging the dragons to find him.

Neba felt the pitiful howl the moxal set up right down to his toes. He'd known the poor thing was alone, but the depth of the longing wounded Neba's heart. Raising the deia again, he blew, this time with more force. Again and again he blew. Finally, his was the only 'dragon cry' in the clearing.

Moxal stared in confusion at the two-legged creature. He'd just been sharing space with it and it was certainly no dragon. No scales, no tail, and a face so flat he must've fallen on it and smashed it in. On the other hand—he sidled closer—it was the same creature who'd been nearby when he heard a mother dragon cry a few days before.

Neba changed the fingering and blew again. The moxal's ears pricked. However, despite Neba's best efforts, the dragon refused to come any closer. Likewise, when Neba thought to go to him, he dropped into a crouch and bared his teeth, growling as menacingly as a goat-sized dragon can.

"Come on," Neba coaxed, wishing he'd held back a few musker fruit. "We can start with something easy, like learning how to retract your claws. It won't take long, I promise." A few minutes later, he dropped back onto the log, scowling at the stubborn dragon. "Fine. Stay over there." He tossed the deia onto his bedroll and folded his arms across his chest. "I should let you scrounge for your own supper, too." His heart softened instantly at the sound of another, much more fearsome growling. That of an empty dragon belly. He seemed to notice the dullness of the scales afresh, a sure sign of malnutrition or illness in a dragon.

"Alright," he sighed. "You win. Just don't follow too closely." He took up his bow and arrows. "You'll scare off the game."

He spent the next few hours stalking the moxal's supper. Much to his surprise, the dragon *did* follow him. And a lot more stealthily than he'd expected. Apparently he'd learned some things the hard way.

They lucked into a medium-sized buck on the far side of the clearing. Claiming the hide and a single steak for himself, Neba headed back to camp, thinking hard. He'd seen tracks further up the stream of a much larger hooved animal. A schelch, he thought. He hoped he was right. Daily hunting to fill the belly of this silly moxal would drive the game away. If they could get a single, large kill, then they could start working in earnest.

Chapter 9

The sound of snoring roused Neba from his own deep sleep early the next morning. Clearly the dragon had found its way back to camp last night. He grinned a little, reminded of waking up to Leuna's rather more delicate snoring. Something he'd never forget was how adorable she looked when she'd just woken up. The sleepy expression on her face, the mussed hair, the shawl wrapped haphazardly about her shoulders… He'd only seen her that way the one morning that they'd both been startled awake by the commotion outside her house, but the picture remained indelibly impressed on his mind. The cheery song of a morning bird called for him to get up and was answered by half a dozen other birds, interrupting his reverie.

Rolling out of his blankets, Neba munched on biscuits from last night's supper while he put together a small pack. The smell of smoke and human would do a lot to discourage the average scavenger from bothering his supplies while they were gone, providing they weren't gone too long. Taking up his bow and quiver from where they waited just inside the tarp, he tied the flaps closed and slipped off into the forest.

The birds didn't cease their singing when he passed silently beneath their nests, his woodcraft having improved immensely under Jartz' short tutelage. He stopped occasionally to listen, as much to acquaint himself with the noises of the forest as to check for any unexpected or out of place sounds. He also savored the fresh smell of morning. The logale flowers, refreshed from their night of rest, were unfurling their vivid yellow petals, sharing their fragrance with the world. Dozens of smaller animals rushed about, collecting nuts and berries. Their industry reassured Neba that he was alone, for the warier forest creatures always stilled as he passed by, a foreigner in this wooded realm.

The temperature dropped a few degrees as he neared the stream. Easing the pack off his shoulders, he leaned it carefully against a tree. The breeze was coming from behind him, so he angled off to his right. If his prey was there this morning, the last thing he wanted was for them to scent him. He heard the water chuckling softly along before he finally came into view of it. Taking great care where he placed his feet, so as to not create the slightest sound, he came to the bare edge of the forest and stopped dead. Lowering himself into a crouch, he observed his quarry.

A small herd of majestic schelch grazed on the lush grass by the stream, their frost-white fur glistening in the morning sun. The does were as tall as Neba, with the clean lines and compact muscles of runners. Two long-legged offspring gamboled about their legs, oblivious to the dangers for which the canny old bull frequently tested the air. Even as he lowered his head to crop a few bites of grass, his eyes roved the area, wary of predators. Only Neba's stillness and caution prevented his detection and probable annihilation under a flurry of pounding hooves.

As Neba saw it, there were three potential outcomes.

Ideally, he got a kill shot on his first try and the bull dropped where he stood while the others fled to safety in the meadows across the stream. Less ideally, he wounded the majestic fellow and they all got away together. The third and least appealing scenario also involved wounding the bull, which then chose to attack him instead of escaping with the others. The slender saplings that formed the edge of the forest here would provide no protection whatsoever. He would have to be ready to move—quickly—into the thick of the forest or suffer the well-deserved fate of making a mistake in the wild.

Sliding two arrows from his quiver, Neba straightened slowly. While his blood resumed its normal flow and coursed through the veins in his legs, he inspected his arrows carefully for incidental damage to the fletching. The high-grade steel blades that tapered back from the tip of the arrowhead were razor sharp and hopefully, up to the job at hand. Holding one arrow in his left hand, he fitted the other to the bowstring.

Inhaling and exhaling evenly, he drew the string back, aiming just behind the bull's shoulder, where he knew the heart and lungs were located. Time slowed as the bull lowered its head for a bite. The second arrow followed the first as quickly as he could loose it.

The bull stumbled forward a half a dozen steps, his sides laboring as he tried to draw breath. His knees folded and a terrible gasping sound filled the clearing. The does were long gone, racing away as rapidly as they could herd their young along once they scented blood.

"I'm sorry." Neba stepped forward and made eye contact with the schelch, magnificent even in death. "I need what you have, or I never would've harmed you."

The schelch's head tipped ponderously to one side, then seemed to dip forward as if in acknowledgement of Neba's words. Releasing a final, shuddering breath, his suffering ended.

Not until Neba stood by the carcass, knife in hand, did it occur to him to wonder if he would know what to do next. Knowing he must do something, he reached out tentatively with one foot to nudge the beast. Should he roll it over? But no, he found himself clambering aboard the broad back and moving toward the nape of its neck. In short order he had slit the hide from neck to tail and peeled it so that it lay flat on either side of the animal.

Using the hide to set the meat on, he worked quickly and reflexively, removing choice cuts from around and under the spine for his own consumption. He rinsed and stored the bulk of the meat using lehorra bags, named for the plants whose fibers were used in a tight weave to make a perfectly waterproof material. Lowering the bags into the icy water, he secured them to a broad stump that must once have anchored a forest monarch on the edge of the stream.

It was a great relief to finally wade into the edge of the cold stream and wash the blood off. Taking a few deep breaths, he submerged himself, letting the cold water take the heat from his tired shoulder and back muscles. It was amusing to bat at the curious fish for a moment, watching them hastily retreat, only to come back almost immediately. He was about to surface when something caught his eye. A glimmer of something buried in the silt at the bottom of the stream bed.

A few powerful kicks carried him easily over to the site and he stared curiously down at the small rocks that had caught his attention. Unbidden, his hand reached to pick one up. Then another, and another, until he was scrabbling in the muck to dig out all he could find. Only when he was sure he had them all did he surface and suck in huge gulps of fresh air, his lungs aching from the delay.

Opening his hands enough to see the rocks he held, a vague sense of disappointment struck him. They were common ash stones, washed downstream from some distant volcano. Pouring them from one hand to the other, he stirred them with his finger. There were gray, black, and even a few dark red stones, all of them riddled with tiny holes and flecked with worthless crystals. He held one up to the sun, watching it glitter in the sunlight.

The thought that there were surely more such stones in the stream bed seized him and he had to exert all his self-control to keep from diving back in to investigate. Stiff with cold, he waded ashore, stumbling as he navigated the uneven terrain. Carefully, he set the stones on the largest rock of his campfire ring. Shoving his wet hair out of his face, he sat down in the sun to think. It was urgent that he set about preserving the schelch meat, but he couldn't get the ash stones out of his mind.

He thought about them even as he loosely lashed the tops of three saplings together, swiftly stringing them with the thin rope he'd brought along until it looked like an addled spider had been at work. With a green wood fire underneath them and spreading boughs high above to thin the smoke, he sharpened his knife and sliced up the leaner meat, setting the strips on the rope to dry.

Only after completing the entire process a second time did he kindle another, smaller fire with fine, dry wood, and set a steak to roasting for his lunch. The familiar tasks had at last settled his mind, leaving him free to focus on what must be done. He was still concerned by his reaction to the stones; he simply had other things to do.

"Now for the fun part." He began by forcing a few rib bones free for later use in working the hide. With the help of some convenient rocks and a great deal of effort, he was able to prop the considerably lighter carcass up off the ground. Kneeling beside it, he separated the rest of the hide from the body and dragged it free. Hauling it into the stream, he stretched it out hair-side down and weighted it with large rocks. Tiny hortz fish instantly darted in and began nibbling at the fat and meat.

He was just—finally—sitting down to consume his lunch when the dragon bolted out of the forest and gleefully flung himself on the schelch carcass.

"Eat hearty." Neba leaned back against a small tree and cut his steak. "Once we've got basic dragon etiquette down, you're going to have to earn your food." He frowned at the dragon, who was hissing and snapping at him from a safe distance atop the shoulders. Between bites, anyway. "You've all the manners of a hatchling. Mark my word, you silly moxal, you're going to learn to behave!" He paused. "As long as I'm going to be working with you, you'd better have a name of some sort. Just so you know when I'm talking to you, that sort of thing."

His eyes traveled over the scrawny dragon, noting that his rib cage wasn't quite as visible today as it had been the first time they'd met. The broad chest, long tail, and clean lines told Neba that, with proper care, this dragon would grow into a fine mount. Only time would tell if the foolish behavior could be corrected and how quickly he learned.

"Moxal." He tested the word as a name and shook his head. "That won't do, you won't be a baby much longer." Lifting the deia from where it hung on his belt, he blew a warning signal. "You're eating too rapidly. You'll make yourself sick."

Rising, Neba shooed him away from the carcass, issuing commanding blasts on the deia each time the dragon snapped at him. Finally, his tail lashing violently, the dragon retreated to a sunny patch and crouched there.

"That wasn't too terrible," Neba laughed. Picking up a partially gnawed leg bone, he tossed it over and the dragon pounced on it. "A few minutes in the sun with a full belly and you'll be fast asleep." He stroked his chin thoughtfully. "Maybe I could call you Sleepy. Or Terrible." Still chuckling, Neba added fuel to the smoke fires and finished his lunch.

The sound of snoring drew his eyes to where the dragon lay passed out, leg bone between his teeth, swollen belly protruding slightly.

"Feels good to be full for a change, doesn't it? Guess I can't call you Hungry, either." He eyed the unresponsive beast. There was still plenty of meat on the carcass, enough for the dragon to eat his fill again and again. "Finding a name for you is going to be a real problem."

The world tilted suddenly and he felt himself sliding off its edge. The air became stifling hot, so hot he began to sweat all over. Rough board planks were under his hands and he could just barely see over the top of one of them into a roomy cave. A grand female dragon was spread across the floor, an indulgent expression on her face as four newly hatched dragons scampered around and over her. One of the babies was larger than the others, dull red in color with gold stripes crisscrossing his back. Tiny tufts of soft gold feathers protruded from behind his ears. Neba couldn't seem to take his eyes off it.

The name must suit the dragon, a voice said. He tried to turn his head, to see who was speaking, but he couldn't move.

"Bikain." The whispered name jolted Neba free from the memory—for what else could it be?—and he shivered. *Bikain…majestic.* The red and gold baby dragon had been his. Though Neba hadn't actually left the bank of the stream, it actually seemed cold now. Abandoning thoughts of working on the hide, he curled up by the fire, needing its warmth as well as the sun's rays to chase away the chill.

He must've slept, for he dreamed. Disjointed images, mostly dragons, played before his mind's eye. Something kept pushing him along before he could really look at any of them. Somehow, he knew they weren't paintings or carvings despite how still they were. So many of them! Small dragons, big dragons, young, old, and…dead. Why were they dead? His own cries roused him and he lay, panting, by the smoldering coals of the fire.

Something pressed against his shoulder and he recoiled, nearly rolling over the fire pit in the process. A soft whuffling sound was followed by another nudge. He relaxed. The fire popped and hissed, sending sparks up into the air.

"Sparks." Neba managed a weak smile. "Just like this fire began with sparks, dragons may be the sparks my memories need." His thoughts returning to the dragon beside him, his smile broadened. "That's your new name, fella. Sparks." The dragon thrust his head over his shoulder as though in response.

"Thank you." Neba reached up and stroked the dragon's soft nose, then scratched under his chin, using only his fingertips. Sparks put a paw on Neba's hip so he could stretch his neck out farther and Neba took the hint, running his palm vigorously up and down the sleek column. Sitting up carefully, he smiled when Sparks stormed onto his lap, demanding more attention.

"You really have been lonely, haven't you, fella?" Neba indulged him for a few more minutes, even knuckling the area at the top of his shoulder where a parent dragon would nuzzle him. When he was as relaxed as he was going to get, Neba set his own curved fingers on top of the nearest paw and dug them into it, just hard enough to prompt a muscular reaction that would retract the claws.

Sparks sprang to his feet, holding that paw up off the ground and sniffing at it. Neba watched him cock his head to one side before testing his weight on it. Then he looked back and forth between his front paws, one with the claws out and one with the claws in. Neba chuffed encouragingly, which drew the dragon's eyes to him. Abruptly, the claws on all three of his remaining paws retracted.

Neba's eyebrows jumped to his hairline. "Well. Aren't you the clever one." He watched a little uneasily as Sparks stalked, stiff-legged, back and forth in front of him, arching his back and tossing his head. His claws extended and withdrew repeatedly. Then, abruptly, he shook himself and began prancing in place, wriggling all over with joy. Neba threw back his head and laughed, relieved.

"Glad you've decided to stick around." He reached out to rub Sparks' head. "You've got a *lot* more to learn than how to retract your claws." Rising, he forced still-shaky hands to obey him as he stoked the smoke fires again before retrieving a steak from one of the lehorra bags in the stream. Sparks glared at him as if he'd stolen it, then launched himself at the carcass with a great deal of growling and ferocity.

"Relax, my friend." Neba checked the sun's position in the sky. "Eat your fill, but no more. Your days of hunger are over for now." Stirring up the cook fire and adding fuel, he fried the steak to his liking and ate it out of the pan. Flexing his hands, he assessed his physical condition. The strange dream and memory left him feeling like a freshly washed dishrag, drug up and down a washboard and wrung within an inch of its life. The food helped, naturally. However, he wasn't sure what to do next. If he slept, he might dream again. If he didn't, what was there to do besides think? It would be dark in an hour.

A large poggybird perched on a limb at the edge of the woods and screamed at Sparks for not sharing the carcass. It was several minutes before he fluffed his feathers and flew off in a fine snit, still protesting. Occasionally bits of tree drifted past the camp, carried along by the stream's current, most likely coming from the small colony of beavers Neba'd spotted upstream.

Reluctantly, he dug the journal Leuna had given him out of his bag. He'd brought it along to keep track of Sparks, or so he'd told himself. Now he filled half a page with an account of the dragon cave. He even attempted to draw the images he'd seen, giving up only when he discovered a talent for drawing that allowed him to recreate them in all their horrible detail. Stuffing the journal back into the bag as if he could magically trap the images there, preventing them from tormenting his mind, he ran his fingers through his hair.

Tomorrow would come no matter what he did, so

he decided to at least try to sleep. Sighing, he stretched out on the sweet-smelling grass between the two drying racks. The smoke would keep the worst of the night insects away and anyway, they didn't seem to bother him the way they did Jartz.

After a few deep breaths, he slept. Twice he awakened, once to add sticks to the fires and once to find a sleepy little dragon curled up by his hip. He reached down to gently scratch the top of Sparks' head and he mewed in his sleep. Sparks must not have been as tired as Neba, though, for he was the first to wake in the morning.

"No." Neba tried to sit up, but the dragon had a forepaw on each of his shoulders. "Sparks, no!" Twisting and turning his face to avoid the inquisitive sniffling and licking, Neba took him by the middle and tossed him aside. As he'd expected, Sparks landed on his feet, wheeled to face him, and began scolding him in high-pitched squeals.

His searching fingers closed around the deia and Neba blew a piercing cry. Sparks froze, dropped on his belly, and pulled in his neck so that his ears were touching his shoulders.

"That's right," Neba confirmed. "I'm the aitak, the dominant member of this kabi. And if it wasn't almost sunrise," he sat up quickly and winced, "I'd be even more upset." Judging by the way his back was complaining, it had been quite a while since he'd butchered a large animal. Rolling to his knees, he arched and popped his back.

"Better! Now, let's teach you about open spaces." He liked the way the dragon's ears twitched when he spoke. It was a sure sign of intelligence. Opening his mouth wide, he exhaled a deep chuff of welcome to let him know they were friends again.

Instantly, Sparks was on his feet, wriggling and prancing in place. As soon as Neba got to his own feet, Sparks darted toward the carcass, only to drop to his belly again when the same dragon cry sounded.

"We don't rush across open ground," Neba informed him, bending down to stroke his ears. "First," he dropped to one knee and gestured with his free hand, "we look to the right." He surveyed the surrounding area for as far as he could see. "Then, we look to the left." He repeated the process to the other side, glad to see the dragon studying his face and looking where he did. "And last of all, we look up. If it's safe," he rose, "that's when we move." A soft chuff and hand wave sent the dragon scurrying toward the carcass. He was making good progress on the carcass, including sharpening his teeth on some of the larger bones. "Not that you'll need to worry about predators from above for much longer."

"Anyway." Neba picked up his bow and arrows. "Behave yourself while I take a look around, alright? I'll be back in a bit." He was pleased to see Sparks taking his time and chewing instead of gulping down one bite after another.

His back relaxed as he moved through the forest, scouting for half a mile around the camp site on both sides of the stream. Finding a high spot on the far side, he crouched down and waited. Eyes and ears open, he observed. The land remained mostly empty, the smell of smoke from his drying racks warning the skittish wild game off. Thankfully, he couldn't actually see the smoke from this distance.

A small red bird perched in a bush a few feet away and scolded him briefly. When he didn't respond, it cocked its head to one side, studied him, then took off. His patience yielding nothing useful, Neba rose. Flexing his leg muscles, he continued studying the area around him for as far as he could see. Once feeling had been restored to his numb feet, he finished his circuit and returned to camp, gathering wood for the insatiable fires on his way back, still careful to leave as little sign of his passing as possible.

"Did you miss me?" he called when he reached camp. Sparks cocked his head at him, swallowed his mouthful of meat and resumed eating. Neba laughed out loud and went to add some of the fuel he'd gathered to the smoke fires.

As he tested the meat on the lower rungs, the vivid images from yesterday's dream returned to haunt him. What bothered him the most was that so many of the dead dragons had been in such gruesome poses. Violent deaths all, heavy arrows protruding from some, others permanently contorted from the pains of poison. If those *were* memories, *his* memories, then what was he? He didn't want to believe that he'd had anything to do with the…*carnage*.

He came to his feet, strode over to the schelch carcass. Walking rapidly around it, he glanced into the stream, reassuring himself that the bags of fresh meat were there. Pacing back and forth in front of the carcass, he compared what he saw before him with the images. He'd stripped the schelch of its hide and all the meat he could reasonably expect to preserve and consume before it spoiled. Sparks would take care of the rest, including a goodly portion of the bones.

The dragons in his mind's eye, however, were in various stages of decomposition. Killed and left to rot. Except… He focused on an individual image. Then another. Where were the enormous bull dragon's tusks? The teeth of the swift and deadly ebaki? On the velour dragons, only their wide bellies were skinned, exposing the untouched muscles beneath. In fact, the more he thought about it, the only attempt at harvesting the meat had been with the sapid dragons, small, plump beasts known in some areas as being delicious. He fought down the bile rising in his throat. If he understood his memory correctly, there'd been an entire kabi of plump sapid dragons, a perfectly harmless species, destroyed for a few steaks. For they hadn't taken the time to harvest the entire animal…just the best, the most *expensive* parts. And by 'they,' he meant poachers. The scum of his known world.

Chapter 10

The next few days passed peacefully. Sparks ate and slept and grew while Neba tended the drying racks and worked on the schelch hide. He was able to tease the dragon into wrestling almost daily, which was how baby dragons learned the basics of combat in the wild.

"Good thing you're such a runt." Neba threw himself on the grass to rest after one of their bouts. Sparks was *quick*. "Otherwise you'd already be getting the best of me." He rolled onto his side, bracing himself on his elbow. "Runt. How's that for a nickname?" He laughed as Sparks charged the schelch carcass, startling the birds who'd been sidling up to it while they played.

"You'll grow out of that, too," he admitted, "but we won't need it for very long. You'll be back up on the crags before bruma and I'll be…" He hesitated. He'd be what? Back at Herrixka with Leuna? In Gertuk, trying to trace down whatever leads Jartz hopefully uncovered?

His memories were all about dragons so far. He could now recall an entire stable full of live, healthy dragons—including the red and gold one from before. He sensed happiness each time he mentally walked through the stable from his memories, so he supposed dragons had always been an important part of his life. And yet, it puzzled him that there was nothing else.

"I'm going after more firewood," he told Sparks, who was waiting for the birds to return so he could chase them again. Neba chuckled to himself and wondered how he was going to teach him that his playfully-lashing tail was clearly visible above the rocks where he was lying in wait.

The cold stream water refreshed him as he waded through it, and he allowed his mind to wander a little. Surely he had parents. Perhaps even siblings. Possibly a wife and children of his own...his thoughts strayed to Leuna's tempting lips and he had to haul them back. He bent to gather some wrist-thick branches, loading them into his arms. How was it that he couldn't remember *anything* besides dragons?

He made a second trip across the stream for firewood, then set a pot to boil with a slice of musker fruit and a few crushed phyla leaves. His pant legs and boots dried in the sun while he baited a line with some grubs from the wood he'd gathered and caught fresh fish for breakfast.

"Jartz said it's a five day walk from Herrixka to Gertuk," he told Sparks while he prepared the fish. "Add a day for the walk from the clearing. Maybe another day to gather his gear and pelts. He probably won't even arrive in Gertuk until today." He set the fillets in the pan and sprinkled salt over them. "So that's what, a little over two weeks? Thirteen days, give or take, just to get from here to there and back again." *And how much longer to hear anything useful?*

Shaking off his melancholy, he drizzled a fine line of musker juice over the fillets. He'd rather have used vinegar, as it was less tart, but he'd make do until Sparks had finished with the carcass. His mouth watered slightly at the thought of all the tasty ingredients waiting for him back in the clearing.

While he ate, he found his gaze straying to the woods where he'd just been. Vivid yellow leaves adorned the horia trees that grew nearest the bank, while the crimson leaves of the taller odol trees lit the forest canopy afire. Flashes of blue and purple accompanied the whistles and trills of the local songbirds, with an occasional glimpse of the shy white txori, who had the sweetest voice of all.

Leaning back against the tree, Neba sipped his musker juice while the breeze off the stream ran its fingers through the grass and giggled through the trees. The more he relaxed, the more a concrete need began to form in him. Without knowing exactly what he was about, he set down his cup and got to his feet. Crossing the stream again, he wandered into the woods and leaned against an old father, its rough bark digging into his shoulder as he studied the scene before him.

To one side, a narrow game trail led deeper into the forest, most likely the trail that the deer used when they came to drink from the stream. An old, sprawling raspberry bush had untxi fur on its lower thorns, as well as being bereft of its berries for the lowest third of its branches. Looking further to his left, Neba felt himself drawn toward the bare bones of an old, fallen tree. Time and nature had stripped it of its leaves and most of its bark. Only half its branches remained intact and these inexplicably drew his interest.

Running his hands over the branches, he selected a straight one about two fingers thick and used his belt knife to weaken its base so that it snapped off when he pulled on it. It stood taller than he was, tapering off at one end. A great feeling of impatience swept over him now and he jogged toward his camp. Scoring the branch at just above chin-height, he broke off what would've been the leaf-end and added that to the fire. Settling himself cross-legged, he took another sip of the musker juice.

He spent the better part of an hour removing the bark, smoothing the shaft, and rounding out the ends. But when he was done with that, he was puzzled. How badly did he need a walking staff that it had drawn him away from the unpleasant thoughts plaguing him before? Rising, he hefted it, balanced it. Twirled it around his fist. And thrust one end out in front of him.

His muscles continued moving him, one step at a time, through what he realized must be a drill, something a warrior might do. Strike, parry, dodge, roll. Front jab, overhead block, two steps to the right. The drills kept coming until he began to sweat from the exertion.

He seemed to hear other feet stamping the ground besides his own, the breathing and grunts of a dozen or perhaps a hundred others moving around him, ghosts of his forgotten past going through the drills alongside him. At first, his thoughts whirled with him. By the time he struck down his final imaginary opponent, however, his mind had cleared and a conviction coursed through his swiftly moving blood that he was no slaughterer of dragons.

"I am Jerl Karruan," he told Sparks proudly. "Dragon Soldier of the first order. Just mustered out because..." His smile faltered. "Because..." He shrugged. "Well, never mind why just now. The important thing is, I have plenty of time to train you." Sparks showed his intense excitement by sniffing hopefully at the bones of the carcass, which was all that was left. Setting the quarterstaff aside, Jerl reached for his bow instead.

"I'll be back shortly," he promised. Indeed, he did not have to go far in the nearly untouched woods to find what he was after and fetch it to the stream bank. Blowing on the deia, he announced his triumphant return. Sparks leapt up from where he was dozing in the sun and pranced over to see what was going on.

Jerl chuffed at him softly, then lifted an untxi from his game bag. Holding it where Sparks could see and smell it, he watched his reaction intently. Sparks shoved his nose in close, snuffling rapidly and with obvious interest. But when Jerl set it on the ground before him, Sparks pranced a few steps backward and looked up at him with a quizzical expression on his face.

"I suppose you never managed to catch one of these for yourself, did you? Too fast afoot for an untrained hatchling. Well, let's see how quickly you learn this." Jerl squatted beside the untxi, knife in hand. He let Sparks examine the knife briefly, then made a straight cut down the untxi's belly.

Instantly, Sparks began crying for the meat he could smell. He whined and looked at Jerl as though asking for permission. Jerl chuffed again and Sparks pounced. His ignorance was plain to be seen as he ate only the exposed flesh before beginning to paw anxiously at the carcass.

Jerl blew a soft note on the deia, then held out his hand with his knife blade protruding from between his fingers. Sparks approached slowly, nose first, and then looked down at his front paws. All eight of his claws extended at the same time and he turned back to the untxi. Pleased, Jerl watched as he discovered the rest of the flesh and devoured it with gusto.

"Nice snack, eh?" he chuckled at the dragon. "Not nearly enough to fill your ever-growing belly. Here," he lifted a medium-sized antzara bird from his game bag. "Get a whiff of this." Sparks repeated his performance from before, snuffling and whining and clearly having no idea what to do with it. "Another animal that I imagine eluded you, assuming you even realized you could eat it. Here." Holding the bird down with one hand, he plucked feathers from its breast to reveal the meat beneath, then shifted out of the way. "Afraid you'll have to use your teeth, m'lad."

It took Sparks considerably more time to consume the antzara, which was about twice the weight of an untxi. From where he sat, cleaning and dressing his own bird, Jerl couldn't help laughing a little each time Sparks sneezed feathers.

"Don't worry," he consoled the dragon. "You'll get better at it with practice." Sparks somehow managed to sneeze once more—and with great finality—then buried the bill and feet before trotting over to nap in the sun.

Ravenous after his drills and elated at his returned memories, Jerl roasted antzara and wild potatoes on the same spit. The fire flared up now and again as the grease from the bird dripped into it. He worked at sacking up the smoked meat while his lunch was cooking, ate heartily, then followed Sparks' example, sprawling on the grass to nap.

He would've slept right through the supper hour, had Sparks not begun pawing at him. Smiling, he rubbed the sleep from his eyes and went to the bags he'd been keeping in the stream. They were considerably lighter now, as he'd been adding to the drying racks from time to time.

"Here you go." He handed a twenty-something pound piece to Sparks, who sat down and began eating it right there. "Too bad there aren't any bighorn roaming the lowlands. They should be pretty common up on the crags, and it'll take a little know-how for a fireless dragon to capture one." He scratched the back of his neck. "Although…you are at least three fists taller than when I first met you. I was already planning to measure you when we got back to the clearing," he hung the empty bag up to dry, "but now I'm starting to wonder if I guessed your age wrong."

For his own supper, Jerl ate leftover bird from his lunch. With the last of the day's light, he pulled out the journal. There were no mirrors handy, so he polished his hunting knife on his pant leg and leaned it against his bag. It was crude, but effective. In short order, he'd transferred the image he saw in his blade to the page. He waited, pencil hovering to the side of the drawing of his face, for another image to surface in his mind. Any image would've done, even a face he didn't recognize. Slowly, he added a quarterstaff to the picture. Only…it wasn't a quarterstaff. It was too tall, too narrow. And what was that forming at the top?

His hand began to shake as he drew the outline of a flag at the top of the pole. He pressed down so hard in his effort to stop the shaking that the pencil tip snapped right off when he tried to draw the symbol that should be centered in the flag. He rose suddenly, letting the journal slip off his lap and into the grass. But where was he going? Leuna's medical case was safely stored under the tarp at the clearing. Pressing his fists against his head, he struggled to breathe.

Noticing his distress, Sparks cowered even as he crept closer. Desperately wishing to help, he tentatively nosed Jerl's elbow. And nearly bolted when Jerl dropped to his knees beside him.

"It hurts." Beyond reason, Jerl looked pleadingly at the dragon. "My head *hurts*."

Sparks, regaining his nerve, shoved his head into Jerl's chest and held it there. Succumbing to the pain, Jerl allowed himself to be pushed onto his side. Sparks curled up almost on top of him, his tail draped over Jerl's legs while he licked his face, which tasted strangely salty. They remained there for hours, Jerl unable to move and Sparks unwilling to. The small dragon growled menacingly at any forest animal that dared come to the edge of the forest, and at quite a few harmless shadows as well. The setting sun soon left them wholly in shadow, and Sparks' head drooped wearily. But he never slept.

"Here now." Jerl reached up to stroke his head. It would have been an exaggeration to say it was dawn already, yet the stars were slowly fading from view. "Have you been up all night? Protecting me?" Sparks' yawn was his only reply. "You'll make a fine aitak someday when you've finished growing up. Yes, perhaps even with a kabi of your own." Sparks mewed sleepily and nuzzled his shoulder, uninterested in the distant future—even if it did feature him as the overseer dragon of his own extended family. His sleek, lustrous scales and almost pudgy body were a pleasant change from the scrawny, dull creature who'd been raiding Jartz' trapline.

Jerl lay there a while longer, scratching at Sparks' favorite spots and watching the sky grow light. He supposed he might have felt worse before. He was glad he couldn't remember, though, for what was worse than aching as if he'd been trampled by a schelch?

"I think it's time to go back to the clearing," he decided aloud. "If remembering things leaves me weak as a motherless kaleko, I'd just as soon be a bit closer to help."

After giving Sparks the last chunks of schelch meat from a bag in the stream, Jerl spent the morning gathering up the rest of the smoked meat to be carried back to the clearing. He'd be carrying well over a hundred pounds of meat back in its dried form, which was considerably lighter than the raw meat waiting in the lehorra bags. For now, though, he was so hungry that he snacked on it while he worked, which had an oddly familiar feeling to it. The saplings sprang back into position when he released them from the twine, some of their branches seeming to wag chastisingly at him as he rolled the twine into a ball again.

He'd no sooner straightened from tucking the twine away in his pack than Sparks, who'd been stalking him semi-patiently, pounced.

"Ooof!" Since his claws were already retracted, Jerl indulged him in a short tussle, the sort of thing Sparks should've been doing daily with his parents. Catching him by the wings, Jerl held on long enough for him to realize they weren't always an advantage in a fight. Releasing them, he nodded in satisfaction when Sparks tucked them flat against his body. Too late, he recognized the stance of lowered head and bent knees.

Again the wind was knocked from him as Sparks drove his head into Jerl's conveniently-located stomach. His momentum carried them both along so that Jerl landed on his back in a pile of schelch hair left over from scraping the hide. With a *poof* of joy, the hairs surged up into the air and drifted down on top of them.

Sparks, not liking it at all, leapt away and bounded across the clearing. He growled at each clump as it fell off him, then sniffed at one, sneezed, and plunged into the stream to clean himself off.

Spitting and swiping at his face, Jerl looked over at where Sparks was splashing away. Wearily, he rose and followed suit, wading into the water.

"Well done," he mock-complimented Sparks,

who by now was sunning himself on a large boulder. "You'll have to remember that move." Supremely disinterested, Sparks spread his wings and wrapped his short tail as far as it would go around the boulder. Jerl's eyes narrowed. That tail wasn't nearly as short as it had been a few days ago. Just how much had Sparks grown?

Shivering even in the late morning sun, he stirred up the fire and started cooking a light meal of wild greens, wild onions, and nuts from a nearby tree. He added a thin slice of musker fruit for flavor, but plucked it out as soon as it began to shrivel in the heat.

"Hey." He looked at Sparks in surprise. "This isn't bad." Leaning back against a tree, he lifted another forkful and let it cool. "Maybe I worked as a chef before joining the Dragon Soldiers." He chewed thoughtfully. "No, that doesn't seem right. Cooking feels more…personal. Somehow."

Filling the pot once more, he thoroughly doused all four fire rings, then gathered the rocks and tossed them into the stream. The shriveled leaves on the inner branches was the only trace of his passing that remained by the time he'd finished, and they would be replaced by new growth soon enough.

"Don't suppose you'd like to help carry?" He grinned at Sparks, who was drinking from the stream and keeping an eye on him at all times. The schelch hide alone was over fifteen pounds. The dried meat weighed considerably more. "Good thing I didn't bring anything else along," he grunted as he swung his pack into place. "I'll be lucky not to get hung up on a tree branch as it is." Bow in hand, he scanned the campsite a final time. And saw the ash stones.

He couldn't take his eyes off them. It was Sparks' whine that snapped him out of his trance. Bending at the knees, he scooped up all of the ash stones, holding them tightly in his hand as he headed back to the clearing. He still didn't know why they were so important to him. He only knew he couldn't leave them behind.

Chapter 11

"I'll bet that tastes good for a change," Jerl laughed as he watched Sparks bound into the clearing and begin gleefully gobbling up the ripe musker fruit that had fallen in their absence. "I should warn you." He shifted the pack to the ground by the tarp and stretched his back. "Tomorrow, training begins in earnest."

He made short work of stowing his gear, then strode off in a new direction to gather firewood. The birds scolded him as he went, warning him to stay away from their young. And their young, who had spent the summer learning to fly and be independent, scolded him because everyone else was. A plume-tailed scuriday leapt between branches above Jerl's head, risking her life for sheer curiosity. She'd never seen anything like him. She stared right back at him, green tail twitching anxiously, when he paused to look up at her.

He didn't mind her curiosity. Scuridays were excellent barometers. She would know before anyone else in the forest if the weather was going to be bad. Plucking several sugarberries from a convenient bush, he left them on a branch in the tree where she was pretending to hide. Hopefully, she'd stick around.

Finally satisfied that he had enough firewood to last for the next few days, he noticed the lengthening shadows. His eyes adapted automatically as the light about him dimmed, allowing him to see quite clearly so long as even a little light remained. He was almost relieved to find that it was growing late, given how tired he felt.

He was shaking out his blankets when he realized he had no idea where Sparks was. Casually, he glanced around the clearing. A long, blue tail stuck up through the undergrowth between the trees and Jerl had all he could do not to laugh out loud.

Patiently, he took his time laying out his blankets while Sparks stalked him. At the last second, as Sparks lunged with a roar, Jerl sidestepped, flinging the blankets into Sparks' face. Startled, confused, and effectively blinded, Sparks howled as he raced off into the forest.

Jerl watched his blankets disappear into the shadows with him. "That…didn't go quite as expected." Sighing, he took off after Sparks, following his trail of broken bushes and paw prints easily. Whistling for him on the deia brought no response, so Jerl kept going, his stomach growling at him because he'd forgotten to bring even a handful of jerky along.

"How in the world…" Jerl stared in awe at the lehorra cloth he used as a ground cloth. Try as he might, he couldn't quite grasp the corner that beckoned him from where it hung on a tree limb. He was getting ready to climb the tree when he spotted a broken branch at least as long as his arm. Carefully, he used that to extend his reach and wound it in the cloth until he'd taken up most of the slack. A gentle flick of his wrist lifted it free from where it had snagged and it floated down to him.

"Well, at least it's not damaged," he muttered to

himself as he examined it. He couldn't say the same for the blankets when he found them. Groaning, he tugged them out from the hole where Sparks had tried to bury them. He could put his head through several of the neatly-sliced holes Sparks' claws left in self-defense. "He's never going to trust me again."

Shaking his head, he wound them up together and stuffed them under his arm. Tired from the long walk hauling everything back to the clearing, he hesitated between two ideas. His devotion to Sparks won out, and he lifted the deia, playing a series of coaxing little trills.

"C'mon, fella," he called. "Fresh fish for supper tonight." He took a few more steps down the trail, then stopped. Sparks had apparently overcome his fright almost immediately after divesting himself of the blankets, for the trail disappeared on the far side of a huge old tree. The darkening shadows suddenly felt a tad more menacing. Resolutely, he walked to the end of the trail.

"You won." He held up the bedraggled roll of blankets. "They surrender!" Somewhere in the distance, a tree frog chirped that the weather was fine. "Are you coming?"

The ground to his left came alive with screeches and strangely percussive calls as a colony of ground birds poked their heads out of their burrows to scold him for waking them early. He nearly jumped out of his socks in his hurry to leave the area. Apparently not content with his efforts, several of the birds harried him along, swooping silently over his shoulders and grabbing at his hair with their claws as they spread out to do their night's hunting.

Finally, he dropped and rolled, hunkering down at the base of a huge old tree until the last of them glided past. Shifting into a more comfortable position, he ran his fingers through his hair. Somehow, against all odds, he'd held onto what was left of his blankets during his mad dash, and he put them behind his head now.

"What a day." Wiping sweat from his upper lip, he relaxed there, considering his options. The sun was nearly set, but that wouldn't bother the fish. If they were hungry, they would bite. On the other hand, *he* was starving. And Sparks? He was full of musker fruit and probably somewhere near the clearing. Where was the clearing, anyway?

Rising, Jerl looked around doubtfully. Sparks' trail had woven through the forest at random for several hundred yards. His own trail, while fleeing the ground birds, was anything but straight. No real beginning or destination, for that matter. Sighing, he squinted up at the canopy, where the thick foliage denied him a view of the sky's constellations

Inhaling and exhaling a deep breath, he began to backtrack himself. He lost his own trail when he came to a rocky patch, and cast a wide loop around it until he found a handful of crushed plants with a heel mark from his boot beside them. He was hesitating at the bramble bush he'd somehow managed to skin through before when he heard the ground birds again.

Walking to one end of the bramble bush, he checked his location against the noise. Ideally, Sparks' path was over… He sighed in relief upon spotting it. Sure, he could've wandered around the forest hoping to bump into a landmark or—if he was extremely lucky—the clearing itself. While backtracking took a little more time, it guaranteed the desired result. Namely, food.

He headed straight for the bags of jerky as soon as he arrived back at the clearing, ate his fill, and curled up under the edge of the tarp. The nights were still pretty warm, so he didn't bother making a fire. His head had no sooner hit the sack of flour than he was fast asleep. His dreams ranged wildly from hunting a very wily piece of jerky to soaring high above the clouds with no visible means of support. They took an even weirder turn when it began raining. The raindrops slid off his face at first. Then they began to bounce off his face. Except for those that stuck to his face?

Coming half-awake, he took a half-hearted swipe at the air, which seemed to encourage whatever was hovering silently around his face. Something landed on his forehead. He could feel the weight. He could also feel it starting to…slide? Opening his eyes while he reached up to touch his forehead, he was shocked to find a bit of fresh musker flesh in his hand. Rubbing at his face, he dislodged half a dozen pieces of musker peel and stared at the ground where they fell. Was he still dreaming?

He looked up. Nothing. Not even a bird perched on the ropes he'd hung between the trees. Slowly he scanned the edge of the clearing. *Thwack!* Something hit him on the back of his head. Leaping to his feet, he whirled to face the direction he thought it had come from.

"Sparks?" Stunned, he stood there while Sparks used his incredibly flexible and dexterous tail to fling twigs and bits of musker—and apparently whatever was available—at him. "Sparks!" He reached for the deia, but couldn't find it. Snatching up his blankets, he shook them out and held them up as a shield between himself and the deluge. Big mistake.

Sparks howled angrily as he recognized them and begun hurling larger objects.

"Ouch!" Jerl dropped the blankets as a whole, green musker fruit, the size of two fists and hard as a rock, caught him on the nose. "Spawks!" He glared at the dragon over the top of his hand as he tried to staunch the flow of blood. "You've made youh point, ok?!" Sparks' well-aimed kick sent the blankets sailing under the tarp, where they were out of sight.

Sniffling and wiping at his nose, Jerl sighed. At least Sparks had stopped.

"Awright." He grimaced at the strange sound of his own voice while he kept pinching his nose. "If youh awe done causing twouble, I think it's time to catch ouw bweakfast."

Sparks followed at a distance, then perched near the stream while Jerl waded in. If he was curious as to why Jerl chose to dunk his head in the chilly water, he gave no sign. In fact, his whole focus seemed to be on finding the perfect spot to bask in the sun. Preferably one that left his back to Jerl.

"Giving me the cold shoulder, eh?" Jerl was shivering, for the sun hadn't yet begun to warm the stream water, but at least his nose had stopped bleeding. "Too bad. You'll miss an important lesson."

The fish were sluggish that morning, also affected by the cold. Careful to stir the water as little as possible, Jerl made his way over to where two or three were dozing in close proximity. Using a two-handed grip, one for the head and one for the tail, he was able to pluck them out of the water and toss them onto the bank without disturbing the others.

Sparks, hearing the fish flopping about on the bank, swung his head around to see what was going on and almost fell off his rock in surprise. Leaping to his feet, he hurried over to the fish and swallowed them whole. Licking his chops, he sniffed around on the bank to make sure he hadn't missed any. And looked up, as if hoping a few more might fall out of the sky for him.

"I guess you didn't fill up on musker fruit last night after all," Jerl observed conversationally. He timed his words with a toss so that Sparks, who'd finally decided to look at him, was able to snap the fish out of the air.

Sparks turned to face him directly now, eyes wide as he studied Jerl.

"Trying to figure out where I got the fish from, are you?" Jerl chuckled. Gliding slowly upstream, he approached a second group of fish. These were fat yellowfin, Sparks' favorite. Working his chilled fingers to be sure he had the dexterity and grip he'd need, Jerl took the plunge.

Three…four…*five* yellowfin landed in Sparks' wide open mouth. He munched them happily and danced in place, eagerly anticipating more free food.

"Alright." Jerl rubbed his hands together and stuck them under his armpits. "Now that you've seen how it's done, let's see if you can do it for yourself. We know your tail is agile enough if you want to do it that way." A pair of medium-sized flat fish waited patiently a few steps upstream and he could already taste them.

Sparks drooped in disappointment as Jerl stepped out onto the opposite bank, flat fish in hand.

"No." Jerl spoke firmly when Sparks began to whine at him. "This is something you have to learn to do for yourself."

By the time he finally got a fire going, Sparks had tentatively entered the stream. His wings and ears were folded tightly back and he was glaring at the water. There were supposed to be fish in there and all he had found so far was slippery rocks.

"Look," Jerl encouraged him. Holding a finger against his own head at eye level, he turned his head to the right and to the left. "Look for the fish." His other hand held the second flat fish, which he was getting ready to clean, and he slowly moved it in front of him in a rough imitation of a swimming movement.

Sparks cocked his head to one side, decided Jerl still wasn't going to give him the fish, and resumed glaring at the water. Abruptly, he lunged forward. And got a mouthful of cold water.

"Alright, hold on." Jerl finished setting his fish to cook. "You're supposed to catch them alive, not scare them to death." Breaking off a longish reed, he held it over the water, pointing at another small group. Signaling for stealth, he waved Sparks forward.

It was always risky to approach from upstream. The silt Jerl stirred up with his two feet might easily spook the fish into swimming away. Sparks, with his four paws, was at a distinct disadvantage. One of the fish, a fat old gent, sensed danger in the water and began swimming toward a rock overhang where he should be safe. The others, too comfortable in the slowly warming water, stayed where they were, ignoring the very same signs. Alas, one was all that it took to spur Sparks into action.

Jumping forward with a roar, he snapped in all directions, usually within scant inches of the fleeing fish. Yet in the end, all he caught was a chill.

"Come on." Jerl shook his head. "Come up here with me, now. We can share my fire and the sunshine, alright?" He reached out to rub Sparks' head, but he ducked away and refused to look at him. "Now don't be embarrassed, fella. You surely don't think I got through my first attempt at tossing fish without a dunking, do you? It's all part of growing up, I promise."

Soothed by his voice, Sparks shoved his head into Jerl's hands and mewed softly.

"That's right." He guided Sparks over to the fire, mindful of his breakfast, and settled him in the sun. "Let's warm up and dry off, alright? Then we can try something simpler, like learning how to catch an untxi on the go." He hummed a little as he stroked the sleek body with one hand and turned his fish with the other. "Speaking of growing up, fella, take a look at yourself will you? I think you've doubled in size since we first met."

He was making a mental reminder to measure Sparks once they got back to camp when he noticed something odd in his mouth, which was hanging slack while Jerl knuckled his shoulder.

"Is that…?" Jerl leaned in to look more closely, then recoiled. "Ugh! Talk about your morning fish breath!"

Sparks grunted and flopped onto his belly, effectively putting his mouth out of easy view and leaving Jerl wondering if he was imagining things. Gailens, like most of the larger dragons, were born with a full mouth of teeth. Baby teeth, too small to do much more than finish chewing what their mothers fed them. As a dragon aged, it grew larger teeth, much like humans. However, while humans got new teeth only once in a lifetime, dragon teeth routinely fell out and were replaced, keeping them always fresh and sharp.

Except…that shouldn't be happening with a three or four month old gailen. Jerl checked his fish, which were almost done, and decided to do more than measure Sparks back at the clearing. He hadn't bothered looking for other age identifiers before, assuming he'd had all the available information already. Now, however, he wasn't so sure.

After his rather dull breakfast, Jerl tossed a few more fish for Sparks, the last they'd be able to get that way until the sun went down again. Then they headed back to the clearing, where Sparks dozed in a semi-standing position while Jerl measured him and recorded it in the journal.

"That's a good fella." Setting the journal aside, Jerl scratched under Sparks' chin and slipped a finger inside his mouth. "Now don't take this the wrong way, fella. I just want to count your teeth, alright?" Holding his breath so he wouldn't gag as Sparks obligingly opened his mouth, Jerl did a quick count and stepped back. "Fifty-three mature teeth, a couple of younger sprouts, and what looked like five locations ready to erupt with brand new teeth any day now."

Writing down his findings so he wouldn't forget them, Jerl decided there was enough evidence to justify looking further.

"As long as you're being so cooperative," Jerl stroked his head briefly, "how about letting me take a look at your hind legs? I can tell a lot from your leg spots." It didn't take much coaxing to get the drowsy dragon to lay down and offer his belly for a rub. "There we go," Jerl crooned. He automatically noted a handful of dry, patchy-looking spots on his torso and started his scratching there.

"Should've brought a rock from the stream," he muttered when the stubborn scales stayed loosely attached despite his best efforts. "I had no idea you were old enough to be casting your scales." He shook his head and examined the leg spots.

A three or four month old gailen should've had bright white spots covering almost their entire inner thigh. As they aged, the spots faded to match their scale pattern until most of them disappeared altogether. Sparks still had dozens of visible freckles, most of them still pure white. There were so many in various shades of blue, though, that Jerl quickly added four months to his age estimate. Maybe even five. Sparks must've hatched very, very early in the year.

Whistling softly, he sat back. "You just became a lot more trouble," he thought aloud.

Sparks' paws twitched slightly. He was asleep.

Chapter 12

While Sparks slept, Jerl set to work. He'd expected to have Sparks back up on the crags, hopefully settled in with a kabi of wild dragons, *before* his fire needed lighting. Now he knew that simply was not going to happen.

At approximately nine months of age, Sparks was in a delicate stage of his physical maturation. His body was preparing to nurture and sustain his fire. He would continue growing by leaps and bounds over the next month or so, but he needed to be able to hunt for himself. To be able to find sustenance any hour of the day or night as his body demanded it. Even the pounds of dried schelch meat wouldn't satisfy that and Jerl knew it.

Worse still was the fact that they had a limited time frame in which to light Sparks' fire. If they missed it, the indar sack would dry up. Permanently. Forever a cold dragon, Sparks would be doomed to a life of domesticity, unable to survive in the wild where dragons fought for dominance, for food and shelter.

Jerl built and placed his untxi live traps with care, then killed three and took them back to the clearing with him. He used the carcasses to lay three separate trails, zigzagging through the grass in a standard untxi evasive pattern away from Sparks. Finishing just as the dragon woke from his nap, Jerl silently climbed the nearest tree so he'd have a good view of what happened next.

Sparks, who'd begun twitching in earnest the last time Jerl'd approached with an untxi, yawned once and bolted upright, nostrils flaring. He started to follow one of the trails, hesitated, and turned toward the other trails. Jerl smiled wryly as the dragon's head swung back and forth. During a real hunt, hesitation like this gave the prey ample time to escape.

Sparks finally settled on a trail, following it nose-to-the-ground all the way across the clearing. His tail wobbled as he tracked left and right, then stood at attention, telling Jerl he'd located the first untxi. He was smacking his chops when he backed out of the foliage and it was several seconds before his head suddenly cocked to one side.

Trotting back to where he'd been napping, he lowered his nose to the ground and inhaled deeply. Jerl ducked back behind the leaves of the branch where he was hiding in time to keep from being spotted, and had to hold back a chuckle. He hadn't been sure Sparks would connect his scent to the untxi trails, yet the dragon was clearly aware that something was going on. Either that or he now thought untxi hid in trees.

Snorting, Sparks followed the second trail, moving more quickly this time. Halfway along it, he lifted his head from the trail. Confidently, he barreled into the foliage…only to make a sharp left. He'd assumed the trail continued as it began, heading toward one section of the clearing's edge. Except it hadn't. He still got his reward, but hopefully he'd learned something in the process. Trails weren't always as straightforward as they seemed.

Loping across the clearing, Sparks' nostrils flared.

He was enjoying this game. Picking up the third trail easily, he kept his snout at a safe distance from the ground and barely slowed. Reaching the edge of the clearing, he pounced!

At that precise moment, a loud rustling sound erupted from beneath his descending paws. The untxi shot away into the brush, rounded a tree and disappeared from view. Bewildered, he stared for a whole heartbeat before bounding after it.

Meanwhile, Jerl lowered himself to the ground, rope in hand, and hurried toward his tent. Halfway there, he was brought to an abrupt halt. The rope jerked in his hand a few times, no doubt the result of Sparks tugging the carcass free of the loop at the other end, then lay still. Sparks burst triumphantly out of the forest, the third untxi clenched in his jaws.

"Well done!" Jerl grinned and began coiling the rope. Untxi sometimes hunkered down, hoping to go unnoticed. If that failed, at the very last second, there remained one last, desperate dash to escape. "Oh, not that well done." He laughed at Sparks as he opened his mouth and roared his success.

The forest went dead silent for several seconds, then exploded with twitters, grunts, cheeps, chuckles, and chirps as everyone assured each other that they were alright.

"Live untxi are much more difficult prey," Jerl promised. "If you catch *them*, that will be something to celebrate."

He busied himself making a fry dough and helped himself to some jerky. Noticing how intently Sparks was watching the fire, Jerl used a couple of sticks to lift out a red hot coal.

"Want it?" he asked. Sparks edged closer, his tail wagging slightly. "Alright." Jerl took a deep breath. "Here you go." Clumsily, he threw the coal.

Sparks' head shot forward and to the side, and he snatched it out of the air. He crunched it happily, swallowed, and looked at Jerl. His tail wagged in earnest now as he cocked his head to the side, panting slightly. Jerl expelled a relieved breath.

"Alright, here's one more." He threw this one higher and Sparks caught it easily. "Now, no more until after I'm done with the fire. And you can get those yourself."

While he ate the fry bread, Sparks dug through the ashes for coals, crunching and savoring each one he found. There was still time. Sparks was old enough to handle the fire, yet his indar sack hadn't ignited. Nor was he belching smoke, whereas a fully grown gailen was capable of lighting his own saliva on fire. One of their showier fighting tactics, it allowed them to literally spit flammable liquid from a distance in addition to scorching their opponent at close quarters.

"Tonight we'll try letting you catch your own supper," Jerl decided aloud. "Tomorrow, for the sake of the local untxi population, we'll try fish tossing again."

Sparks belched, rolled onto his back, and squirmed. The soft grass proving entirely ineffective, he rolled back onto his stomach and tried to reach the offending itch with his hind paws. Then with his teeth.

"Hey." Jerl stood, but the dragon ignored him. "Hey!" He spoke a little louder that time and got his attention. "Come here." Placing his back against a tree, Jerl pretended to use it to scratch his back by bending his knees and rocking his shoulders.

Sparks watched him with a doubtful tilt to his head. After Jerl 'finished,' he sauntered over and took his seat, doing his best not to look directly at Sparks, who had begun sniffing at the tree. The dragon circled it twice, reared up on his hind paws as if to inspect the trunk, and awkwardly turned around, still on his hind paws only.

To keep from laughing as the dragon awkwardly began doing his best back-scratching shimmy, Jerl shoved his head under the tarp and surprised himself by coming up with the journal in hand. If he hadn't had other things to do… Reluctantly, he put it back and reached for his bow instead.

"Stay here," he admonished Sparks, who was scratching almost in rhythm with the sound of musker fruit thudding to the ground around him. He was a *much* larger dragon. "I'll be back in a bit."

Keeping clear of the untxi thickets he planned to take Sparks to later that day, he cast a wide loop around the camp. It was nearly an hour before he came across fresh antzara scratchings. There were no clear foot prints in the soil, but judging by the amount of scratch marks in the dirt, it looked like a decent-sized flock had passed through earlier that day.

Not far from the scratchings, he found a loblong bush that was stripped clean of its fall berry crop.

Perfect. Any animal would have a difficult time escaping from the thickly-branched bush. Of course, even antzara birds wouldn't bother trying to force their way into an empty loblong bush. So next, he returned to the sugarberry bush he'd visited the day before.

Plucking a broadleaf, he twisted it into a cone and filled it with enough berries to bait his trap. Sparks found him as he was strategically scattering the last of them in the middle of the bush, and Jerl scrambled for the deia just in time to keep him from destroying the bush to get the sugarberries for himself.

"Trust me," he shooed Sparks away from the trap. "You'll be much happier with what's in there tomorrow." Sparks sulked all the way back to camp, where Jerl eyed the ground around his scratching tree. "You mean to tell me that you finished eating all the musker fruit you knocked down and still wanted sugarberries? I'm going to have to introduce you to gozoa root." He didn't try to suppress the grimace as he remembered the painfully sweet 'treat' Jartz and the others had persuaded him to try. Shuddering, he reached for his staff and began drilling.

The staff moved in his hands like a live thing as he parried, thrust, dodged, and struck at his hypothetical assailants. Only when he noticed the shadows beginning to lengthen on the night side of the clearing did he stop, winded but at peace. Actually, it seemed that he was disturbed only as he tried to remember more about himself.

"Alright, fella." Jerl dropped a few handfuls of

jerky into a small sack and fastened it to his belt. "Let's see if we can find some untxi." Sparks' ears pricked up at the word 'untxi' and his tongue lolled out. "No, I didn't bring you any." Jerl laughed. "Tonight you do your own hunting."

As they neared an untxi thicket, Sparks began sniffing the air with interest, immediately identifying the untxi scent. Memories came back to him of mornings and evenings spent watching such thickets from low-hanging branches. At the time he hadn't realized the hopping, fur-covered…things tasted good. The few times he'd tried to catch them or play with them, they'd disappeared into their underground burrows faster than he could react.

As they neared the thicket, Jerl slowed, then stopped, but Sparks continued on, apparently oblivious to his presence. The dragon dropped to his belly, slowly squirming closer until he had a good view of the thicket. He held perfectly still even after spotting his first untxi. If memory served, there should be more of them, busy feeding before it was time to return to their burrows for safety during the night.

His tail quivered as he painstakingly pinpointed the location of each floppy-eared morsel. Unlike his experience back in the clearing, his choice seemed obvious. Soundlessly, he edged toward the nearest one. His tail and wings pressed against his body and stirred not a leaf as he crept into range. Finally in position, his tail shot forward, breaking the neck of the nearest untxi.

Jerl's jaw dropped. He'd been prepared to shoot

an untxi for the sake of the dragon's supper if he startled all of them into hiding, but he absolutely hadn't anticipated this.

Not content with one untxi, Sparks set his catch aside and eased toward his next target, pausing each time the untxi, uneasy somehow, stopped feeding to look around. He hesitated after his third catch, but the same instinct that had been guiding him stopped him now that he had enough for his own supper. He didn't think in terms of preserving his food supply, or leaving enough untxi to care for their offspring. He simply knew he had enough to fill his belly. And that was enough.

Silently, he withdrew, his nimble tail retrieving the fallen untxi as he went.

Jerl followed at a respectful distance. He'd been so fascinated that he'd even forgotten to munch on the jerky he'd brought along. So far as he knew, this was Sparks' first successful hunting trip. He knew he hadn't taught him the skills he'd seen tonight. Not all of them, anyway. Were they common among gailens? Perhaps Sparks just needed a few pointers, like learning to keep his wings tucked and that his tail could pick things up. One thing, however, seemed fairly obvious. It wouldn't be long before he was ready to be on his own.

He was so preoccupied with thinking about what remained to be done that he almost didn't notice the smell of food cooking. Sparks, who'd been leading the way, slowed, then stopped. Uttered a growl deep in his throat.

"Easy," Jerl whispered, moving up beside him.

They were close enough that he could see a fire and someone sitting on the log by the supply tent. "This is either the worst ambush in the history of ambushes, or a friend." As he watched, the figure straightened, looked around, and rubbed the back of her neck. *Leuna.*

Glancing down at Sparks, he frowned. Of all the times to have a stranger in camp! Stepping out from the tree line, he began walking up to her as casually as he could. Hopefully, Sparks would follow his example.

"Kaixo!" Leuna grinned up at him from where she was stirring a pot of soup, her cheeks flushed from the heat. She disciplined a grimace at the startled expression on his face. Was her Marroi rustier than an old nail, despite her efforts? She'd dug out her old college manuals and dictionary after he left and felt fairly confident till she was looking him in the face. Admittedly, even back in the day she'd never had a very good accent. It still seemed like the best way to check on his memories, though.

Jerl stopped and stared at her. Unless he was hearing things, she'd just said 'hello,' though he didn't know in what language. It was foreign and familiar at the same time. Comforting, somehow, like when he woke to find Sparks' wing draped over his shoulder. As hard as he tried, however, he couldn't come up with a response in the same language. His hand began to hurt and when he glanced down, he saw that he had his bow in a death grip. With a little conscious effort, he managed to loosen his hold.

"Hasi nintzen kezkatu duzu." She tried again, waited for several anxious moments before he responded… But not in Marroi?

"You don't have to worry about me." He smiled and set his bow aside. He was vaguely aware that Sparks had opted to slink off instead of joining them, which was probably for the best. Dragons with fresh meat could be unpredictable creatures at best. Motioning for her to take a seat on the log, he joined her. "We were just out hunting for Sparks' supper."

"We've all been worried about you, silly." She switched to Lurrakian and tugged on the small braid that had fallen over her shoulder. It wasn't a style, exactly, to wear most of her hair in a bun and a little in a braid. It just gave her something to fiddle with while her mind whirled with questions, most of them medical in nature. She settled on what she hoped was one of the more neutral options. "Sparks? Did you name the dragon?"

"Why…yes. It felt odd, him not having a name." He studied her, adding up the signs. Her tone of voice, the words 'worried' and 'all'… The way her eyes strayed to the shadows gathering around the far edge of the clearing. "We're fine, I promise." Leaning over the cookpot, he inhaled appreciatively. He was glad to set the pouch of jerky inside the supply tent in favor of her soup. "I don't think I quite recognize this dish."

"I'm surprised." She smiled, giving him her full attention again. "It's a pretty humble meal, really. Lentil soup."

"Hmm." He swirled the spoon around the pot a

few times, then sampled it.

"I tried waiting until you got back, but I was restless, so I raided your supply tent and kept busy." She laughed to hide her nerves. What had she been thinking, making lentil soup? "Jartz told me about what happened with the gozoa roots. So I thought I'd try something savory instead." She bit her tongue after that to stop herself from rattling on.

"It's delicious," he assured her. The pan of flatbread looked like it would be even lighter than his own. And the soup! He didn't have to know exactly what was in it to appreciate the rich flavor. "If you're looking for the dragon," he took another taste of the soup, "he's off somewhere enjoying some untxi."

"Oh." Hearing the disappointment in her own voice, she tried again. "Jartz said he wasn't much bigger than a goat, or maybe a year-old calf."

"He's more than twice that size by now." Jerl smiled. "Another month or so and he'll be large enough to ride." He frowned slightly, hoping he wouldn't actually be training Sparks to the saddle. His intent was—and ideally would remain—to teach survival skills and join him to a kabi. "Wait until you see the sunlight gleaming off his scales. It's positively breathtaking."

"I don't understand," she objected. "How could he get so much bigger so quickly? Or are you exaggerating?" She grinned at him, half believing that he was.

"No, it's the simple truth," he asserted. Opening the journal, he showed her his record, such as it was.

"I took these measurements our first day together. But these," he tapped the second set, "I took earlier today."

"That's astonishing! I can't imagine…" She closed her eyes and shuddered. "What if children had growth spurts like that?"

He hooted with laughter. "You must understand," he said when he'd gotten control again. "Best guess, he's somewhere around nine months old. While he was living alone, he was barely surviving. Which is part of why he began raiding Jartz' trap line." She nodded slowly. "Lately, however, he's been getting plenty of food, uninterrupted rest, and growing by leaps and bounds."

"So." She frowned in concentration as she tried to understand. "Dragons can remain small if there isn't a sufficient food supply. And once they're full-grown?"

He shook his head. "They can't go back at that point. And, to be strictly correct, any dragon that remains as small as he did for as long as he did," his face darkened, "is in grave danger of dying."

She swallowed hard, more upset than she cared to admit. She hadn't even seen the dragon yet and Neba's frank declaration had her anxious for its safely.

"Do you think he'll come back? Even if I'm still here?"

"I promised to take him fishing in the morning." He winked at the skeptical expression on her face. "He'll be back. You can get a good look at him and report back to Zaharre that things are going just fine."

Startled, she didn't respond at once. "I did promise to bring a report back to Zaharre, but how did you know?"

"I knew because Zaharre's more than the oldest man in your village. He's the one everyone turned to that night." He leaned back against the tree. "He's the one who agreed to let me try this, *after* he considered the danger to the village. He's also the one everyone will blame if it goes badly."

"Yes," she nodded. "I see what you mean." She leaned back against the tree, too, her shoulder brushing his. "Ten years ago, he would've come in person."

"I'm sure of it."

"I'm not just here as Zaharre's eyes and ears, though." Shifting so that she was more or less facing him, she inquired, "Zure oroitzapenak itzuli??" She felt silly now. Some of his memories must've returned, or he wouldn't be able to understand her. He hadn't even known his own nation when they first met.

"Ah, you've also come as my doctor." He nodded at the clearing. "First time I've ever heard of a doctor making a forest visit." He chuckled and she made a face at him. "I have remembered some things, yes."

"For example?" she prompted.

"I've remembered that my name is Jerl Karruan." His fingers strayed to the pile of ash stones and he picked them up. Holding them seemed to help ward off the headaches that came whenever he tried to remember more details. "I was a Dragon Soldier of the first order until just recently."

She watched him pour the stones back and forth between his hands, an apparently idle gesture. Except something about it seemed… familiar.

"Jerl," she repeated. "I like it." Reaching out, she took one of the ash stones from him, held it up to the fading light as if to examine it. "Weren't you happy as a Dragon Soldier, Jerl?"

"I…" He shrugged and shook his head almost simultaneously. He wanted to change the subject. He didn't want to think about his past or even his future. The present was known, it was safe. "I guess I was. It's all pretty vague still."

Leuna kept one eye on him while she leaned forward to stir the soup. The fingers of his left hand were now curled tightly around the remaining ash stones.

"That smells done to me," he offered.

"I think you're right." She smiled and allowed him to change the subject since her questions were obviously distressing him. Deep down, however, she had a feeling that something was terribly wrong. "It isn't very fancy," she demurred, unfastening her eating kit from her day pack.

His shoulders relaxed as he smiled at her. "Just so long as it's filling." He started to return the ash stones to their place on the end of the log and hesitated. "Could I have that stone back?"

"Stone?" She began dishing up soup for herself. "What stone?" His fist clenched again, knuckles white this time. Something was definitely wrong here. But as hard as she was trying, she couldn't think what it was.

"The ash stone," he prompted, opening his hand to show her the others. He kept his hand close in to his body, as if he was a little afraid she'd try to take another one.

"Oh, that." Laughing, she pretended to squint at the grass between her feet. "Here." Leaning forward as if to pick it up from where she hadn't dropped it, she produced the stone she'd taken. His expression of intense relief set alarm bells off in her mind. It was something to do with a course of study she'd completed at the university. Unfortunately, her memories of it were so hazy that she couldn't begin to know what was bothering her.

The stones settled safely back in their pile, he set the bread aside to cool and filled his own dish with soup.

"Now, let me see." He blew into the soup as he stirred it. "I see the lentils. I think the meat is probably salt pork?"

"From your supplies, yes." She grinned a little guiltily and was pleased with his friendly wink. Whatever was going on with those stones, it didn't affect his entire personality.

"I definitely tasted pepper earlier." He took a bite, chewed, and swallowed. Repeated the process. Shook his head. "There's a flavor here that I don't recognize."

A slow smile spread across her face. "Really?" She took a bite. "It tastes alright to me."

"It tastes fine," he agreed quickly. Gesturing with his spoon hand, he expanded on that to say, "It tastes absolutely wonderful! I just wish I knew what makes it so good!"

"All food tastes better when you didn't have to cook it yourself," she shrugged.

"I disagree." He took several more bites, pausing after each to think. "There is definitely something unique here."

"Eat some more," she suggested. "Perhaps you'll recognize it."

He frowned and playfully pointed his spoon at her. "You're teasing me."

"Perhaps a little." She couldn't stop smiling.

"Tell me."

"You'll figure it out." She winked at him.

Chapter 13

"Fresh tomato chunks." Jerl finished rinsing the pot and set it aside. "I can't believe I didn't recognize the flavor!"

She smiled up at him from where she now relaxed on the grass, reclining against the log. "Not everyone adds tomatoes to lentil soup," she pointed out. Her stomach full and her body tired after her long walk from Herrixka, she stretched her legs out beside the fire and sighed. "It's so beautiful here." The sun hadn't fully set, yet she could clearly see two of the three planets that shared their solar orbit. "I'd forgotten how purple Morea is this time of year."

"It is," he agreed, scanning the forest again before joining her on the grass. While she hadn't complained about how awkward it was for her to look up at him from their disparate angles, his own neck was starting to ache in sympathy. He nudged her elbow. "But don't change the subject. Who taught you to add tomatoes to lentil soup?"

She burst out laughing. "My mother. And she learned it from her mother."

He smiled, enjoying her presence. He hadn't realized he was lonely. Was that why he was so fascinated with her eyes?

"Well, good for them." He added a small log to the fire, not so much because the night was cool as because she seemed to be enjoying it. "Now, what's the other reason you're here?"

She blinked. "What?"

"The other reason." Resting his near arm on the

log, he faced her. "Zaharre could've sent almost anyone to check on me. In fact," he admitted, "I'm surprised he waited this long before he did. Yet you implied you were already planning to make the journey as my doctor." Tapping the site of his cut, he shrugged. "Thanks to your excellent treatment, my wound is completely healed. I don't think I even have a scar. And if Zaharre had sent someone else, why, you could've asked them to check on my memories for you."

"That would've been relatively useless," she interjected before he could take a breath and continue. "Since I was the only one in town who'd spent any time with you before you left. No one else would've known if you'd really made any progress." Not to mention that the average person would never have noticed his near-obsession with the ash stones.

"Nevertheless," he asserted firmly, "had you wanted to, you could've found some other way to assess the state of my memories." He cocked an eyebrow at her. "What's your other reason for coming all this way?"

She bit her lip and looked down at her hands. "Sati."

"Sati?" he repeated. It was familiar, sort of. Probably a name given how she'd said it…ah, of course. A shy, smiling face came to mind. "Your apprentice?"

She nodded. "Her father is still resisting the idea of sending her to university. His latest excuse is that she needs more time with me before she'd be ready for the entrance exams." Spreading her hands, she shrugged. "I told him I was confident she'd pass."

At her hesitation, Jerl guessed, "And he challenged you on that."

"He said that if I was really confident, I'd go gathering in the forest…or take a trip to see my grandparents…or," she gestured broadly, "something. Anything that would leave Herrixka's health in Sati's hands, like my father had done with me." She'd gone off in a huff to Zaharre after talking with Sati's father, only to have him agree! That was when she'd reluctantly decided to come check on Jerl and his dragon.

"Hmm." He drummed his fingers on the log. "This was your compromise, eh? Give Sati some room to prove herself while remaining close enough to be reached in an emergency."

"That's part of it." She drew her knees up. "I also happen to love Herrixka and almost everyone in it. It's my home and I don't like leaving it just for the sake of stretching my legs." She shrugged. "As for Sati, I really have taught her everything that I can. She needs to attend university if she's to progress any further."

"You're worried her father will just find some other excuse, aren't you? Another way to stall?" She didn't have to answer. He could see it in the droop of her shoulders. "Must she become a doctor?" He didn't know quite why he asked that question. It hadn't occurred to him until Leuna clasped her long, slender fingers around her knee.

"I…" Startled, she hesitated. "I think that's a very good question. When my father died, I assumed the role of her teacher as much to fill my own time as to see to her continuing education. But that was years ago. She may have changed her mind since then." She searched his face and eyes, struck by his insight. "I'll ask her as soon as I get back."

"She very likely still wants to become a doctor, given how much time she's put into it." He smiled. "But leaving her home and moving to a large, busy town with strange people and stranger ways will be much easier for her to do after she has found the need within herself and shared it with her father."

"You're right." Leuna shifted to give her side a break from the bark digging into it. "I had my grandparents for support, letters from home. Some of my professors remembered my parents, too."

"Yet you still felt like a stray kaleko at times." His tone softened and he found himself imagining her at Sati's age. Fresh-faced and sheltered, venturing into a slightly larger world for the first time. Had she been frightened? Excited? Probably a bit of both, as brave people often are.

"Yes." She smiled at his reference to their conversation and a friendly silence settled over them. Her thoughts transported her to her first year in Ibilia. Until then, she'd never known a single city could hold so many people. Oh, she'd gotten lost countless times in the massive city, to the point that her grandfather had begun drawing her detailed maps or sending a footman with her whenever she was going somewhere new. Of course, that long ago he'd still been heavily engaged in the banking business. He was retired now. She chuckled at the image of all six and a half feet of him trying to relax at home, getting underfoot more often than not. When was the last time she'd written him? Too long ago, no doubt.

As Jerl watched the emotions and firelight playing across her face, a warm, contented feeling settled over him that he didn't try to identify. He simply accepted it.

The fire crackled hungrily as it consumed the logs, splashing its light and warmth over their faces. The songbirds had already settled into their nests and the forest was quiet save for an occasional ground bird or tree frog making conversation with their neighbors. It was a rustling sound that made Leuna tense.

"Is that him?" she whispered, easing her legs out straight before her. "The dragon?"

"Perhaps." Jerl shrugged, remembering Sparks' stealth in the untxi thicket. "If it is, he wants us to hear him." He studied the shadows near where he thought the sound had come from. He hadn't been sure Sparks would come in at all tonight. She was the first human besides himself Sparks would officially meet, should he deign to grace them with his presence.

"And if it isn't him?" Her left hand strayed to her wrist catapult, which she'd set beside her day pack. Useless against anything larger than an untxi, it was still her nearest weapon. That or a stick of firewood.

"I haven't seen any signs of larger predators in this area. Sparks' arrival, and then my own, has driven most of the larger animals elsewhere." Jerl was still trying to outthink the dragon. Would he be angry? Territorial? Jerl frowned. It might be better if the dragon decided to sleep elsewhere tonight after all.

"Oh." She loosened her grip on her wrist catapult. "Do you think we'll see him tonight?" She almost screamed as a shadow detached itself from the nearby bushes, crystal blue eyes glowing in the darkness.

"Company manners, fella," Jerl admonished, gripping her shoulder and wishing he'd had a chance to warn her. Even with his excellent night vision, he'd been fooled by Sparks' trick of moving the bushes near the end of his tail. It was a neat trick, diverting a seeking gaze to where he essentially was not. "We have a guest tonight." Without taking his eyes off Sparks, he reached into the supply tent and brought out a handful of sugarberries. "Allow me to introduce my friend, Leuna."

Following her arm down to her hand, he gave her the sugarberries. "He'll probably come close all of a sudden, so try to be still. Let him smell you. When he finds the sugarberries, just lay your hand as flat as you can without dropping them." He kept hold of her wrist, worried that she was going to squish the berries.

"Alright." Her voice shook ever so slightly as she spoke, but her entire body twitched as Sparks abruptly moved forward and stood over her.

"Easy," Jerl soothed her. "I know it's frightening, I do." He gently stroked the inside of her wrist with his thumb, worried by the rapid pulse he felt under his fingers. "He has no intention of hurting you, I give you my word." He was glad she didn't ask how he knew that.

She held perfectly still while Sparks shoved his face in next to hers, his breath stirring her hair as he sniffed her. He delicately touched his cool nose to her forehead, then rubbed his head up and down against her cheek.

Jerl chuckled. "How about that. He likes you."

Gingerly, she lifted the hand that held the sugarberries, grateful when Jerl continued holding her wrist. It kept her hand from shaking.

Sparks, scenting the sugarberries, shivered with delight and nipped them out of her hand, his snout tickling her palm in the process. Then, he turned around twice, and collapsed beside her.

She stared down at the dragon head in her lap, stunned. Tentatively, she rested her hand on top of his head, hardly noticing that Jerl had released her. Running her fingers lightly over Sparks' scales, she was astonished at how soft he was.

"He's glittering," she whispered in surprise. The firelight rose and fell, making his scales change color as if he was a living, breathing extension of the fire.

"It's a trait of the gailens," Jerl explained. "Any light at all makes their scales glitter."

"I had no idea he'd be so…beautiful." She found the feathers behind his ear and stroked them gently. She lifted her hand clear when his ear twitched, then laughed. "You said his scales were so strong they'd shatter a bone arrowhead. Can he even feel my hand?"

"He can feel your warmth alright. If you want to give him a good scratch, like a kaleko or a dog, you'll need something harder than your fingers. You don't have to push," he cautioned, passing her a piece of firewood. "Just run it over his scales like you were doing with your fingers. There isn't much flesh between a dragon's skull and his scales, so it's actually a lot like brushing the sensitive legs of a horse or a mule."

Obediently, she took the stick and gripped it in the middle, like she might a curry brush. Keeping her fingertips clear of contact with Sparks' head, she scrubbed the stick along where her hand had gone the first time. His head lifted slightly, pushing against the stick the way a dog or kaleko leaned into a desired scratching.

Jerl watched, bemused, as Leuna overcame her fear of the enormous, scaly creature who'd all but climbed into her lap a few moments before.

"I was expecting a wild, ferocious beast." She shook her head, laughing at herself. "Why, he's basically tame!"

Jerl frowned. The images he'd pushed away into the back of his mind surged forward, like a wave cresting on a beach and drenching everything in its path. Only there was something new this time. Sparks. Prancing and shimmying up to poachers, unafraid because he was tame. Then dead, because he wasn't afraid. *And it will be my fault.*

"Jerl?" Her head snapped toward him in response to his gasp of pain. "Jerl, what is it?" His only answer was to grab at his head with his hands, his facial features contorted in agony. "Jerl?" She grabbed his shoulder, shook him as hard as she could. Nothing helped. He was in the throes of some internal battle. "No!" She tried to hold him upright, but she wasn't strong enough. "No, no, no! Stay with me!" Desperate, she slapped his cheeks. "Neba!" He didn't respond.

By that point, he'd slid right into her lap on top of Sparks, who scrambled out of the way. She stared at the dragon as he began to whine and paw the ground beside her. Leaping lightly over her legs, he curled up beside—practically on top of—Jerl, and looked at her out of his huge, sad crystal-blue eyes.

"Has this happened before?" Too late, she remembered she was talking to a dragon. Nevertheless, he didn't have to use words to answer her. While she knew next to nothing about dragons, she recognized the look on his face as he scanned the edge of the forest for danger. In fact, at that moment, he reminded her a great deal of her mother's favorite dog, Kume. He hadn't been nearly as pretty as Sparks, but they shared an intense devotion to their humans, and Sparks' protective intent was plain.

"He'll be alright," she promised, bringing Sparks' eyes back to her face. "We'll make sure of it, you and I."

Smoothing Jerl's hair, she assessed the situation as calmly as she could. His legs still extended out toward the fire, then he bent in the middle so that his head and shoulders were on her lap. She might've been able to reposition him if Sparks wasn't in the way. Could she…?

Struggling out from underneath Jerl, she knelt and stroked Sparks' head. "Hey, big fella." His ears pricked up a little and he looked at her. "Could you move, please? He can't help himself right now, and I need to move him so that he'll be able to, well, breathe. More easily, I mean."

Patting her legs, she backed away a step at a time from man and dragon. Her shoulders sagged in relief when Sparks gave a deep-throated groan and reluctantly got to his feet to follow her.

"Thank you, thank you!" She said the words over and over again, stroking his head and doing her best to scratch under his chin when he offered it to her, dog-like. "Now, if you'll just wait right here, please." Grabbing Jerl's legs, she froze mid-pull at Sparks' growl. "I'm only trying to help him."

But Sparks wasn't growling at her. His ears were laid back so that they were almost invisible against his skull and his eyes were fixed on the near edge of the forest, staring down at something she couldn't even see. She bit her tongue to keep from asking a question he couldn't answer. There was no sense in distracting him, either. She still almost screamed and climbed on top of the foot-high log when he lunged into the shadows.

"Get a grip," she commanded herself. Since she already had a grip on Jerl's legs, she hauled on them, pulling his body into a more-or-less straight line. Surprised that she'd managed to accomplish it in one try, she lowered his legs to the ground and took up his bow, which was currently the nearest weapon. And found that she lacked the strength to pull the bowstring back properly.

Rather than fighting with it and probably shooting something she didn't want to, or getting a wicked slap to her own arm with the string, she put it back into the supply tent. Snatching up a burning log from the fire pit, she raised it high in time to see a narrasti shrink back from the illumination. In time to see Sparks strike a death blow with his mighty claws, neatly decapitating the narrasti.

Going to her knees for the second time that night, she sagged against the log.

"Good boy," she murmured when he came to her, whining and nuzzling her shoulder. "Such a good boy." The energy which had surged through her only moments before abandoned her now, leaving her as limp as a boiled noodle. "I'm…going to take care of Jerl now, alright? Will you stand guard, my big, beautiful dragon?"

Sparks had gone strangely stiff under her hand, his eyes fixed on the burning log she still held.

"Do you want this?" she asked, offering it to him flame first. She'd have picked him every sugarberry in the forest if it wasn't dark, so a single flaming log seemed a small price to pay. He was a dragon, after all. He wouldn't be injured by such a small amount of fire as this, would he?

Sparks came up on his toes like a kaleko getting ready to run, opened wide, and bit the log in half.

Dazed, she could only watch as he crunched the log up, swallowed, and belched smoke.

"You *eat* fire, too?" She didn't recognize her own voice as it squeaked out of her mouth.

His sides began to glow. She blinked and scrubbed at her eyes with the palms of her hands, convinced she was seeing things. The glow became brighter, causing the shadows cast by the fire to deepen still further.

Rearing back on his hind legs, Sparks spewed fire into the night sky. His triumphant roar shattered the silence, rousing hundreds of forest animals who huddled closer together and looked fearfully into the darkness.

Leuna had closed her eyes against the dazzling display and only when the clearing went relatively dark again did she dare open them.

"Why do I get the feeling," she asked as Sparks licked his chops and came over to nestle between her and Jerl, "that I've just done something I wasn't supposed to?" She pushed her sleeves back and lifted her hair up off her neck. "And are you always going to be this warm?"

Chapter 14

Pain thundered behind Jerl's eyes even as he forced them open. There must be a nutcracker nearby, given the sharp cracking sounds that had woken him. He winced and sat up.

Crash. Crash. That wasn't right. Nutcrackers were large, purple birds who dropped rocks on nuts so they could eat the meat inside. But unless they were dropping boulders, something else was making that infernal noise. Something close by. He looked to his right, cringed at another *crash*, and gingerly turned to his left.

Leuna sat a few feet away, cross-legged, in front of a large, flat rock that she must've hauled in from somewhere, since it hadn't been there before. For some bizarre reason, she was smacking a smaller rock against the surface of the larger one.

Shaking his head to clear it, he squinted at the large rock. Was she cracking nuts? No, whatever was there was too small to be a nut worth the effort. He sucked in a breath as he suddenly realized what he was looking at. Her hand rose and fell, smashing an ash stone to dust.

"No." He lunged to his feet, staggered woozily, and fell into the cold fire pit. "NO!" He almost screamed it as he saw her hand rising again. "Please!" He didn't bother trying to get up this time, opting to launch himself at her instead.

Rolling to one side and over her shoulder, she came lithely to her feet. Tensely, she waited for him to decide between pursuing her and checking on his precious ash stones. She took a step back, knowing it was cheating to try to keep his attention but desperate to be wrong.

Sparks appeared between them, crouched and ready to do battle on her behalf.

Jerl recoiled from the smoke pouring out of the dragon's mouth. Panting, he leaned on the rock he'd come up hard against. He snatched up the ash stone and held it close to his chest.

"They're all there," she said, hastily reaching out to stroke Sparks' shoulder. "I didn't actually smash any of them, I promise." Sparks, somewhat mollified by her tone, sat back on his haunches. "Count them."

He hesitated, eyeing Sparks wildly, then moved up on his knees and did as she'd suggested. Finding them all there, he held them tightly and slumped back against the log. Rubbing his shoulder, which had begun to ache from where he'd struck it on the rock, he closed his eyes.

"*What* is going on?"

Leuna relaxed. Patting Sparks soothingly on the back, she murmured to him and tossed a musker fruit for him to chase.

"That was a test," she told Jerl. Picking up a freshly-filled water skin, she knelt beside him. He was soaked with sweat and his pupils were still dilated. "Here." Opening the skin, she helped him take a drink.

"What were you testing?" he asked, his eyes going to where Sparks had gathered a handful of muskers on the ground and was gleefully roasting them. "Which one of us he likes better?"

She laughed mirthlessly and settled beside him,

resting her elbow on one, upright knee. Poking through the mess of tins and vials at her feet, she found the one she wanted. "Roll up your sleeve." With a light touch, she began massaging the numbing salve into his injured shoulder. "I tried some of this on you last night." She laughed tiredly. "I tried a little of everything, I think." Closing her eyes, she shook her head against the memory and took a deep breath. "If it helps, Sparks took me completely by surprise just now."

He groaned and scrubbed his free hand over his face. "It doesn't." Jerl shook his head, his heart sinking as the implications of Sparks' fire being lit came to weigh heavily on him. "Look at him." It was barely a whisper. Clearing his throat, he went on. "He should've been safely with a kabi of wild dragons by now. Their aitak," he gestured vaguely, "the dragon in charge of the herd, should've been the one to light his fire as a ritual of acceptance."

She shifted guiltily. "Sorry about that."

"Why should you be sorry?" He turned to look at her, puzzled.

"Well, last night I…" She took a deep breath and got it over with. "After your attack, Sparks killed a narrasti on the prowl. Then he wanted a stick from the fire and I thought it would be alright, so I, um, gave it to him."

"You gave it to him." Jerl took the water skin from her and poured some into his mouth. Swishing the water around, he held it for a moment before swallowing. "You just," he shrugged, "gave it to him?"

"I didn't know," she reminded him spiritedly. "I decided it wouldn't hurt him so, yes, I just gave it to him." Noticing that his shoulders had begun to shake, she glared at him. "Are you laughing at me?"

"I am laughing," he agreed, the action bubbling into his words. "But only because at this point, it's all I can do."

"Here." She dropped a water skin into his lap. "Have some more water. What you didn't sweat out with your mind fever, Sparks wrung out of you with his heat."

"Mind fever? What's that?" He took a deep breath to quell his laughter, then a big gulp of water.

"That's where someone's mind is suffering so badly it shuts their body down." She watched his face, half-expecting him to collapse again.

"I…see."

"Will he be alright?" She became absorbed in wiping her fingers clean of the salve. "I didn't actually hurt him, did I?"

"He'll be fine." He frowned a little as he remembered something she'd said. "But I do need to take him to the stream."

"Are you sure you're up to it?"

He managed a genuine laugh at that. "Some breakfast would help. And don't think I've forgotten my question." He held her gaze while he forced himself to loosen his grip on the ash stones. "What were you testing?"

"Here." She gave him a chunk of bread from last night. She wasn't sure she should answer that question yet. Mind fever sufferers needed time to recover between attacks. "And I found this in the supply tent." She held up the small bag of jerky.

"What? You're not going to offer me a fresh narrasti steak?" he teased.

"Oooh, hmm." She folded her arms across her chest. "I don't think that's a good idea."

"Sparks got to it first?" he guessed.

"Oh no, that's not it. It's just that I don't recommend eating venomous narrasti's."

"Venomous?" He was too tired to keep the skepticism out of his voice.

"Mmhmm. The brilliant scarlet stripe down its back serves as fair warning." She leaned back, crossing her ankles. "It's the first time I've ever seen one outside of one of my father's books but my best guess is that it's the deadly po zoia, whose venom is so potent that it fouls the flesh."

"Fascinating." Disturbed by the thought that he'd been lying there, helpless, with such a dangerous predator about, he struggled to refocus.

"Let's go." He took a bite of the bread and clambered to his feet. "See if you can get him to come along, will you?"

"Me?" she sputtered. "Have you lost your mind?!" She stopped, blinked, then muttered under her breath, "Why yes, Doctor. However did you know?"

Sparks sprang past her, eager to go with them. He paused to touch her hand with his tail and whine at her.

"Don't be silly." She made a face at him. "Of course I'm coming, too." It was at that moment that

Jerl missed a step and nearly fell. "Hey, wait for us!" She kept her tone light, as though nothing was wrong. As soon as she caught up with him, however, she slipped her hand through his arm to steady him.

"Before I forget, I have to ask. What bizarre happening shredded your blankets?" She needed to get his thoughts away from the mind fever for a while before she posed the questions she still needed to ask. To that end, she listened, wide-eyed, to his story. Whenever possible, she requested details, keeping his mind occupied during the walk.

"I suppose I have two choices." He tucked the empty jerky bag into his belt. The bread was long gone. "I can either try to repair the blankets or ask you to ask Jartz to bring me a new set."

She laughed and relinquished his arm as he bent to splash water from the stream on his face and hair.

"I have a better idea. I'll leave mine when I go back to Herrixka." Looking out over the stream, she took a deep breath. He'd told her a bit about his adventures with teaching Sparks and she was curious. "How exactly does one teach a dragon to fish?"

"Watch." He winked and stepped into the stream. "And learn."

Amused, she picked a sunny spot and settled into a cross-legged position. The cold water would do them both a world of good. She bit her lip uneasily, worried about how he would react when she shared what she'd learned. That was probably half of the reason she was stalling. For now, though, she allowed herself to be entertained by the shenanigans of man and dragon.

She couldn't hear what, if anything, Jerl was saying, but that only made the hand gestures funnier. And the splashes as Sparks accidentally slapped the water with his tail. And the subsequent splashes as he decided he'd rather play than work.

"I forgot to tell you," she called after one particularly effective splash drenched Jerl. "I came here before you woke up this morning and filled the water skins."

"Yes?" Jerl's tone contained more than polite curiosity. "What else did you do?"

"Nothing much..." She shrugged disinterestedly. After watching Sparks miss repeatedly at trying to snatch a fish out of the water, she'd guessed that he didn't have a clue that water bent light. "I could tell that he was having trouble with his water perception, so I," she drew back fractionally when Jerl took a step in her direction, "sort of taught him how it worked. He's quite good at it now."

"You taught him how it worked." Jerl slowly approached the bank. His intent must've been pretty obvious, because she was already gathering her legs under her. "Thank you so much." He stepped onto the bank, the water pouring down his legs and squelching in his boots. "For telling me." He made a grab at her, intending to throw her into the creek, but she ducked, rolled, and moved out of reach.

"Now wait." She held out her hands placatingly, fighting to get the smile off her face. "I didn't mean any harm."

"Of course you didn't." He advanced only to have her dodge and escape. His feet slipped in his boots, warning him that a high-speed chase was out of the question. He smiled mischievously. There were other ways. "I know that."

"Then you're not mad?" She frowned warily. He'd taken a slightly sideways stance, yet he seemed to be gradually closing the distance between them.

"Mad?" He shoved his hair out of his face and squeezed some of the water out of it. "Why would I be mad?"

She was backing away from him when she realized he was herding her nearer to the bank. Pivoting, she started to dash to safety—and her foot slipped!

"Whoa!" Two long strides brought him close enough to catch her. Once he had her in his arms, all thoughts of getting revenge for his unnecessary soaking dissipated. He absorbed the moment, taking in her flyaway hair, her rapid breathing, the delicious curve of her lips. He could feel her heart racing in her chest. Their breaths intermingled as he lowered his head.

"Neba." There was barely a whisper of space between them when she managed to speak.

Gently, he caressed her soft, white cheek. "I'm not your brother," he said huskily.

Swallowing hard, she pushed away from him.

She'd gotten lost once in a bruma storm and stepping away from him left her feeling just as cold and alone as she had then.

"Tell me about your time as a soldier, Jerl." If she

was right—and she was sure that she was—he wouldn't be able to.

"What do you want to know?" Frowning, he let his arms drop to his sides. That was a…weird request.

"What color was your dragon?" She took a step to her right while she waited for him to respond. "What unit were you part of?" He shook his head and scrubbed his hands over his face.

"I…don't know." He turned to face her. "Yet."

"Why did you leave?"

"I don't know!" Hearing the anger in his voice, he took a deep, shuddering breath.

"You're not Jerl Karruan." she said quietly. She couldn't deny the truth any longer. The ash stones; the mind fevers; the single, isolated sliver of memory…it all added up to one thing.

"Why would you say that?" Panic twisted his gut. "I remember. I do," he insisted vehemently.

"I'm sorry, but that's a false memory." She shook her head slowly.

"A what?" He almost shouted the question.

"It has to be a false memory. Everything points to it."

"Name one thing!" This time he did shout.

"What, besides the fact that you remember almost nothing besides that name?" She threw up her hands. "How about this? You had a mind fever last night."

"So?" He raked his fingers through his hair. "It's not the first time."

"That doesn't make it normal!" She saw the

confusion and frustration in his eyes and wished she could make it all go away. Instead, she gently took him by the hand. "Come back to camp with me. I'll explain as best as I can." Whistling for Sparks, she picked up the water skin she'd refilled—again—and started back to camp.

"Wait." He tugged his hand free and turned to face Sparks. He'd almost forgotten about him. "Here, fella. Come here." Reaching out, he ran his hand over the dragon's shoulders and back, working his way down to where his indar sack was located. "Feels good to not be so hot, doesn't it?"

"Is that why we came here?" she asked, intrigued. "So he could cool off in the stream?" He knew so much about dragons. And she'd wanted so much to believe that he was Jerl. She was almost as upset as he was, to be honest.

"Pretty much. This is brand new to him. He'll learn to control his body temperature soon enough, but in the meantime, the stream will give him some relief from his fire."

"Then you really aren't upset with me for teaching him about water perception." She gestured toward the stream. "He was still…fishing, I guess you'd call it, when I came back to camp to check on you."

He shrugged and palpated the indar sack. A full sack was a danger to a dragon, especially one as inexperienced as Sparks. He could overheat without ever considering it a danger.

"I set an antzara trap yesterday," he told her absent-mindedly. "It probably has a few birds in it by now, so if I was just worried about feeding him, we would've gone there."

"I'm glad to hear that your deductive reasoning abilities are intact."

He looked up from his examination, puzzled.

"I did more than brush up on my Marroi language skills since meeting you." She managed a light laugh. "When I first examined your head injury, I told myself that it was already healing. You'd had it for at least three days, possibly longer, so while it was small, I told myself that it was obviously the reason for your missing memories."

He frowned and straightened, his concern for Sparks temporarily satisfied. "You told yourself?"

She held out her hand. "Come on. Let's go back to camp and I'll explain everything there."

"You're worried that I'm going to have another mind fever." It wasn't a question.

"Yes. I am." Opting for a more direct approach, she took him by the arm. "And since I really don't feel up to carrying you all the way back, unconscious, I'd much rather finish telling the story there instead of here." Suddenly a smile flashed across her face. "You're soaking wet. I…I think I forgot." Giggling, she stepped back and beckoned to Sparks.

"Can you do it again, fella? Remember how you helped me earlier?"

"What?" Neba started to ask, then retreated a half-step when Sparks took a deep breath.

"It's alright," she assured him. "He's just going to dry your clothes for you."

"He's what?" Much to his shock, that's exactly

what happened. Sparks emitted a low flame that grazed his clothes without singeing them, raising the water from his clothes as steam.

"That's…" He stared at her. At Sparks. "This is impossible! There's no way he should have this kind of control over his fire yet!"

"Well, turn around anyway," she urged with a laugh.

He obeyed, his expression still that of complete shock. His boots squelched again and he automatically removed them to pour out the water. When he was dry, she slipped her arm through his and they started back to camp.

"What did you mean when you said that Sparks shouldn't have control yet?"

"Exactly that," he answered quickly. "For at least a couple of weeks after a dragon's fire is lit, it rules them, not the other way around."

"That sounds terribly dangerous," she frowned.

"It is!" He pointed back toward the stream. "I should be cooked to a crisp because, unlike a dragon, I have no scales to protect me."

She shivered. "I'm glad I didn't know all of this earlier when he decided to help me."

"It was his idea then? You didn't ask him to dry your clothes?"

"How would I ask him?" she asked with a laugh. "I admit, I thought about how much nicer it would be to have dry clothes on." She paused. "Actually, I did sprinkle him with some of the water from my sleeve. Do you suppose that's why he did it?"

"Who knows?" He threw up his hands. "Who

knows how he has learned so much so quickly?"

She let a moment pass before venturing to say, "I never thought of dragons using fire as anything but a weapon."

He nodded and pushed a tree branch aside for her. "That's the common portrayal, to be sure. And it isn't wrong. A war dragon, for example, will be specially trained for accuracy, heat level, distance firing, and much more."

"A war dragon," she repeated. "What other kinds are there?"

He shot her an amused look. "Dozens. Dragons range in size from as large as a castle to pets small enough to wrap their tail around a child's wrist and ride on their arm. Most of them whistle or cry, but some breeds are talented music makers." He held out his hand, palm up. "While any wild dragon is dangerous, there are a handful of breeds that are possessed of vicious natures, preferring to fight in nearly every situation. Amongst themselves, against other breeds…" His words trailed off into silence. *Dead dragons…*

"Tell me again what breed Sparks is?" she asked quickly, sensing distress.

"Sparks?" He cleared his throat. "Sparks is a gailen, the largest and finest of all mounted dragons."

"Mounted dragons?" She giggled. "That makes it sound as if they're hatched with riders on their backs."

"Not quite," he chuckled. "But the domesticated lines have waiting lists for their hatchlings, including some riders who already have a gailen. They add their names back to the lists as quickly as possible so that they need never be without one." As the camp came into sight, he found his steps slowing. He wanted—no, he *needed* to know exactly why she thought his memory was false. Yet the implications alarmed him.

"There's so much more to dragons than I ever thought!" She squeezed his arm and seated him on the log by the supply tent. "Now. Much as I'd rather hear more about them," she forced herself to continue even as the animated light faded from his face, "we need to talk."

"As doctor and patient," he surmised unhappily. He could still feel the warmth of her in his arms.

"Yes." She swallowed a painful lump in her throat. "And as friends." Even if they hadn't nearly kissed, she would've had no trouble reading the dissatisfaction on his face at her choice of words. It matched her own feelings, though she kept a strictly straight face.

"I've already mentioned your head wound," she began briskly. "However, since I had ample evidence that you retained some abilities, such as being able to cook, I was confident that your memories would return on their own."

"And now you're not." He reached for the ash stones.

"Now I am certain that they cannot." She held up her hand to prevent him from asking questions she was in the act of answering. "I spoke with Jartz before he left for Gertuk. What he told me made me curious. You seemed to be basically intact, clearly possessed of opinions and skills. Yet after approximately five days, you still couldn't recall the slightest thing about yourself."

"But I did remember," he pointed out doggedly.

"And that's when the mind fevers began," she countered, taking a seat beside him.

"How did you know that?" He frowned, wondering for the first time if he'd missed something during his scouting trips. Had she been watching him?

"It makes sense given what else I know, little as that is. Your mind fever last night was very revealing." She bit her lip on all that she might've added. She hadn't understood most of what he'd said in his sleep, anyway. Besides, it was better to stay focused on one thing at a time. "Mind fevers aren't common. I hunted through the better part of seven years' worth of university notes before I found them in a small section of notes on mental health."

His brow furrowed. "Small section? Then not much is known about mind fevers?"

"As I said, they aren't common." Shifting away from the knob of wood digging into her hip, she continued. "One primary cause of a mind fever is overwhelming guilt, such as might be experienced after a heinous act." She hesitated when he flinched. She had dismissed that as a possibility for him, yet he seemed ready to accept it. Why? "At other times, they're a complication of a grave illness, lingering for weeks after the patient is otherwise healed."

"And which of those do you think has caused mine?" He spoke so softly she could barely hear him, but his white-knuckled grip on the ash stones again betrayed his anxiety.

"Neither." She put her hand on his and leaned a little closer. "Your fixation on the ash stones was the final clue that you're experiencing the effects of the third—and almost unheard of—reason for mind fevers: the process of logura. Mind manipulation."

His eyes slammed shut against the crushing pain and he rocked forward. He thought he heard Leuna call to him, her voice warped and faint as if she was a long, long way off. He wanted to answer. He wanted to open his eyes and tell her it was alright. Only he couldn't. He could barely breathe, let alone speak.

Leuna nearly fell off the log in her haste to respond to his distress. One hand closed over a half-empty vial and the other over the rag she'd used the night before. It took all of her strength and body weight to roll him onto his back so she could administer the treatment. Draping the rag over his nose and mouth, she added a few drops of oil of the wild egin flower from the vial. None of her treatments for pain, and she'd tried them all, had any effect on him last time. Sleep had been his only respite, and that was from the pain, not the fever.

Chapter 15

"Shh," she murmured, mopping his face with a cool, damp cloth. It wasn't terribly helpful, but it was fractionally better than sitting idly by while he moaned and writhed with the pain of his mind fever. She hadn't used enough oil to put him completely to sleep this time. Just enough to allow her, she hoped, to access his inner mind. "Listen to my voice. You know my voice. You know you can trust what my voice tells you. You control your mind. No one else."

She repeated the words over and over, speaking as rhythmically as she could. Her voice grew hoarse but she persisted. Hope surged through her as his eyes turned toward her.

"You control your mind," she croaked. "No one else." His lips moved in unison with the words, as they had the last several times. She was trying to decide which would be worse for the treatment, stopping to clear her throat or take a drink of water, when he began whispering the words himself.

With each repetition, his voice grew stronger, his gaze more clear. Slowly, he pulled himself into a sitting position.

"Logura?" He coughed and took a deep breath. "I think I remember…a little."

"Here." She shoved the journal and a pencil into his hands. "Sketch it." If he told her about it, the risk of the mind fever returning increased tremendously. By drawing what had happened to him, he might be able to trick his own mind into thinking it was just seeing it again.

She watched anxiously as he drew a poorly-made table and cheap chairs that seemed to fill the room they occupied. No light came in through the windows he added and only a single lamp rested on the table. He struggled with a figure on the far side of the table, drawing it first as a lumpy rectangle and grumbling in frustration.

The third time he had to erase an unrecognizable blob and start it over, he took a deep breath and began reciting the words Leuna'd taught him. Gradually, and with great effort on his part, a person started to take shape. At first it was just a smallish person. He added detail, including a wrap about the shoulders and a jangle of bracelets on the person's left wrist.

"Enough." She put her hand on his, blotted sweat from his forehead. "It's enough." It was actually amazing. In the demonstrations she'd seen while at university, not once had a subject tried to draw the doctor who'd performed the logura. It was always as though the doctor wasn't even there.

"It's not recognizable." His hands shook as he surrendered the journal and pencil anyway. "The face, I…"

"It's enough." She ruffled his hair, wondered irrelevantly when it had last been cut. "Trust me, Neba."

He nodded and slumped back against the log, breathing deeply.

Putting the journal aside, Leuna quickly assembled a meal of sorts, consisting of fruit and cheese from her own pack, and hardtack from his supplies. It took a bit of coaxing, but he swallowed a fair bit before she wrapped her blankets around him, put a water skin where he could reach it, and allowed him to fall asleep.

The sun was still high, so she spent the next little while studying the sketch. He'd added a stack of boxes with quick, bold strokes, then strained to fill in a simple shipping stamp on their sides. She transferred the likeness of the stamp to a fresh page that she tore from the middle of the book. Something told her it was terribly important.

That left the figure by the table. It had been while he was drawing it that sweat popped out on his face. In her small, neat hand she recorded the defining characteristics: petite and female; fondness for bracelets. Thankfully, doctors who specialized in diseases of the mind were few and far between.

Sparks loped into the clearing just as she was folding the paper. Proudly, he strutted over and showed her the untxi clamped in his jaws.

"Oh my!" She scratched behind his ear. "What a good boy you are, catching your own meal like this!" He basked for a moment in her praise, then bounded off to enjoy his lunch.

Shading her eyes, she studied the sun's position. She'd been too busy to notice, but she was hungry, too. She'd declined as politely as she could when Sparks offered her raw fish for breakfast and by now even the snack she'd shared with Neba was a mere memory.

Rustling in the supply tent, she fetched out some vegetables and set them to simmering in a daub of lard. Before they finished cooking, she added chunks of jerky to the frying pan, a squirt of water, and covered it all with bread dough. Using one of the tin plates as a lid, she spread a layer of insulating ashes, then a layer of live coals.

"Hey, sleepyhead." Resting the back of her hand on his forehead, she was relieved to find that his forehead felt no warmer than it should. "Hey." She smiled at him as his eyes blinked open. "Did you have sweet dreams?" Her gut clenched at the memory of his troubled sleep the night before. He'd spoken several times, always in Marroi, and she wasn't sure how much of it was incoherent ramblings and how much of it she'd simply been too frazzled to catch.

He chuckled. "You tell me. I was busy sleeping." Seeing the tightness of her answering smile, he became concerned. "Did I say something or do something to worry you?"

"Here." She gave him her hand and helped him sit up, then seated herself on the log. "You slept well just now."

"But not last night." The way her eyes flicked to his and then away confirmed his guess.

"Last night," she clasped her hands in her lap, "I tried everything I had to help ease your pain. At the last, I administered egin oil to put you into a light sleep. Usually, it allows my patients to slip into a deeper, natural slumber on their own."

"I didn't?" He frowned, wondering why she was so uncomfortable.

"No. Quite the opposite, in fact." She gave a weak laugh. "Once you slipped from full consciousness, I believe your true memories tried to surface."

"You're sure?" He leaned forward sharply. "How is that even possible?"

"I couldn't say." She shook her head and drew a folded paper from inside the journal. "Despite that, I was able to copy down a few words here and there. Most of your mumblings were in rapid-fire Marroi, and completely lost on me." She held out the paper, but held onto it long enough to say, "You control your mind. No one else."

He nodded and took the paper with both hands. "Koroa," he read aloud. "Nire. Berdin." He looked at the rest of the words and growled in frustration. "I have no idea what these words mean!"

"From the way you said them, I think Nire and Berdin are names, probably people of importance to you," she suggested. He'd called out for Nire several times, and wept a little, too. Leuna looked down at her hands, thinking of how close she'd come to allowing his kiss at the stream. She would have to be stronger going forward. She couldn't accept his affections before finding out exactly who Nire was—and what she was to Neba.

"Names." He frowned. "And Koroa?"

"That's the Marroi city of governance."

He laughed bitterly. "Awake I remember nothing at all. Asleep, on the other hand…" He slapped the paper face down on the log.

"I've been thinking about that," she nodded. "Logura is an extremely complex subject and I'm not an expert." She spread her hands almost apologetically. "However. It seems to me that there are two logical possibilities. The first is that what you remember while sleeping didn't concern the doctor who performed the logura." It would've been simpler to refer to the doctor by their discipline, as was the custom, but she wanted to be sure Neba understood her.

"Doctor?" he interrupted with an angry snort. "What kind of doctor would do this to someone? And why?"

She cringed away from his censure. "I've given that a lot of thought, too." She took a deep breath and looked him squarely in the eyes. "I don't know why this happened to you. Or who did it. But the second possibility is that the doctor planned to restore your access to your memories."

He sat in silence for several seconds, trying to sort out what she was saying.

"Why didn't they?" he asked through clenched teeth.

"I think you mean, why did you wake up, alone, in a remote area." She raised both of her eyebrows at him. "I know you've thought about that."

"I've found no answer," he returned. "As you say, these woods are remote. There's no chance that I just happened to wake up here instead of elsewhere." He shrugged. "Except that I was injured, so I might've escaped, but from whom? Where were they going and what were they doing and how was I involved?" He ran his fingers through his hair and squeezed his head between his hands. "I only have questions. No answers."

"Which is where I come in." She tugged his hands away from his face. "I can help you find out who did this. No, it's true," she answered the skeptical look he gave her. "The field of mind manipulation is *very* carefully regulated. Only a handful of doctors are actively practicing logura and if more than three of them are women, I will eat a raw musker." He rewarded her with a half-smile.

"You mentioned that mind fevers can also come from guilt." His eyes dropped from hers as he thought of the slaughtered dragons he'd remembered. "Yet you seem certain mine are from this least likely source. Why?"

"Several reasons, including the selective nature of your memory loss." She gestured at the paper. "You are Marroi. I had to tell you about your own nation when we first met and you still have no idea what the governing city is. I spoke to you in Marroi and you understood, yet you responded in Lurrakian. And while I may be a poor judge of your skill with dragons, you clearly are not a novice. However, you can't remember the simplest thing about Jerl Karruan." She picked up an ash stone. Instantly his eyes were fastened on her hand. "Then there's your obsession with these ash stones."

"A master of logura can make a subject believe almost anything. While I was at university, I saw my professor use an ash stone to 'trap' a secret for his volunteer." Handing him the ash stone, she continued, "See how the surface is riddled with holes? He told her to tuck her secret into one of the holes and leave it there."

"What, forever?" Neba looked up from his examination of the stone, surprised.

"He gave her the ash stone after the demonstration, instructing her during the session that she merely had to crush the stone to retrieve her secret."

"Which is why you were pretending to crush the stones this morning." His fingers curled protectively over the stone he held.

"Exactly." She debated briefly, then stated the obvious. "You weren't given the same release."

"Hardly. I fished these out of the stream, so there's no chance they hold any secrets of mine. And yet I was outraged at the thought of crushing one of them." He grimaced. "I don't understand how you can suggest that my memories were meant to be restored."

"It's possible I'm being overoptimistic," she agreed reluctantly. "I just can't help believing that no practicing doctor would leave you without a release, some way to regain your memories. I suppose I need to believe it. The alternative is unthinkable."

He chuckled dryly at her pun, and then they both laughed.

"Anyway. We must go to Ibilia and consult the records. Once we know where this doctor is living and working, it should be a simple thing to find her and ask her to give you the ash stone she used."

He nodded, eyes trained on the ash stone he was now rolling between his fingers. "It's that easy?"

"I would like to promise you that it will be." She met his gaze directly when he raised his eyes to hers again. "But even if it isn't, you *will* have to find the original doctor in order to get your memories back."

"You mean, the only one who can help me is the

one who did this to me. Wonderful." Taking a sip from the water skin, he changed the subject before he gave in and made the disagreeable remarks swirling around in his mind. "What about Herrixka? What will they do for a doctor if you and Sati are both gone?" He guessed that she would combine the two trips.

"Well, it's only an eighteen-day round trip from here to Ibilia. Once I get Sati settled and you on your way, I'll come right back." That sounded horribly lonely and she paused to take a deep breath.

"Anyway, you don't need to worry about Herrixka." She grinned impishly. "That's one of so many things I love about my village, actually. The people there haven't yet come to rely on others the way that city dwellers do. We have a butcher and a seamstress and a laundress and a doctor, it's true. But every child is still taught how to dress chickens, how to sew and wash their own clothes, and yes, even to tend their sick."

"They sound excessively independent," he interjected, an amused tilt to his lips. "No wonder they live at the extremes of Lurrakian territories."

"Yes, exactly." She gestured at nothing in particular. "Where else could they have this kind of freedom?"

"But if that's all true, then why were you so concerned about leaving Sati there on her own?" he asked, confused.

"Because I remember the first time my father left me in charge while he returned to Ibilia for his recertification." She nudged a pebble with the toe of her boot. "I was eaten alive with the anxiety, worried about broken legs and gashes and rashes and not having anyone to turn to for help." Shrugging, she leaned forward to brush the ashes and coals off the plate.

"I won't say I was disappointed that nothing bad happened, medically speaking, while he was gone. That experience did, however, give me a lot to think about."

"Why did you become a doctor?" he asked, her story having sparked his curiosity where before he'd simply accepted it as an established fact.

"There's no easy answer to that." Using rags to protect her fingers, she got a careful grip on the tin plate-lid and lifted it clear. "I wanted to be like my father, ready and able to help whenever and wherever I was needed. I also can't stand to watch someone suffer." She stirred the food with a long-handled spoon. "But I also didn't want to give in to the fear of making a mistake. So…I guess I became a doctor to prove that I could."

Sensing a deep dissatisfaction in her words, he decided to change the subject. Sniffing the mouth watering food appreciatively, he joked, "I hope you made something for yourself."

"Is that supposed to mean you're hungry?" She couldn't help being a little amused. He'd been through a lot and was bearing up quite well. And she was grateful. Still, it'd been a long time since anyone had asked her about her chosen profession. Her answer always felt…inadequate. Like a potion mistakenly prepared without a key ingredient.

"Starving is more like it."

"I should probably make you fend for yourself now that you're feeling better," she teased, holding his plate just out of reach.

"I'll cook supper," he promised quickly. It was his turn to grin as he accepted the plate, loaded high with the savory vegetables and rehydrated schelch jerky, topped with melt-in-your-mouth biscuits. He took one long, deep breath, relishing the scents wafting up from the food. "You are a woman of many talents."

Laughing, she busied herself with filling her own plate, though she only took about half as much as she'd given him. Still, she was flattered to note that he didn't shovel the food into his mouth. He stopped occasionally, eyes closing as he focused on the flavors, and still finished his portion first.

"You missed Sparks' triumphant return," she told him, nodding when he looked hopefully at the rest of the food in the frying pan. His hunger was a good sign, especially after back-to-back attacks.

"Oh? I suppose he caught some untxi?"

"That's right." She smiled, took another bite. "I've been meaning to ask why you decided to call him Sparks. It sounds like a lot of name for a dragon you're not planning to keep."

He squeezed his eyes shut in anticipation of an attack that didn't come. He remembered the large cave, the mother dragon and her hatchlings, all without a twinge of pain. *I control my mind.*

"Are you alright?"

"What? Um. Yes." He nodded. "Fine." Trading his empty plate for the frying pan, he hesitated. "You're sure you don't want any more of this? It's terribly good."

"Thanks, but," she showed him her plate, "I'll be lucky to finish all of this."

Shifting to a new position against the log, he dug his fork into the food in the pan. "I admit, it was a pretty big name for an awfully small dragon." He flashed her a smile. "I no sooner decided to name him than I had this…powerful memory." He squinted at the dying cook fire, grouping his thoughts.

"I was in a cave somewhere. I think I was pretty short at the time it actually took place, because when I looked through the wooden fence between myself and a nest of new hatchlings, there were more planks above my hands than below them." He took a few more bites, then shook his head. "I heard a voice telling me that the name should suit the dragon. I couldn't turn to see who was speaking, couldn't turn my head away from the dragons at all. Sparks sprang to my lips, and I've been calling him that ever since."

Looking over to where Sparks was burying what he wouldn't be eating, she wondered aloud, "Sparks of what, do you suppose?" Their eyes met and neither of them could shake the solemn feeling that settled over them.

Neba finally offered a one-shouldered shrug. "Sparks to re-ignite my memory." He hadn't known at the time that his memories had been intentionally taken from him, of course.

"So you've been around dragons since you were small," she concluded, skipping over a chance to rehash the logura.

"It seems that way." He shrugged again. "Not always pleasantly, though." He chafed a little under her curious gaze, but since he was the one who'd brought it up… "In addition to that memory of the hatching cave, I've been plagued by images of slaughtered dragons."

"Slaughtered?" She raised a skeptical eyebrow.

"Only parts of them were harvested, parts that," he swallowed, "could be sold quickly. For a lot of money." He dropped his fork, raised his hand to his forehead. Almost inaudibly, he began reciting Leuna's mantra.

She put her hand on his head, tugging lightly at a bit of his hair. "When was the last time you cut this?"

He looked up, laughed. "At least two weeks."

"Well, hurry up and finish your dinner," she admonished. "I just happen to have a pair of scissors in my medical case."

Sparks bounced in and out of the clearing at will the rest of that day. Intrigued by the sight of something falling to the ground between them, he sniffed at the pile of Neba's hair once, but it was enough like the schelch fur that he snorted and backed away. The sun was setting when he stopped to shake off the last of the stream water on them. Much to his delight, Neba sprang to his feet and challenged him to a wrestling.

Chapter 16

"I still don't quite understand what we're doing," Leuna confessed as she gathered the muskers that had shaken loose from the stalk when it hit the ground. She was thrilled at the idea of helping to train Sparks, who wasn't yet ready to be on his own. It was a completely brand new experience for her for one thing. For another, Neba had refused to leave for Ibilia until Sparks had been accepted into a dragon kabi on the crags.

"Tonight I'm going to introduce him," Neba pointed at Sparks, who was watching them impatiently from just a few feet away, "to hunting live antzara birds." Plucking three muskers from the stalk, he began to juggle them. "They are surprisingly fast on their feet and have the advantage of being small enough to elude a dragon this size by darting through an opening he's too large for."

"You could be describing an untxi," she pointed out. She'd never learned to juggle and now she watched him a tad enviously as he deftly tossed the fruit around.

He chuckled. "For the most part. Untxi's, however, have predictable feeding habits that make them more susceptible to tail strikes." He fired two of the three muskers at Sparks, who caught them easily and munched on the treat. "Antzara birds are the more challenging prey. What makes them more desirable is that there's more meat on them."

"Alright." She handed him two more muskers

and he resumed juggling. "How does this help?"

"Well," he lobbed two muskers at Sparks, one to the dragon's right, the other to his left. It took Sparks by surprise and he almost missed the second one. Neba quickly took three additional muskers from Leuna and began juggling all four. "Untxi's run a pretty standard zigzag pattern. If he had to chase one, I'm confident it wouldn't take him long to figure that out and use it to his advantage." Raising one leg, he fired off a musker underneath his knee. Sparks, taken completely by surprise, had to chase that one down.

"Antzara birds," Leuna began to understand, "don't have a pattern. They just flee."

"The entire flock flees, which means there are birds going every which way." He grinned and fired off all three remaining muskers at Sparks. He aimed high this time and Sparks managed to get all of them before they hit the ground. Musker juice bubbled through his teeth as he 'grinned' at them.

"I think he likes this game," Leuna laughed.

"Good." Neba took four more musker. "Because we're hunting antzara birds tonight and he needs the practice."

"Why the juggling?" she couldn't help asking.

"Makes things more interesting. Makes it harder for him to tell what's going to happen next, which musker I'll throw where with which hand." Neba grinned. "Speaking of which. Why don't you toss one this time?"

They worked through two stalks of muskers before Sparks began to lose interest, but by that point he wasn't dropping any, either.

"Think he's ready?" she asked eagerly.

"He'll be fine." Neba shook the water skin to see how much was in there and offered it to her. "Let's go to the stream for a while."

She drank while he gathered a few things from the supply tent, then they all headed for the stream, Sparks joyfully bounding ahead.

"I've never seen anything like that," she marveled after they made a brief stop at Neba's worming ground.

"Neither had I," he laughed.

Sparks, completely uninterested in learning how to hunt worms, had run ahead and was belly-rubbing on a shelf of exposed rock.

Neba snapped his fingers. "I'm a blockhead!" he denounced himself. "I completely forgot he was having trouble casting some of his scales."

"Casting?" she repeated.

"Yes. Dragons cast their scales several times during their lives, shedding old, weaker scales and growing fresh new ones."

"Oh, dear." She looked at Sparks anxiously. "Will he be vulnerable until the new ones finish coming in?"

"Thankfully, it works the other way around. The new scales itch pretty fiercely as they push the old ones out of place. Scratching like that," he nodded to where Sparks had turned around and was trying a new angle, "just dislodges the old one. A new scale hardens after about an hour of fresh air."

"Amazing."

"If you want to help," Neba suggested, "grab a fist-sized rock. He's a sap for belly rubs and you can work the rock around the edges of his old scales until they fall off. You can push as hard as you like, too. Plenty of meat under those scales."

"He'd let me do that?" she asked.

"He'd consider it a favor," he promised. "Like I said, those new scales itch terribly until they harden." He continued baiting his line as casually as he could while keeping an eye on her. Predictably, Sparks dropped what he was doing to see what she was up to. She eventually must've found a rock that suited her, because the next thing Neba knew, she was bending over a belly-up dragon.

She went at it with a will and was still at it when Neba began cleaning four fat fish. He sprinkled them with the spices he'd brought from the supply tent, stuffed them, and set them aside. Cutting some reeds, he skillfully split them partway and wedged the waiting fish into the gap. When they were all ready, he daubed on some lard as a finishing touch.

"I hope that's supper," Leuna called, dropping the rock and shaking out her tired arms. "I'm famished."

"It will be in a minute, assuming Sparks wants to play." Neba held the fish up and Sparks looked them over. "Don't worry, you don't have to eat these," Neba laughed as the dragon took a step back. "I just need you to dry them, alright? Just dry their clothes. Can you do that?"

Sparks wriggled all over and opened his mouth as wide as it would go.

"Sparks." Leuna's tone was reproachful. Every time he did that, the fire was bonfire hot. "Play nice."

Sheepishly, the dragon shifted its weight, then tried again. A low but intense flame curled around the fish till their yellow flesh turned a deep, golden-brown.

"That's enough, fella." Neba stabbed the bottoms of the reeds into the ground to let the fish cool. "And here's your reward." From the stream, he pulled out a stringer with five fat fish. "All for you, big fella."

Leuna stepped carefully around where Sparks had plopped himself to consume the fish and admired Neba's work.

"I never would've thought of cooking with dragonfire," she admitted.

"Then this will be a first you'll never forget. The dragonfire does something to the food, no matter what you're cooking. Adds a unique flavor or enhances the flavor or something, I've never figured it out," a brief flicker of pain crossed his features. "I just know there's nothing else like it."

"Let's see." She felt a little silly picking up one of the reeds like it was a giant fork, and even sillier when he cleared his throat and lifted a different fish free of the reed nearest him. She did her best to keep a straight face, to act as if it had always been her intention to take her fish out of the reed in her hand. "Mmm." Her first bite exploded with flavor. She was too involved in the experience to even think about chewing.

Equally entranced by the rapturous expression on her face, Neba could've stood there watching her until all the dragons in the world grew cold.

"If I hadn't seen you catch this fish with my own eyes," she blurted out, "I wouldn't believe it was ordinary old…anything! Let alone yellowfin!" She gripped his arm earnestly. "You have to tell me what you did. What you stuffed these with." She looked at the fish in her hand, but couldn't begin to guess what the translucent contents had once been. "There's more than dragonfire at work here."

"That's true," he admitted. "It's the most important ingredient, though." Seating himself on the grass, he crossed his legs and took a huge bite out of his fish. And chewed. When he thought she was going to burst with impatience, he swallowed. "I started by adding salt, pepper, and garlic."

"Garlic," she interrupted through a mouth full of food. "Really? Garlic? I don't taste any garlic."

"Nor should you, not right away." He gestured broadly. "A dish is not about the herbs used in its making. This dish is about the fish. Everything else must enhance the fish, bring out and…and *improve* its flavor."

"You're absolutely right."

Neba laughed, suddenly self-conscious, and lowered his arms to his sides. He'd been waving his hands around as if doing so contributed to the impact of what he was saying.

"But you were asking for the recipe, not a lecture." Smoothing his hair, he took a deep breath. "I had to use what was on hand for the stuffing, so I broke up some of the hardtack and mixed it with ripe, juicy musker." Hastily, he stuffed his mouth full of his fish before he could start babbling about how different kinds of fruits affected the dish.

"That's…" She looked down at the remaining bite of fish in her hand. She'd gobbled it down so quickly that she was probably going to get the hiccups. "Astonishing. I never, ever would've thought of using musker fruit like this."

"It's the whitish part there." He pointed. "The heat changes the color and draws the juices out."

"Uh-huh." She nodded and looked him squarely in the eyes. "I'm pretty sure I wouldn't have eaten this if you'd told me there was musker in it."

He grinned. "That's why I didn't tell you." Picking up the remaining portions, he handed one to her and nodded toward the forest. "Let's walk a bit."

"While we're eating?"

"While he's distracted." He looked over his shoulder at Sparks, who was cheerfully splashing in the stream. "I want to reach the antzara trap first."

"Mmm, I see," she nodded. "Do you really think he'll be interested in hunting tonight? He just filled up on muskers and fish." She missed a step as her eyes dropped to the food in her own hand and she couldn't help giggling. So had she!

"A mere snack for our growing dragon." He

waved his hand dismissively. "However, I'd rather he hunt his first couple of antzara while he's not ravenously hungry. Remember how I said they're fast, smaller than him, and can fly?" He held a branch out of the way for her. "In close quarters like these, he could easily run himself into a tree and break something. It's much better if he gets used to this prey while catching one is a prize, not a dire necessity."

"I hadn't thought of that!" she admitted. "He's grown so much so quickly, he might forget that he won't fit in tight places anymore." Frowning, she asked, "But wouldn't that kind of a collision do more damage to the tree than to him? His scales shatter arrows, don't they?

"A direct hit to a scale will shatter an arrow, yes. Even a boulder would bounce off a time or two before the dragon began to show any ill effect."

"Trees are different?"

He laughed. "No, the tree would definitely lose the contest. However, when anything that can be broken rams into something solid at full tilt, there is going to be damage done. And whether it's a broken shoulder or a trunk-sized bruise, I'd rather not put him through it."

"Of course." She smiled up at him. Realizing they'd stopped, she looked around. She heard the faint gobbling noises before she saw the trap. "Jartz would be so jealous!" Moving closer, she counted. "Four in a single trap! Whatever did you use for bait?"

"Sorry, that secret's not for sale." He winked at her. "Four should be enough. Even if two get away, he'll have a full belly."

"Alright, we've reached the trap first. Now what?" She gasped softly when he caught her around the waist and lifted her onto a chest-high tree branch.

"You should be safe up there," he announced, turning back to the trap once he was sure she wouldn't fall. "I need to ask you not to make a sound."

She opened her mouth to ask him why, then closed it slowly and nodded instead. From everything she'd seen, he knew what he was doing. So she could trust for now, and interrogate him later.

Neba forced a small rock between two of the thicker stems, creating a hole in the trap wall. It wasn't large enough to let them escape, just large enough to get their attention. Three huddled on the far side of the trap, oblivious to the fact that they were mere inches away from the entrance to the tunnel they originally entered. The fourth puffed out his chest feathers and spread his wings to make himself look bigger than he actually was. Strutting over to the hole, he pecked at the rock inquisitively.

"Not yet, tough guy." Neba shooed him off to the far side of the trap, where he stood, glaring and fluffing his feathers in empty menace. Looping some twine around the stems, about half-way up, Neba tied a simple bowstring knot.

Some of Leuna's questions were answered just by watching him test the arrangement. When he pulled the loop tight, the stems and branches inside it were all smashed together, significantly widening the original hole. She guessed he was planning to use that hole as a chute, releasing the antzara one at a time, giving Sparks yet another advantage.

She yelped and almost fell out of the tree when a paw brushed her leg.

"You startled me," she hissed at Sparks, who gazed up at her adoringly. "No, I'm not going to pet you. You're not even supposed to know that I'm here!"

"Go ahead." Neba stood a few feet away, arms folded across his chest and biting the inside of his cheek to keep from laughing out loud.

Sparks nudged her elbow and she sighed in defeat.

"Little monster," she accused as she ran her hand down his neck. "Spoiled little monster." She did her best to sound severe, but Sparks snuggled into her side anyway. They both looked up at a whistling sound.

Neba pressed a finger to his lips, requesting her silence as Sparks dropped his front paws to the ground and padded over in dutiful response to the signal from the deia. Even as he came, his ears suddenly pricked up and his head swung toward the trap.

Neba used the deia again rather than calling to the dragon with words. Obediently, Sparks stopped where he was. Pointing at the trap, Neba used the string to open the hole wide enough for a bird to escape. He'd dropped a few sugarberries near the opening and the stupid birds were more interested in them than the dragon.

It was touch-and-go for the next half an hour as the dragon stalked the antzara birds. The first bird inexplicably ran straight into Sparks' waiting paws. The others learned from his mistake and proved that their speed and sheer unpredictability more than made up for the size difference between prey and predator. One escaped by changing direction at full tilt to run lightly across the top of a sandy patch.

Leuna, who'd been silently cheering Sparks on, watched in shock as he skidded to a halt and sniffed the ground suspiciously. Gingerly, he tested it with his paw, then jerked back, shaking his paw vigorously to free it from the wet, boggy mix that would've sucked him in. By the time he'd found a substitute route, the bird had disappeared into the undergrowth.

Neba called him back with a soft whistle and released another bird. The last one headed pell-mell for a tree, only to spread its wings and hop over a low branch. That gave Sparks the idea of trying the same thing. For several seconds, he was airborne. Claws extended, he plucked the bird off the ground, killing it instantly.

"Three out of four." Leuna broke her silence. "Not bad."

"Not bad at all." Neba knocked the trap apart and retrieved the twine. "I think I'll spend tomorrow working on the schelch hide I told you about. See how he fares doing his own hunting for a whole day."

"And if he does well?" She looked around, trying to figure out which way would take them back to camp. She was usually pretty good at finding her own way, but Neba had a way of diverting her attention. Like right now, as he lifted her down from the tree limb, his hands warm on her waist.

"Then he's ready to return to the wild." Neba absent-mindedly took her elbow, shifted her a quarter turn to her right, and began walking.

"Oh." Somehow that was all she could think of to say. "What about flying?" she asked a few yards later. "Won't he have to fly up to the top of the crags?"

"That's true." He lifted her over a knee-high log. "Of course, you saw what he did just now. With that last bird?"

"Well, yes. But that wasn't flying. Not *really*."

"It's nothing compared to what he'll soon be doing," he agreed. "However, he was born to fly. He won't need my help with learning to fly the way that he did with learning to hunt and fish."

"I don't understand." She paused under a tree, her forehead puckered in confusion. "Every year I see birds teaching their young to fly."

"Yes, in a way." He pursed his lips thoughtfully. "If he'd grown up in a kabi, like he should've, he'd have seen the adult dragons taking off and landing several times a day. He and the other hatchlings would have naturally imitated their behavior, strengthening their wings in the process. A lot like birds," he conceded. "However, Sparks doesn't require that example. Now that he's large enough, an inborne desire will drive him to fly, to soar."

They walked in silence briefly before she asked, "What will you do? Once he's up on the crags, how will you get back down?"

He smiled and released her elbow as they stepped into the clearing. "I don't know yet."

Chapter 17

Leuna was brushing her hair when Sparks dashed into the clearing. She inhaled sharply as he pranced over, but relaxed when she saw that he was feeling friendly. That was alright until his nose hit a ticklish spot on her side. Startled, she gave a shriek of laughter, dropped her brush, and tried to shove his head away. Taking that as an invitation to play, Sparks promptly dumped her on her back and resumed his unwitting tickling.

Neba looked up from where he was writing in the journal, grinned, and sat back to watch. It only took her a moment to duck under Sparks' head, crawl under his belly, and get trapped under his wing. Neba could've sworn he heard the dragon snickering as Leuna poked and prodded his wing, looking vainly for a way out.

Whistling softly, Neba called for it to end while it was still fun for them both. Sparks, noticing him, left Leuna in favor of challenging Neba to a wrestle. Neba got a glimpse of a beautifully disheveled Leuna over Sparks' shoulder, then focused on Sparks.

Leuna exhaled in relief as Sparks' wing folded itself. It hadn't been exactly pitch black under there, but too close for her comfort! Her mild irritation at having her hair thoroughly messed up faded as soon as she saw what had drawn Sparks away. She hadn't been able to budge the ornery dragon, yet Neba somehow got his shoulder under Sparks' chest and, straightening his bent legs, threw the charging dragon off.

Neba raced to the center of the clearing, where there was less risk of either of them running into something, and issued a taunting whistle, the dragon equivalent of, *I was there. Where were you?*

Delighted, Sparks puffed smoke, wheeled and raced toward him. He spread his wings this time, intending to trap Neba under one of them the way he had trapped Leuna. He was getting close when Neba abruptly began running away from him—backward. Surprised, Sparks sped up so he could catch him before Neba disappeared into the trees. Neba switched directions as soon as he did, faked a leap into the air, and dove under the outspread wing, rolling to his feet well behind the dragon.

"Come on, big fella. Try again."

Sparks rose up on his hind legs, using his wings for balance, pawed the air, and lifted off. He rapidly closed the distance between himself and Neba, but wasn't exactly in control of his landing. Neba evaded him easily. The shadows grew long while they played, shouts and growls punctuating their mock-battles.

Neba was executing another hair's-breadth evasion when he felt the toe of his boot slip. Off-balance, he threw himself to the side. Sparks' shoulder caught his, sending him spinning. He saw grass-sky-grass-sky and landed with a *thud* in the grass.

Sparks, who'd spun to face him, nearly planted a paw on his chest. He teetered dangerously over his fallen friend before settling his weight on his three other paws. Whining, he nudged Neba with his snout.

"Easy." Leuna gently pushed Sparks aside. "Let me in there, big fella." Leaning over Neba, she put her hand on his shoulder. "You did this on purpose, I assume." Her flippancy was rewarded with a strained smile.

"Of course," he agreed, struggling into a sitting position. "He'll get discouraged if I win all the time."

"Here." She brushed his hand off his injured shoulder and performed a cursory examination. "It's dislocated." Seeing that he was also having trouble breathing, she reached down to touch his torso. He flinched and she frowned. "I hope you haven't broken anything."

"I'm too stubborn to do that." His smile looked more natural this time.

"Ha. Ha." She glared at him as she dropped to her knees. "Take this." Giving him the wrist of his injured arm, she began a deeper probe of his injury. "You should've stopped sooner."

"It's good for him to be challenged." He tried to shrug and hissed sharply in pain.

"You should probably hold still right now. Your shoulder muscles are tight with pain." Skillfully, she started to knead them into a more relaxed state. "Almost ready," she promised after he'd reached up to wipe the sweat off his brow.

"Alright. Lift your arm." She continued massaging until his shoulder slipped back into place. Sitting back on her heels, she wiped sweat off her own face. "That's going to be sore for a while," she informed him in her best business-like tone. "Let's get you over to the tent and I'll take a closer look at your ribs." Helping him to his feet, she slipped under his good arm. "Are you favoring your ankle?"

"I…rolled it when I fell."

Holding in an exasperated sigh, she let him lean on her while he hobbled over to the tent.

"For the record?" She lifted his shirt over his head. She didn't see any swelling on his torso, which was a good sign, but she could already see half a dozen smaller bruises forming. "You are *not* a dragon." Prodding his side, she watched his face. "Take a deep breath." He complied with only minor flinching and she smiled. "Not broken, just bruised. Stay there."

Retrieving her medical case from the tent, she slipped her hand inside, enjoying the touch of the cool glass bottles on her fingertips. Bypassing the bottle with the raised, rounded dots on its side, she searched through the rest for a square bottle with a pattern of only three dots. Finding it, she lifted it out along with a small, three-sided metal vial.

"Hold these, please." She handed him the bottles and shook out two lehorra cloths. "Thank you." Taking the square bottle, she sprinkled some of its contents in the centers of the cloths. Filling her palm with water, she let it trickle into the small mounds until they began to expand. Folding the first cloth carefully, she tied it into a bundle. "Where does it hurt the most?" she asked, touching his side again.

"Up a litt…" He inhaled sharply. "There." She set the bundle on his skin and he inhaled sharply. "Whoa!" He stared down at the bundle. "That's cold!"

"Good." She used a bandage to loosely bind the bundle in place, then inspected his ankle. "Could've been worse." She gently set his foot back on the ground. "Could've broken it." She prepared and placed the second cold bundle to help prevent swelling on his ankle as well.

"I don't think I've ever broken a bone." He frowned, pushing back at the mental fog. As always, there was some pain, but it only nipped at the edges of his mind instead of crashing down on it like a boulder on a glass egg. "I don't *think*," he reiterated with a sheepish grin.

"You almost broke several just now," she observed quietly. Pouring a drop from the three-sided vial into a tin cup, she added water and swirled. Satisfied that they were mixed, she filled the cup the rest of the way. "Drink this down. It will relieve some of the swelling around your injuries."

Obediently, he gulped it down, his mouth puckering instantly. He tried to speak, but his mouth would not cooperate.

"I know," she told him, refilling the cup. "It's a little bitter." She almost laughed at the expression on his face as he guzzled the second cup of water. "And you'll need to take it for a couple of days. Maybe that'll teach you not to play so hard with Sparks."

At the sound of his name, the dragon, who'd been watching anxiously, shoved his head between them in a blatant bid for attention.

"Yeah." He worked his mouth and jaw a few times before shaking his head. "I told you, he needs to be challenged." He tried to stand, but a stabbing pain in his side drove him back down on the log. "I know more about dragons than you do."

Turning away from him, she allowed her eyebrows to rise thoughtfully at his aggressive tone. She hadn't particularly enjoyed her required classes on mental health, but now that she needed them, she was glad of them.

"I still think you pushed it too far," she needled. She hated to do it, but sometimes you had to cut into a patient in order to reach what was embedded beneath their skin.

"And what would you know?" Irritated by her patronizing tone, he glared at her back. Why wouldn't she look at him? "This is the first dragon you've ever seen! Now you're trying to tell me how to train one?"

She replayed his words in her mind while she arranged firewood in the pit. There was definitely something else fueling his anger. Something deeper.

"It's alright to admit it when you're wrong." She dusted her hands off on her trousers and took a seat on the log, leaning back against the tree to make observing him simpler.

"What?" He leaned forward, changed his mind and straightened carefully. "*I'm* wrong? After what you did, how dare you sit there and tell me to admit that *I'm* wrong?!" The vehemence in his voice pressed her further back against the tree. "**You lit his fire**."

She looked sharply at Sparks, who'd retreated a little as Neba's voice got louder. He looked alright, but really, what did she know? Had she hurt him?

"That's a special event in a young dragon's life." Neba continued in his anger. "It means the older dragons have judged them ready for the responsibility. That they've been fully accepted as an adult member of their kabi."

"I didn't know." She couldn't stop the excuse that sprang from her lips. Anyway, he wasn't really angry about that or he would've said something sooner. The facts of how she'd come to light Sparks' fire were irrelevant. Unlike the anguish that wrenched her gut as Neba went on.

"You didn't know? Well, that makes it alright. I'll just explain that to the aitak, make sure he understands this was an accident, and he won't challenge Sparks to a fight to the death. You didn't know!" He hurled the tin cup into the woods. She winced at the sound of it bouncing around. "I don't know! I don't know anything and I…" He blinked, seeing the tears in her eyes for the first time. His focus shifted to something else he didn't want to see, something inside. "I don't…" He shook his head. "I don't know who I am or why someone took my memories. I'm sitting here, a six day walk from Gertuk, the closest place where somebody might know something about me, yelling at the only friend I've got about something that can't be changed because," he took a deep breath despite his bruised ribs, "I'm scared." There. He'd said it.

"There's nothing wrong with being scared." She blinked back her tears, determined to remain professional despite the feelings his raw vulnerability evoked in her. "You're extremely vulnerable right now. I'd be concerned if you weren't a little scared and a lot frustrated."

He looked down at his hands. "I feel so helpless, sitting here when I should be there, at Gertuk with Jartz. I can't ask him to make a second trip, give up another eighteen days, minimum." He shot a look at Sparks, wishing he had a saddle dragon so he could just fly to Ibilia. Instead they would have to walk to

Gertuk, charter a boat to go upriver, and then travel another day by some sort of rail conveyance.

"Why can't you?" She edged a little closer, trying to get him to look at her. She'd certainly want Jartz along if she were him, both for the companionship and for the backup. Neba could hardly be expected to simply trust the logura doctor at this point. To be honest, she was tempted to go along herself, just to be sure the doctor didn't try anything sneaky. "Neba. Why can't you ask for help?"

"I already have." He finally looked up. "You've helped me. Jartz has helped me. You're planning to go out of your way to help me find the doctor of logura who did this to me." He dug his fingers into his thighs. "I can't ask for more than that."

"First of all." She tucked a strand of hair behind her ear and tried not to care how she probably looked. "You saved my life. You put an arrow through a narrasti who was planning to have me for its main course." She held up her hand to stop him when he tried to wave it away. "It might seem like a small thing to you, who most likely always hits what you're aiming at. But to me?" She drew her knees up to her chest and wrapped her arms around them, remembering the sunlight glinting off the narrasti's cold eyes. "I'm alive because you did something 'simple'."

He ducked his head a little.

"Secondly, about Jartz? You found his trapline robber." She tried to point to Sparks and stubbed her finger on his hard head. Snuffling at her, he came in close and rested his head on her knees, his back completely blocking her view of Neba.

"Vicious beast, isn't he?" Neba managed a small chuckle.

She laughed and lowered her feet to the ground again, leaving room for her to see over Sparks while she stroked him. "Not exactly. My point," she softened her tone and maintained eye contact, "is that you helped us first. There is nothing shameful in allowing us to do something for you. So ask Jartz to come with us when we go to Gertuk. Let him decide for himself."

He nodded slowly. "I can do that."

"Good." She tickled Sparks' ear feathers lightly. "Do you think you can be patient as well? He'll be back in a few short days, hopefully with answers."

"Yes, I think I can. However, that isn't what's holding me here." Reaching out, he tugged on Sparks' ear. "I promised to take care of him, fly him up to the crags, which he won't be ready for until well after Jartz' return." He blew out a breath. "So really, I'm angry at myself. It's my own fault that I'm not at Gertuk right now. That I have to wait for Jartz to return instead of being there to hear the answers immediately."

She set her hand lightly on his. "And if the mind fevers had begun after you left? What then?"

"Things could've turned out much worse," he agreed slowly. His exasperation hadn't vanished, never to be heard from again. But at least now he had something to combat it with the next time it struck. Without thinking, he lifted her hand to his lips. "Thank you." He adored the way her cheeks pinked when she was flustered.

"You're welcome." She withdrew her hand and resumed stroking Sparks.

He looked at the woods, then at his bandaged ankle. "I'll get the cup in the morning," he promised.

She laughed. "Good idea. It's time to go to sleep."

"Yes, another day gone." He allowed himself a moment of regret over the loss of his blankets.

"Which means Jartz will be back in Herrixka in just three or four days." She smiled.

"Perhaps with information." His return smile broadened at the sight of her trying to stifle a yawn. "Come." He started to rise and remembered his ankle. The medicine had done its work, though, leaving him able to put his weight on it with only bearable discomfort. "Where are your blankets? I've cleared a spot over there," he indicated the spot by the fire, "of most of the twigs and rocks."

"Then you should sleep there." Scooting Sparks' head off her lap, she got up as well. "I'll sleep over there." She pointed to the far edge of the supply tent. Untying her blanket roll from the top of her pack, she marveled at all that had happened in such a short time. Had it really only been two days since she'd left Herrixka so Sati could try her wings?

Walking around the fire pit, she made it halfway to the supply tent before she was intercepted by Sparks. His neck was pulled in a bit with his head raised, reminding her weirdly of Ama's chickens. His wings came out from his sides next, making the resemblance even stronger as he brought them to shoulder height, their trailing edges almost touching the ground as he moved toward her.

"Neba?" She took a step back. Another. "Neba, what's he doing?"

Neba looked up from where he'd been untying the bandage around his ankle. "He's herding you. Somewhere." Hastily unwrapping the bandage, he set it and the lukewarm bundle on the log. "Hey, big fella." He hobbled between them. "What's the idea?"

Sparks bobbed his head in approval and moved forward again, shooing them toward the edge of the clearing.

"Neba?" She asked again.

"I don't believe it." He shook his head, hoping the deepening shadows hid his expression from her. "He's herding us. He knows it's nighttime, time to sleep, and he's herding us into a logelak."

"A low-geh-lack? What's that?"

"A place to sleep. A safe place," he qualified his original statement, "for a kabi of dragons to sleep."

"So he thinks we're dragons?"

"Whatever he thinks we are," Neba shrugged, "he's decided we're his."

"Oh. How sweet. I guess." She watched in concern as Sparks dropped to his belly and whistled at them. "He won't…roll on us will he?" she asked worriedly.

Neba shouted with laughter. "No, I promise he won't. In the first place," he bent and began moving a few of the larger rocks and twigs that littered the area around Sparks, "he knows we're not eggs to be hatched. In the second place, this behavior is typical of an aitak, the kabi's guardian dragon. Once we're arranged to his liking, he'll barely move a muscle until morning."

"Guardian? You mean," she tentatively stroked Sparks' head, "he's trying to protect us?"

"Exactly." He nodded. "He has no other family and we must seem pretty puny to him." He noted the adoring way Sparks gazed up at her.

"I never thought of that," she chuckled. "Well. So…what do I do?" She lowered her hand and Sparks nudged her with his nose, then raised his near wing again.

"He'll position you," Neba explained. "When he stops, it's time for you to lie down." He grinned at little at the clumsy dance they were performing, Sparks nudging her with his head—an inch to her right…no, a quarter inch back to her left…and so on. At last, Sparks gave a tremendous sigh. Neba caught her eye and nodded.

Gingerly, Leuna dropped to her knees. Sparks watched her so closely that she almost laughed. It was all so reminiscent of a hen with her first batch of chicks!

As soon as she was settled, Sparks began herding Neba into place, too. However, for propriety's sake, Neba gently but firmly refused to lie down at her side, opting instead for a spot nearby that would give Sparks plenty of room to settle between them.

Sparks fussed and whined and nudged, all for naught. Finally, he dropped his head sulkily to the ground between them. Carefully, he spread his wing over Leuna, causing her to catch her breath as she realized just how large he was.

"Ow!"

"Neba?" She tried to look at him, but Sparks was in the way. "Are you alright?"

"Oh, I'm fine." His tone was laced with irritation. "Sparks just smacked me in the face with his wingtip."

"Really? He didn't even come close to touching me," she responded, puzzled.

"He's not mad at you," Neba pointed out with a touch of humor. "I'm being punished for sleeping over here instead of where he wanted me."

"Oh." Leuna bit her lip, not sure whether to laugh or blush. "I'm sure he'll forgive you."

"Probably. In the meantime, though, I'm not sleeping with his elbow in my diaphragm."

Leuna did laugh then at the sound of them tussling lightly. It wasn't long, though, before peace settled over the clearing.

"Do you hear that?" she asked after a while.

"Hear what?"

"That odd thumping sound." She listened again. "It's so rhythmical, it's almost like…"

"A heartbeat?" Neba inserted.

"Yes, exactly. Except…not quite."

"It's heartbeats, alright. The difference you're hearing is because Sparks has two hearts."
He paused in case she wanted to say something. "They beat at almost the exact same time, so it sounds strange at first."

She laughed lightly. "I suppose you've slept like this many times."

"I suppose," he chuckled back. "Will the sound keep you awake?"

"No, I don't think so. Now that I know what it is, in fact, listening to it is making me a little drowsy." Reaching out, she patted Sparks' side, then let her hand rest there. He was so warm. She yawned, much more loudly than she meant to, curled up on her side, and fell fast asleep.

Chapter 18

Sparks was the first to rise the next morning, shaken awake by a rumbling deep in his empty belly. Coming to his feet, he arched his back, stretched his neck, and licked his chops. He nosed Neba, who swatted him away; then snuffled at Leuna, who just smiled in her sleep when his breath stirred her hair. Worried, he looked back and forth between them a few times before his stomach made up his mind for him.

With a final sniff of the breeze to check for predators, he hurried off. The sun was already rising, after all. They would be fine while he caught a breakfast of fresh fish. Had the breeze been blowing from a different direction, he might've caught wind of a strange scent and gone to investigate. As it was, the source of the scent approached undetected.

Leuna finally stirred when Neba's mutterings got loud enough. Rubbing the sleep from her eyes, she looked over just as he sat bolt upright, startling her into doing the same. Her breath coming in frightened jerks, she scanned the clearing. Nothing appeared amiss. Neba resumed speaking, coherently this time, drawing her attention back to him.

"Nire! Itxaron nazazu!" His fingers gripped the grass beside where he lay. "Kontuz ibili!" Staggering to his feet, he started off at a run.

"Neba!" Grateful she'd kicked off her blankets during the night, Leuna surged to her feet and tackled him. She winced as they landed, her on top. "He's never going to heal at this rate."

"What…?" He blinked and looked around. "Are you alright?"

She sighed. "Oh, fine." Scooting back a few inches, she rolled onto her side and propped her head on her hand. "How are you?"

"Me?" He brushed a loose strand of hair out of her face. "I've been worse." Dropping his hand to the grass between them, he tapped his index finger against the ground a few times. "So…what happened?"

"You were dreaming."

"Dreaming?" he echoed.

"It sounded like a bad dream." She bit her lip, willing herself not to betray what she'd just learned. "You were shouting." *Nire!* She remembered his words. She understood them. *Wait for me!* Then, the horrified, *Look out!* She feared the worst for Nire, but how could that help him? Actually. It could make things worse. Mind fevers could do permanent damage if they ran unchecked. It was reasonable to assume that was also true of back-to-back mind fevers.

"Shouting." He glanced around, easily spotting the area of flattened grass where Sparks had spent the night, and the two smaller places on either side.

"You started running."

His eyebrows shot up. "Running."

Without thinking, she put her hand against his chest and shoved, knocking him onto his back. She'd been through a lot the last day or two and wasn't in the mood to be mocked.

"Running," repeated a new voice, startling them. "And shouting. And dreaming."

"Jartz!" She bounced to her feet and hugged him. "What're you doing here? I mean, so soon? We weren't expecting you for a few more days!"

He chuckled and hugged her back. "That's a long story to tell before breakfast." He frowned a little at Neba, noting his stiff movements.

"Fair point." Neba grinned. "Let's go down to the stream. We can catch some fresh fish and..."

"No need for that," Jartz interrupted, taking off his pack. "Figured you might be running shy on supplies, so I packed out a slab of bacon and a few other things."

"Bacon?" Leuna grinned from where she stood by the supply tent. "I'll make some biscuits to go with it."

Neba heated some canned beans and boiled water for their musker while Jartz sliced the bacon. Daubs of honey on the fresh, hot biscuits rounded the meal off beautifully.

"I didn't realize I was so hungry." Leuna grinned sheepishly as she scraped up the last of her beans.

"Bacon can do that." Jartz winked, belched a little, and set his tin plate in the pot of boiling water. "Now, first things first. You'll be glad to hear Herrixka's doin' just fine for now. Sati's keeping up with her studies, which ought ta give you an idea of how busy they're keepin' her."

"That's a relief." Leuna smiled, her thoughts reverting back to her conversation with Neba.

"Figured it might be." Jartz nodded. "As for my trip to Gertuk," he picked up a green stick and began peeling the bark off with his thumbnails. "It wasn't any use at all."

Neba paled slightly. Of all the possibilities he'd considered while waiting, this hadn't even crossed his mind.

"Why not?"

"They had good reason." Jartz shook his head. "I'll start at the beginnin', sort of lay it out for you. That's probably the simplest way." Shifting so that they more or less formed a triangle, he took a deep breath. "I hadn't gotten two days out from Herrixka when I ran into a cadre of soldiers from Gertuk." Without meaning to, he began drawing his journey in the bare ground around the fire pit. "They were on special duty, burning any structure that wasn't on their map."

"*Burning* them?" Leuna spluttered.

Jartz nodded soberly. "Every trapper's cabin and hut and shack that they said didn't belong got put to the torch. I asked 'em," he shrugged with his hands, "if it was a good idea to do that with bruma comin' on. They just grumbled and said they had orders."

Leuna sat back, her lips tight with annoyance. She'd spent more than one night in a traveler's shack and knew how the people in the area depended on them.

"I made like I didn't care, even helped where I could, and they give me leave to ride in the cook's wagon. Arrived at Gertuk just a day later."

"Where nobody wanted to talk." Neba squirted water into his dry mouth, held it a moment, then swallowed.

Jartz nodded. "Those soldiers were just a small piece of what's been goin' on over there. Here." He drew in the river that brought Gertuk its prosperity and prominence in the region. "Over here," he tapped on their side of the river, "is Lurrak. Over there, is Marroi." He scratched an *x* on the other side. "Seems poachers from over there have been killin' dragons and smugglin' the hides and whatnots over here for the black market."

"That doesn't make sense." Leuna frowned. "Our scientists proved long ago that owning a dragon tooth or tusk doesn't actually make you stronger or wiser or live longer or..."

"Maybe not." Jartz interrupted. "But even if everyone in Gertuk has the good sense to *know* that, they might just be foolish enough to want to find out for themselves. And besides all that, the one thing I did learn is our criminals and theirs have wised up, started workin' together."

"Neba?" Leuna looked over at him, wondering at how still he was.

"I'm awful sorry, Neba." Jartz turned his attention to the dishes, lifting them clear of the water and setting them to dry. "Between the soldiers and the city guard, folks was mighty tight-lipped." He snorted in disgust.

"Neba." Leuna moved closer to him on the log. "Do you think you found some poachers or the smugglers? That would explain some of what you've told me."

"So you've done some rememberin' of your own, then." Jartz nodded. "Good."

Neba barked a laugh, startling them both. "Good? That's…" He tightened his grip on the ash stones he'd picked up when Jartz began talking. "That's debatable."

A shadow skated over the group, startling Leuna so badly that she jumped to her feet.

"Sparks!"

"Not you, too!" Jartz scolded Leuna. "I know I taught you better than to name an animal you can't keep."

Sparks landed in the clearing and pivoted to face them. He arched his back, extended his claws and wings in an instinctive effort to make himself appear larger. He recognized the scent of the newcomer. He'd trailed it to a stream and the first decent meal he'd had in weeks. He'd even seen him a time or two, from a distance and always from concealment. What was he doing here?

"Easy, fella." Leuna surprised herself by stepping forward. "He's a friend."

Jartz whistled softly, inadvertently drawing Sparks' attention back to himself.

Neba moved between Jartz and Sparks, who was watching them closely. "Hold still," he advised calmly. "Both of you. Give him a moment to decide what to do next."

Tail lashing side to side, Sparks stalked over to their group. The newcomer stayed where he was, a little behind the others. He seemed very small, even compared to the others like him, but Sparks knew better because he'd seen the others make themselves just as small. When he was close enough, Sparks nudged the female aside with his snout. He hesitated a little at the non-dragon. Much to his relief, that one stepped back on his own, giving him a clear view of the stranger.

Jartz held himself poised and ready to move quickly in case the dragon decided to see how he tasted. His grip on the hilt of his belt knife tightened as the snout was shoved into his chest. His shirt was pulled away from his body by the dragon's inquisitive sniffs. The snout moved to one side, then came back.

Sparks nosed further in, following an intoxicating new scent. It was meat of some sort, he was almost certain.

Jartz twitched. "He's licking my hand." The tongue was surprisingly dry, and felt like a baby narrasti crawling over his hand.

"Which hand?" Leuna asked quickly, unable to see Jartz at all around Sparks' broad shoulders.

"Which…my right hand!"

Leuna giggled, half at the irritation in Jartz' voice and half at what she'd deduced. "Bacon! You ate your bacon with your right hand!" Sparks drew back and looked at her. "I think he wants some," she laughed.

"Bad idea," Neba warned. They all looked at him. "He's a wild animal," he reminded them. "If we feed him human food, we'll make a thief out of him." He looked pointedly at Jartz.

"But…"

"No buts," Jartz cut her off. "He's right. He's already stolen from a trap line, so he'll most likely go back to robbing humans given the chance." He rose slowly, watching Sparks with the eye of a man who'd spent most of his life around animals. "Folks might tolerate a peace-loving dragon what lives on wild game. Animals what preys on livestock are chased off or killed."

Thoroughly chastened, Leuna dropped her gaze. The thought of Sparks dying, or worse, ending up locked in combat with humans, made her ill.

"Now that we're agreed, we need to distract him." Neba hesitated, then made up his mind. "Jartz, there's a leather bucket in the supply tent. Will you take it to the stream and fill it, please?"

"Why do we need a bucket of water?" Leuna looked on in surprise as he reached for her field case and began riffling through it. "You still haven't retrieved that cup, you know."

"We need the water in case we accidentally set something on fire." He showed them the metal flask he'd found.

"Paraffin oil?" Leuna was more confused than ever. "You need water in case you accidentally set something on fire while using a flammable oil?" She half-turned to look at Jartz for help, but he was already slipping between trees, bucket in hand.

Neba laughed. "It'll all make sense in a minute."

Leuna shrugged and pitched in, helping him cut his damaged blankets into strips and tying them into loose, fist-sized knots. Sparks was, as planned, thoroughly distracted by their sudden busyness.

"Oh, Sparks," she protested when he grabbed one end of the blanket and tugged. "Not now!"

"Here, fella." Neba tossed a few musker and Sparks gleefully chased them across the clearing.

"I guess he still doesn't like blankets," she grinned.

"Apparently not," he laughed.

"What's he got against blankets?" Jartz walked into camp and hung the bucket from a stunted branch. Spotting a tin cup glinting in the foliage, he stooped to pick it up. It was badly dented, but still serviceable, so he brought it over when he joined them. Wisely, he kept his questions about it to himself.

"That's a funny story," Leuna grinned as she finished her blanket. "Here, give me that," she took the other blanket from Neba, "and show Jartz how to tie these ridiculous knots while you tell him what happened."

The clearing rang with laughter as Neba recounted his misadventure with Sparks, who had come back over and stretched out beside Leuna without a second glance at Jartz.

"I'd say that was a waste of a good blanket," Jartz wiped laughter tears from his eyes, "if you hadn't figured out you could use them for…well, whatever these are." He tossed his latest knot on top of a pile of them.

"These are for fire training. We don't have a lot of room here, now that he's so big." Neba nodded at Sparks, who by now had begun practicing picking up twigs with his tail and was dropping them in Leuna's hair like a mischievous child. She scolded him, of course, it just didn't do any good. "Still, I think we can teach him a few things he'll need to know."

"And the oil?" Leuna asked, still mystified about that.

"That's for me." Neba kept a straight face despite the shock on theirs. "I'm going to breathe fire."

Leuna's jaw sagged as her shock jumped a few notches.

"*You're* going to breathe fire?" Jartz threw one of the knots at him. "Stop your fooling."

Catching the knot easily, Neba grinned at them both. "Wait and see." Using Leuna's bandage scissors, he made dozens of cuts in each of the prepared knots, hoping that would make them catch fire more easily.

Leuna finished her pile first, her practice with tying bandages lending speed to her fingers in this venture, so she moved over to help Jartz.

"Alright." Neba flexed his fingers and set the scissors aside. "All done over there?" At their nods, he smiled. "I think we're ready." Climbing to his feet, Neba took a thin stick from the pile of firewood, lit one end on fire, and waved it to get Sparks' attention. "Hey, fella. Watch this."

Sparks eyed the torch briefly, but couldn't bring himself to be overly interested. After spending most of his morning watching them destroy his attacker from a few nights ago, he was ready for a nap.

Neba lifted the flask of paraffin oil to his lips.

"You can't drink that!" Leuna gasped, reaching for the flask.

"I won't." He held it out of reach. "I have no intention of drinking this, really." He maintained eye contact until she seemed convinced. "Now. Throw a knot toward the center of the clearing." He poured a little oil from the flask into his mouth.

Biting her lip, she gave one a half-hearted toss. And nearly shrieked when fire seemed to erupt from Neba's mouth, passed over the torch, and ignite the knot.

Sparks *did* howl. What was going on here? Racing over to where the knot fell, he pounced on it. After batting it around, tasting it—just as bland as before, but definitely real fire—and generally mauling it to death, he turned to glare at Neba.

Neba spewed fire again, striking a second knot. The oil must have been highly refined, because he was getting incredible distance with it. Making eye contact with Jartz, he motioned for him to be ready to throw as well.

Sparks stared in shock as the non-dragon blasted two knots in rapid succession. Then his ears went up. That looked like fun!

Neba placed the burning torch in the fire pit and scooped water from the bucket into his mouth, rinsing and spitting until he'd cleared out as much of the oil as he possibly could.

"Why is he whining?" Jartz asked warily. Now that he thought about it, he wasn't so sure that teaching a dragon how to use its fire was a great idea.

"He wants a turn." Neba gestured for Leuna to throw the knot she held, gargled and spat once more for luck, and turned his attention to Sparks.

"He roasted that knot." Jartz swallowed hard. "Ain't even ashes left to hit the ground."

"He's still learning," Neba reminded him. "The other day he dried my clothes without even singing my eyebrows. He's capable of control, given enough time and practice." Selecting a short, knobby stick of firewood, he held it up for Sparks to see. In the other hand, he held up one of the cloth knots. Intentionally exaggerating his movements, he threw them both at the same time.

Sparks torched the knot and casually sent a blast chasing after the wood. The knot was reduced to smoke instantly. The stick, however, landed with a thud and sputtered out as it rolled along in the grass. His ears cocked, Sparks trotted over to it, sniffed it and tried again.

"Let's see how he handles this," Neba whispered, just loud enough for the others to hear.

Leuna bit her lip to control a chuckle. More than once, while teaching Sati, she'd had to take a step back and let her student struggle through something on her own. Never anything involving fire, though!

Sparks tried a few more times, decimating the nearby grass with his blasts. Neba whistled and held up another cloth knot, but Sparks snorted. Clamping his teeth around the stick, he hustled over to Neba and dropped it at his feet, whining piteously.

"That's a relief." Jartz inspected the smoldering stick from a discreet distance. "With a powerful fire like his, I figured he'd be able to light whatever he'd a mind to."

"Like I said." Neba dropped to one knee by the stick. "Give him time." Reaching out, he placed his hand on Sparks' throat. His eyes half-closed in concentration, he worked his way down the neck till he found what he was searching for. Gently, he turned Sparks' head so that he was looking out into the clearing.

Leuna took a slow step back. Something about the way Sparks was standing, so still and rigid, had her fumbling for the handle of the water bucket. Just in case.

The fingers of Neba's right hand dug into the dragon's neck. Sparks coughed, sending a ball of liquid fire flying a few feet before it splatted into the grass.

"Easy." Neba stroked his neck. "That's how you use your liquid fire, alright?" He smiled as he spoke, wondering how many more times he'd have to help the dragon manipulate his glands.

Jartz and Leuna exchanged glances.

"Did you know he could do that?" Jartz mouthed.

Leuna shook her head vigorously. "I wonder what *else* he can do?" she mouthed back.

"Ready?" Neba had already located the second gland. "Here we go."

Leuna and Jartz eventually seated themselves so that they might watch more comfortably while Neba worked with Sparks. As it turned out, the dragon was also capable of breathing thick smoke, spitting liquid fire that wasn't burning, expelling a ball of flame that exploded—they nearly ran for cover that time—and producing a thin stream of flame that was so hot, he ignited the now-cold stick of wood he'd started with.

"That's enough for today." Neba rose, a surprised expression on his face as he rubbed his stiff legs. How long had he been kneeling there, anyway? The shadows that were pooling at the base of trees on the sunset side of the clearing were now battling the sun for dominance in the middle of the clearing.

"We should go down to the stream," he suggested to the others. "He'll want to keep practicing and there's more water there."

"You two go ahead." Leuna looked up from where she was stirring the pot of tinned beans. "I'll be along once the journey cake is done."

"And leave you to carry all that hot metal by yourself?" Jartz scoffed. "Not a chance."

"I agree." Neba scratched his chin. "But I may have a solution."

Chapter 19

The next morning, Jartz and Neba took down the supply tent and loaded the last of the supplies into the tarp itself, securing the bundle with rope.

"It's still a lot for one man to carry," Jartz observed doubtfully, nudging the bundle with the toe of his boot.

"I plan to teach Sparks to carry it for me," Neba said matter-of-factly.

"Simple as that?" Jartz wasn't convinced.

"He did alright with supper last night," Neba reminded him.

Jartz paused, the sight of the dragon carrying the journey cake and beans on his back still fresh in his mind. Zaharre had given him explicit instructions to assess the danger to the village and report back, which he'd assumed would be easy. Now, though, he wasn't so sure. Sparks didn't seem to have a mean bone in his scaly body. On the other hand, a large animal carrying fire in its belly could cause trouble without intending to.

"You were rather impressive last night," Leuna murmured, reaching out to knuckle Sparks' neck affectionately. She still hadn't gotten over the fact that Sparks had been able to heat just the one scale the dishes rested on! Instead of having to start a new cook fire at the stream, they'd been able to sit down and eat right away. "But you're going to have to get up so I can go home."

Sparks, comfortably situated with his head on her feet, didn't so much as open an eye to look at her.

"I think he wants you to stay." Neba squatted down beside him and tugged gently on his ear.

"Well, that's very sweet of him." She swallowed hard against the painful tightening of her throat. "I do need to get back, though. I have to check on Sati. And the triplets. And their mother, Gai. She's probably worn herself to a frazzle while I was gone. She does that when there's nobody keeping an eye on her…" Her eyes met Neba's and her voice trailed off. As a sober stillness settled, she knew that was why she'd been in such a hurry to fill the air with words a moment before. In the silence, she couldn't pretend to be oblivious to the fact that she'd miss Neba, too.

"You're very important to Herrixka, Miss Doctor," he observed gravely, using Sati's title for her.

"No, not terribly." She caught herself smoothing her pant leg as though it was a fancy skirt and quickly brought her hands together in her lap. "I mean, I…"

"Time to go," Jartz called, swinging his pack onto his back. Stomping over a little more loudly than he really needed to, he offered Neba his hand. "Meant what I said last night. You get that dragon taken care of and come on back to Herrixka. I'll traipse along to Ibilia with you; do what I can to help you get your memories back."

"Thank you." Neba gripped his hand firmly, truly grateful for his offer. At his urging, Leuna had explained everything to Jartz over supper, though she'd downplayed the mind fevers a bit.

Leuna cleared her throat. "I could use a little help

here," she remarked pointedly. "I can't believe how big he's gotten."

"Big oaf," Jartz snorted. Truthfully, though, the now-horse-sized dragon was a wonderment to him. He'd never seen anything grow that big that fast.

"I'd say he's just being lazy," Neba stooped and wrapped his arms around the dragon's head, "except that he's actively resisting right now." Relaxing his grip on Sparks, he caught Leuna's eye. "Be ready to move as soon as you think you can, alright?"

At her nod, he bent his knees, tightened his hold and lifted, all in one fluid motion. Catching Sparks by surprise, Neba was able to move the stubborn dragon's head off her feet enough for her to tug them free and swing them around to the other side of the log.

"Don't look at me like that." Neba released Sparks and gave him a friendly shove away from where they were standing. Miffed, Sparks turned up his nose, flounced a few feet off, and lay down right on Neba's pack. "I'll make it up to you, I promise," Neba laughed.

Leuna chuckled and swung her pack onto her shoulders. "Zaindu zeure burua," she murmured in Marroi as they clasped arms in farewell. *Take care of yourself.*

"Bidaia segurtasunez," he returned. *Travel safely.*

Neba watched them leave, marveling silently at his rapid progress since Leuna's diagnosis. It seemed a wonder to him that he was able to communicate at all when his own language had been taken from him by an unknown mind manipulator. Even now, his best efforts at retrieving his language failed miserably unless someone else prompted him. Words like 'deia' and 'kabi' were obvious exceptions, stemming from his close association with dragons. Or so he supposed.

Hoisting the supply bundle onto his shoulder, Neba approached Sparks. "Ready?"

Sparks grunted in displeasure as Neba eased the burden onto his scaly shoulder. Huffing a small cloud of smoke at Neba, he put his head on his front paws and pretended to fall asleep.

"Good idea." Neba stretched his hands up to the sky, then plopped himself down so that he was leaning against Sparks' bulk. "Pays to be well-rested before moving camps."

Sparks rattled his scales the way a dog might twitch its skin to discourage an annoying insect. Neba remained where he was. The dragon shifted to his right, sending Neba sliding limply to the ground beside him. In so doing, he left Neba's pack unprotected.

Neba lay still for several heartbeats. Sparks expressed no further interest in him, so he came noiselessly to his feet and took up his pack.

"It's a beautiful day for a walk," he said loudly, striding to the edge of the clearing while he swung his pack onto his back. "Going to be awfully lonely here for anybody that stays behind."

He played and held a soft, keening note on the deia. Sparks' ears pricked up and he looked around.

"How about it, big fella? Think you can manage that pack?" He shifted his pack as he spoke and nodded at the supply pack still waiting where he'd left it between Sparks' shoulders.

Following Neba's gaze, Sparks turned his head so that he was able to see the item in question. He blew a puff of smoke at it, climbed to his feet, and meandered in Neba's general direction.

"Still mad, eh?" Neba chuckled. "If it helps, I'll miss her…um, *them*, too."

Sparks kept his distance the rest of the morning, but he never let Neba out of his sight. The non-dragon's company was better than being alone again, and Sparks somehow knew Neba was leaving the clearing for good. Sparks perked up when they reached the stream, but they turned upstream instead of stopping, and pushed on clear through lunch.

"Not here, fella." Neba shook his head when Sparks tried to stop at their old campsite. The schelch bones had vanished and there was new grass where the small fire pits were. Rather than stopping to coax the dragon, he continued striding along. As he'd hoped, Sparks whined a bit, then followed.

"Trust me," Neba said soothingly. "You're going to love the place I found while I was out scouting. It's on the far side of the stream and the grassland extends clear out to the crags. Plenty of space for you to stretch your wings." He kept talking and walking until they crested a low rise. "Time to get our feet wet."

The statement proved unfounded as the stream was shallow enough there that he was able to cross without water filling his boots. Further upstream a bit, an ancient flood had cut one bank back far enough that it was now a marshy spot. Brilliantly colored reeds and rushes grew thickly in the soggy earth, providing ample habitat for the dozens of small birds nesting there.

Sparks watched Neba drop his pack on the far side of the stream and followed suit, dumping the supplies unceremoniously beside it. Unburdened, he raced off to explore.

"Oh, for…" Neba rubbed his hand over his face. "Nothing like announcing yourself to the local prey," he muttered as Sparks joyously bounded after the flock of grassbirds he'd flushed from their hiding place.

His eyebrows rose as Sparks spread his wings and followed his, um, playmates into the skies. The birds worked desperately to escape, too frightened to realize that none of them were being eaten. They banked and rose and dove. Their hairpin turns gained them precious seconds that would've foiled the average predator. But it wasn't until a final desperate dive and turn that Sparks, powerful wings beating in an effort to keep up with their delightful game, miscalculated and drove himself headfirst into the tall savannah grasses. Tip over tail he bounced and rolled, finally coming to a halt at the base of a huge old ezcor tree.

"Well." Neba scratched his head. "I doubt he'll forget that lesson."

Sparks' tail end, which had been up, flopped to the ground. By the time his head bobbed up above the grasses, Neba had cut enough rushes to weave a fish basket. Sparks did a little weaving of his own as he wobbled his way over to where Neba sat working.

"Guess I should've warned you," Neba observed as Sparks stuck his head in the cold stream water. "Those grassbirds play a mean game of touch." He chuckled when Sparks ignored him in favor of wading into the water. It was too shallow to cover all of the dragon, but he went belly-down in the mud to get as much coverage as he could.

"You'll be alright by morning," Neba predicted, resuming his weaving. "If you'd hit that tree at full tilt, it'd be another story. Ezcor trees are almost as tough as iron."

Sparks lay in the stream long enough that the fish grew bold again and began swimming around him. A dozen of them fell prey to his nimble tail before he took a final drink and rose, scattering the rest. Refreshed, he wandered over to check on Neba, who was still working.

"I know." Neba slapped his tail away. "I know it's almost time for sleep, just let me finish this first."

They slept then, and lingered there for the next two days, each busy with their own concerns. Sparks spent most of his time in the air, searching for his limits. The grassbirds were constantly showing him new things to try and he reveled in his new-found abilities.

Neba, meanwhile, was drawn back to the schelch hide. It was a constant struggle to keep his blade sharp as he cut and shaped the thick leather. At length, he found himself with two large pieces identical in size and shape. Next, he used an inch-wide piece off the main hide to lace the larger pieces together with a generous three-finger span between them.

"Do you know what I'm doing?" he asked Sparks on the evening of the third day. He had a feeling it was important, so he kept at it even though his fingers were sore from working the hide, but he still had absolutely no idea what he was making. Sparks just nudged his shoulder with his snout. "I know," Neba sighed. "Time to sleep."

They moved on in the morning, Sparks begrudgingly allowing Neba to strap the supply tent to his back before taking off. Neba watched him a moment, admiring the combination of grace and power that was a young dragon. He didn't worry about getting truly separated, confident somehow that Sparks would be able to find him any time he chose. "My mind is my own," he reminded himself, as he did every morning in the hopes of keeping the mind fevers at bay. "I control my thoughts."

The grasses swished around his boots as he made his way along, aiming straight for the crags. They were more than visible now. They filled a larger portion of the sky with each passing hour and would soon dominate the morning view entirely. Then it would be time to fly Sparks up to their top.

It wasn't until he stopped to rest and eat at midday that it finally hit him. Inhaling sharply, he picked up the two leather pieces and stared at them. Spreading his feet a bit, he placed one leather piece against the inside of his leg, his knee a scant inch from the rounded outside edge. The second piece came to rest naturally against his other leg, with the narrower ends of both pieces tapering off about where they hit his ankles.

He was making a jarlekua! A pad to protect his knees and legs while he rode Sparks up to the top of the crags! It still lacked a few things, such as a chest strap, a belly strap, and stirrups, but he could envision each piece as clearly as if the complete article was already fastened on Sparks. He didn't even wait to take measurements before resuming his work with gusto.

He even laughed as he realized that the supply tent was the perfect training tool. Sparks was out there somewhere getting used to carrying a weight on his back. Steering would be an entirely different problem, naturally, yet Neba didn't expect much trouble on that score—they would be going nearly straight up. His excitement carried him as far as a likely camping spot, where he skillfully completed the jarlekua. The stirrups, woven from reeds, were by far the most difficult part and he still had them attached before Sparks rejoined him.

"Of all the nights to stay out till dusk," he complained as Sparks finally touched down. "I've been waiting here for hours!" Sparks looked at him expectantly and Neba started to laugh at himself as he unstrapped the supply tent. "Alright, alright. At least you didn't lose the supplies."

Neba had a hard time sleeping that night, troubled by dreams that came and went without leaving anything to remember, but still he came awake with a start when Sparks got up before dawn. Reaching out quickly, he caught hold of one of

Sparks' scales and was pulled unceremoniously to his feet.

Sparks looked back at him, ears pricked forward as if to ask, *What do you think you're doing?*

"I know it's rude to work before breakfast," Neba apologized without letting go. "So I'll ask your pardon." He hooked a toe through the laces of the jarlekua and dragged it closer until he could catch hold of it with his free hand. "I just need you to wear this today so you can start getting used to it."

Careful not to move too quickly, Neba opened the jarlekua and set it on Sparks' shoulders, lining it up with his spine. He made a point of knuckling Sparks' neck as he brought the chest strap around and secured it, much to Sparks' delight.

"What do you think so far, fella?" Neba crooned, reaching forward to ruffle Sparks' ear feathers when they came in reach. "Just let me fasten the belly strap here and…" He patted Sparks' shoulder. "I'll even carry the supply tent, alright? You get used to this today and we'll be up on the crags by supper tomorrow."

Sparks sniffed curiously at his new gear, then lightly head-butted Neba in the chest.

"I don't think so," Neba laughed, pushing his head away. "You're already too tame. I've handled you too much." He shook his head. "Hopefully your kabi will teach you to distrust us humans." He waved his arms, startling Sparks into taking off.

The supplies were greatly diminished, so after carefully repacking things, he tied it on top of his pack and settled it on his shoulders. The sun rose as he walked, turning the clouds cheerful pinks, but it was barely past midday when the shadow of the crags fell on all about him.

Like the dragons they were named for, the many hues of Firedrake Crags shimmered in even the palest light. The oranges and yellows seemed ready to leap off and dance through the evening air, but even their glows faded with the daylight.

"This is close enough," Neba decided at last, eyeing the weathered granite surface that loomed up before him, dominating the horizon.

Sparks swooped down in a spectacular landing, practically posing, wings half extended and neck reared back like he was going to roar. Except his tail distracted him.

"Daft moxal," Neba muttered affectionately as he watched the dragon turning in circles. "If you ever catch that thing, you'll regret it." Looking up at the crags and down at his pack, he knew he didn't have the heart to take Sparks up that evening. "It's too late to scout a proper campsite up there," he told himself.

Since Sparks didn't seem to mind continuing to wear the jarlekua, Neba ate a little supper before stretching out beside Sparks, who likewise huddled close as if he sensed the coming change.

The next morning, Sparks kept looking back at Neba as he double-checked the jarlekua.

"It's alright, fella," Neba soothed him, rubbing his snout. "We're going to take a little flight together, that's all." Neba put the toe of his boot on the ridge of one of Sparks' scales. Finding handholds two scales further up, he hoisted himself onto Sparks' back and carefully took a seat with his knees just behind the leading edge of Sparks' wings. While Sparks stared at him in apparent shock, he quickly stabbed his boots into the stirrups and took firm hold of the tops of two scales in case of a quick takeoff.

"Easy now." Neba patted the glossy blue neck as Sparks' wings began to spread. He was worried about his pack and the supply tent—which by now was just the canvas and poles—throwing off his balance while in flight. Unfortunately, the equipment was part of his plan for getting back down. "Let's take it easy."

Sparks took one bounding leap forward, then began flapping his wings in powerful strokes that carried them up, up into the rays of the rising sun. Neba gasped as they broke through a line of clouds and soared, almost seeming to hover there, watching the clouds mark time by their changing colors.

"I wish we could stay here." Neba leaned forward, resting his arms on the base of Sparks' neck. "I feel like I'm home."

A savage scream of challenge split the air and sent Sparks streaking toward the clouds.

"Hold, Sparks, hold!" Neba commanded, pulling back on the scales. He looked all around, even leaning forward to check beneath them, and found they were alone. Then, he looked up.

Seized by determination, Neba pulled on the scales again, directing Sparks upward. There were dragons on the crags—right now! He wasn't familiar with the migration patterns for this area, and had actually worried about how long he might need to stay with Sparks on the crags, waiting for a kabi. Sparks humped his back and stubbornly headed for the clouds again, wanting nothing to do with the battle erupting above them.

"Will you trust me?" Neba grunted and leaned closer to Sparks to keep the winds from buffeting him off the dragon's back as they streaked down toward the ground. "I don't want you in a fight any more than you do," he smacked a scale on Sparks' right side with the heel of his hand. Startled, the skittish dragon veered off to his left. "The crags are enormous! We could land anywhere."

It was a fierce battle of wills, but Neba found another skill emerging as he directed the dragon back up toward the top of the crags. Sparks finally stopped fighting him when the battle cries grew more and more distant. The wind whistled in Neba's ears as they flew higher and higher until at last they rose above the crags.

Puffball clouds obscured their view for an instant, then were swept away by a breeze. Sides heaving with exertion, Sparks landed heavily on the rocky edge, where Neba swiftly dismounted.

"Here, fella, here." Hands moving at lightning speed, Neba cut the belly and chest straps, letting the gear fall free. "Try some of this," he encouraged, leading Sparks over to a tall, round belaki plant. Cutting away some of the vines sprouting from it, Neba showed Sparks how to access the spongy inner material so he could slake his thirst. "You'll be eating a lot of new things up here," he murmured, turning to look around him.

Here and there he could see hollows worn in the granite where the wild dragons rolled and rubbed off their old scales. Belaki plants of various sizes stuck out wherever there was a crack or seam in the granite, and further in from the edge, he could see grass and what looked like musker trees.

Tucking what was left of the riding pad under his arm, and with his pack still on his shoulders, Neba hunted out a place to hide while Sparks followed his snout to the rolling hollows. There were plenty of old scales lying about and they captured the young dragon's full attention.

Lifting the deia to his lips, Neba played a cry of greeting. Sparks' head jerked up from the old scales, but Neba was nowhere to be seen. A second cry came from a distance and still a third carried to where Neba had hunkered down to watch and wait.

A purple dragon rushed out from amongst some rocks, followed closely by a gorgeous yellow female who was too young and curious to be cautious. The purple dragon, an old father of many years, reared up on his hind legs and screamed when he saw the strange blue dragon. This was his territory and all who came must acknowledge it or pay the price. Fortunately, Sparks was already in awe of the newcomers and willingly dropped to his belly in token submission.

Neba held his breath as the purple dragon examined Sparks, his nostrils flaring at the strange scents the young dragon carried. Thankfully, the wind was still coming off the plateau, carrying Neba's smell away from them, and the old father decided the cowering newcomer was no danger. Administering a warning blast of flame, the old father shook himself and left, probably returning to his favorite sunning spot. The inspection successfully completed and Sparks having been accepted by their elder, the yellow female butted Sparks in the shoulder with her head, inviting him to play.

If Sparks looked back, Neba didn't see it. The last few days of flying free had done their part in preparing the dragon for this final separation. There might still be trouble ahead. Neba didn't lie to himself about that. The old father was weathered and scarred, much like the crags, yet the battle cry from earlier had come from a much younger dragon. Battles like that probably occurred every day amongst the young males and, eventually, one of them would challenge the old father. Hopefully, the old father would at least last out the cold time, giving Sparks a chance to learn what it really was to be a dragon.

Well hidden in the shadow of a boulder nest, Neba's nimble fingers made short work of repurposing the riding pad into a chest harness for himself. Attaching the lines from the supply tent, he created a makeshift hegan or rectangular flying canopy. For a long moment, he stood at the edge of the crag. Being about to jump off that edge somehow made him want to take stock of himself. After all this time, he still knew so little.

He could shoot down his supper in mid-flight. He could make a deia and a jarlekua and…who knew what else? He knew how to drink from a belaki plant and how to make a fish trap from reeds. With all of those endeavors, he could try again if he needed to. But this…hegan that he was wearing. The canvas canopy would either fill with air and slow his descent—or one of a hundred things would go wrong and he would die without ever knowing who he was.

Taking a deep breath, he squared his shoulders. Gripping the canopy by the leading edge, he stepped off the top of the crag. A strong wind rising up the face of the crag immediately ripped the material out of his hands and filled the canopy, throwing him back up for several seconds until a breeze off the crags caught him and propelled him away, as though it was rejecting him as a non-dragon. He threw back his head and laughed, glad to be alive. It was time to find out who he was.

DRAGON FUGUE Excerpt

Chapter 1

The wooden ax handle was roughly as long as Neba's arm, smooth and worn from years of use. He ran his dark brown thumb along the sharpened edge of the ax head, listening to the ringing sound it made as his skin stroked the burr. There was a familiarity to the feel of the tool and he swung it experimentally.

CRACK. The ax bit into a log of seasoned odol wood, splitting it to reveal the dull red of the wood beneath the bark.

Neba whistled softly and looked at the ax with new respect. Odol wood was dense and thick, making it an excellent choice for firewood on the cold bruma nights the others assured him were coming. Placing another thigh-sized log on the chopping block, he raised the ax and let it fall.

He split another log. Another. When he'd volunteered to chop firewood for his new best friend—and doctor—he hadn't actually been sure he could do it. But like so many of the skills he was discovering, it was just a matter of trying. It could be extremely frustrating, at times, to have no idea who he actually was.

The impact of the ax head against the wood jarred his arms and shoulders. The raw force required and the repetitive motions felt good. It gave him something useful to do with his pent-up anxiety. They were leaving in the morning for Ibilia, the Lurrakian capital. He planted the ax in the chopping block with minimal force and began stacking the wood he'd just split.

He'd turned up on the outskirts of Herrixka almost a lunar ago with little more than the clothes on his back and a cut in his side. Unable to access his memories, he'd nevertheless demonstrated a handful of skills. Leuna had treated him, taken him in. Now she and her apprentice, Sati, as well as a local man named Jartz, were all going with him to Ibilia to try to find the solution to his missing memories.

Wiping the sweat from his face, he finished working his way through the stack of logs, which he restacked as firewood. His next task was to haul water from the well in the backyard, so he started by dumping a bucket of it over his own head. Refreshed, he resumed his tasks with a will. Helping set Leuna's house in order for the winter was the least he could do.

The last two buckets he carried to the house, pausing just outside the back door for a moment to listen to Leuna humming. He didn't have to recognize the cheery tune to enjoy it. She'd been humming all morning while she chopped this and measured that, graceful white hands moving with speed and precision. Her humming was no doubt meant to reassure her anxious young apprentice, Sati.

"Does this look right to you, Miss Doctor?" Sati asked for the dozenth time, holding up a jar of amber-colored tonic water. She felt a little silly for asking, especially when Leuna was doing most of the preparation, but she couldn't seem to help herself.

Leuna shrugged. "Does it look right to you?" She shared a quick smile with Neba, who was just coming in from the garden, laden with brimming water buckets. If Sati was a little more cautious today, a little more uncertain of things, it was understandable. They were leaving in the morning, Sati's first time outside her hometown of Herrixka, and that was enough to addle anybody's brain.

Sati bit her lip, looking younger than her nineteen years. "I…I think so."

"Then seal the lid with wax and set it with the others to cool," Leuna advised gently. Using the rag tied to her arm, she dabbed at the sweat on her forehead. Even with the front and back doors of the cottage open to the breeze, the kitchen seemed to cling tenaciously to the heat the way the five-year-old flowering mahat vines clung to the brick chimney outside.

"I've topped off the wood pile," Neba reported, setting the buckets within easy reach of the two women. Leaning against the wall for a moment, he watched Leuna's nimble white fingers line up a row of dried fruits to be chopped. "Remind me what you're making?"

"Fire tonic," the women answered in unison. At Leuna's nod, Sati explained.

"Fire tonic is a concoction of herbs, hot fruits, vinegar, and honey that, taken regularly, can help prevent sickness during bruma, the cold time."
Sati relaxed a little at Leuna's approving nod.

"It needs a few months to reach full strength," Leuna added, using her knife blade to slide freshly chopped hot fruits into a basket. "So we always make it in uda, when the temperatures are just beginning to cool."

"How can I help?" Neba shifted to a standing position, arms folded across his chest.

Leuna saw his closed posture and tried not to frown. What was bothering him? He was half the reason they were in such a rush to make the fire tonic. If Neba didn't need her help getting his memories back, she could've waited until after taking Sati to Ibilia for her entrance examinations to come back to Herrixka and make the fire tonic.

"We're bumping into each other as it is," Leuna did her best to laugh. An idea struck her. "Maybe you could go check on Jartz? See if he needs help packing the supplies?" He nodded and left her wondering at the sudden change in his attitude. All morning he'd been cheerfully keeping himself busy with one thing or another. Had she said or done something to upset him? She couldn't think of anything.

Chopping the next line of fruits with slightly more force than necessary, she shook her head. Maybe she expected too much. After all, how well could she really know him? Their dramatic meeting (wherein he'd saved her life) was still less a lunar ago. And he'd spent three of those weeks—fifteen days!—in the forest and beyond, working with an orphaned dragon. Since his return after releasing the dragon on Firedrake Crags, he'd been keeping his distance. Including bunking over at Jartz' instead of in her spare bedroom. It was the proper thing to do, of course, yet she found that she missed his company.

"Alright." She meticulously washed the minak residue off and wiped her hands on a clean towel. "I've finished chopping. Let me help you fill the bottles."

Leuna added the herbs and hot fruits, then Sati poured in warm vinegar and honey. Tired of the terrible smells and heat, Leuna began humming a cheerful tune to take her mind off it. With a shy smile, Sati joined in with the lyrics in her sweet soprano and soon they were both singing about the fun they would have skating on the sheets of ground-ice that would cover the land in bruma.

"The trees will glow in the sunshine," sang Sati as she heated enough wax to seal the last half-dozen jars. The tips of her fingernails had absorbed some blue dye from the wax, but she shrugged it off. She'd trim her nails soon anyway so they wouldn't hinder her while she was working. "And cheeks will glow in the cold…"

Leuna stopped to stretch and survey their work. She seemed to feel every moment of the harvesting, drying, scrubbing, and chopping that had gone into the three dozen jars in the muscles of her lower back. She wasn't even thirty springs old yet, but she could feel every one of those, too.

"There." Sati set the last jar in place and beamed at the rows of amber-colored jars with their flat silver tops and ring of rich blue sealing wax. She'd helped in the past, of course, stretching as far back to when she fetched and carried for Miss Doctor's father, but this was the first time she'd been in charge.

Leuna's discomfort faded in her own pleasure at Sati's happiness. Which reminded her… Removing the apron she'd worn to protect her clothes, she hung it on a peg and smoothed the front of her shirt.

"Sati, now that we're done, let's sit a minute. Alright?" She put on a smile, though she was rather dreading the conversation she was about to initiate. There was nothing for it, though. She couldn't put stall any longer or they'd be discussing this while on the trail to Ibilia.

Leuna took her father's chair, as she had so many times since his death, and the leather sighed a little as she curled up in it. Sati was just settling into the other chair when Leuna cleared her throat.

"There's something I need to ask you." Leuna ducked her head, embarrassed at how serious she sounded.

Sati looked up from where she'd been about to relax against the tall, soft back of the other chair. The skin around her soft brown eyes crinkled a little at the corners.

"Have I done something wrong?"

"No!" Leuna reached out to put her hand on Sati's. "No, it's just the opposite." The deepening crinkles on Sati's face warned her that she wasn't making sense. She took a deep breath. "Sati. Tomorrow we're leaving for Ibilia, where you'll take the entrance examinations for the university."

"You don't think I'm ready?" Sati interjected, her fingers closing tightly around Leuna's. "Oh, I knew it! And after you've worked so hard to teach me!" She closed her eyes, thereby completely missing the stunned expression on Leuna's face. "You even promised that I could stay with your grandparents if I got into the medical program." She gasped, her eyes opening as abruptly as they'd closed. "If I go and fail the test, we'll have to tell your grandparents and…"

"Sati, Sati!" Leuna jiggled the hand she still held while adopting her most soothing doctor-voice. "Listen to me, please! You're putting words in my mouth. Yes," she nodded to encourage the faint light of hope in Sati's eyes. "I have every confidence that you will pass the examinations." She smiled and let that sink in for a moment. "If you really want to."

The puzzled look returned to Sati's face. "If I want to?" she repeated.

"I never asked you if you wanted to be a doctor." Leuna dropped all pretense of a casual conversation in favor of the bald truth. Worse than her admission was that she'd never given it a second thought if Neba hadn't brought it up. "You began your training with my father when you were just ten years old, Sati. I continued training you after his death, yet I never asked you if that was what you wanted." They stared at each other, both of them temporarily without words.

"It's your choice, Sati. I needed to make sure you knew that."

Sati smiled. "Thank you for asking, Miss Doctor…but I choose every day. To follow you into the woods to harvest medicinal plants. To spend hours copying your father's journals. Even to practice my sewing skills in case I must suture a wound." She squirmed a little at that. "I want to go to Ibilia. I want to pass the exams."

"Then that is exactly what is going to happen." Leuna started to get up, intending to hug her student, and stopped to laugh when they both winced. "Here, let me show you another stretch."

Across town, Neba was still trudging over to Jartz' two-room cabin, which was located on the far side of the colorful village from Leuna's. He didn't expect to find Jartz there, but that was alright. He needed time to think. About everything. So far as he knew, this would be his first visit to Gertuk, the busy port town five days walk from Herrixka. Jartz hadn't learned anything during his last visit, which they all agreed was due to the Lurrakian soldiers' strange behavior.

Neba kicked a rock and watched it bounce away, then lifted his eyes to the squat cottage at the end of the lane. All of the houses in Herrixka were built from the colorful local hardwoods, so he could predict that the family living there was large. The main wall in this case was purple morea wood, while the new rooms on either side were made with green and blue woods. *What was his own home like?* he wondered.

A friendly whine brought him back to the present and he looked down in surprise at the village dog walking beside him. No one person owned the village dogs; rather, they all shared the responsibility, setting out leftovers and water, and so forth. In return, the dogs kept a constant vigil, alerting the townspeople to new arrivals. Like the day Neba arrived.

"Hey, Akur." He bent to pet the mutt, his brown fingers sliding through its rough gray fur. Their first meeting hadn't been quite as friendly, but by now he'd accepted Neba.

Ordinarily, a larger town like Gertuk kept at least a few secrets from the local law. This time, however, the soldiers were turning over every rock, poking into every hidey-hole, and arresting everything that moved in a concerted effort to stop the smuggling of illegal dragon goods. It was hardly the best time to admit to knowing…anything. Which was where Leuna came in.

"She's the key," he told the dog. He supposed that was better than talking to himself. Probably. "She can find out who the mind manipulators on record are, and where they are." With Leuna's help, he'd been able to remember just enough of what happened to identify the manipulator as a woman. If there were as few female manipulators as Leuna believed, it should be as simple as looking her up in the university records.

Once they found out who had taken his memories, he'd be on his own again. He'd have his bow, steel-tipped arrows, and the few remaining gold arranos he'd accumulated by selling meat to the local butcher. But Jartz would come back to his trapline. Sati would commence her medical courses. And Leuna? She might be as reluctant to part company as he was—they hadn't actually spoken of their near-kiss in the woods—yet she'd be duty-bound to return to Herrixka as its one and only doctor.

Patting the dog on the back, Neba straightened and resumed walking, this time heading straight for Jartz' fur shack. It was the most likely place to locate Jartz at this time of day.

The shack was a smallish construction that looked somewhat like a wooden beast with a fondness for adorning itself with animal pelts. There were no windows, just four well-built walls, a tight roof to keep out the rain, and a door. The door was open now while Jartz worked and daylight struck the dozen or more gleaming new traps Jartz had bartered for during his last visit to Gertuk.

"Need a hand?" Neba offered, eyeing the stack of kastore pelts at Jartz' knee. He wasn't sure why he offered. He didn't know anything about processing hides.

Jartz looked up from the one he was stretching on a wooden board.

"You any good?" he asked bluntly.

"No idea." Neba grinned a little. His amnesia was no secret here in Herrixka. What kept astonishing him was how many things his muscles remembered how to do. Carving, camping, training a dragon… His grin faded as he thought of Sparks, the orphan dragon he'd recently rescued and returned to the wild. He'd done the right thing, but sometimes he still caught himself looking around for the pesky creature.

"Sure, c'mon and give it a go." Jartz' hands continued moving expertly, centering and securing the pelt he was working on. "It's not like you can hurt 'em. Kastore pelts ain't worth much to begin with. Wasn't for the bounty, I wouldn't even bother with the sharp-toothed vermin." He didn't object to getting paid twice for them, naturally: a bounty for each head and a pittance for each pelt.

"Looks like you're keeping busy," Neba remarked as he turned a bucket over and seated himself on it. Jartz had spent almost two weeks away in Gertuk, trading furs for supplies and keeping an ear open for information about a missing Marroi man matching Neba's description. "Despite having your trap lines robbed." He sighed and picked up a pelt. That was how they'd found Sparks, a scrawny little thing that ate the carcasses from Jartz' line to keep from starving.

Jartz shrugged. "Kastore always run thick through these parts. The village dogs keep 'em out of town, but they're plentiful elsewhere." Jartz kept an eye on Neba as he clumsily tried to spread the pelt on the wooden board. He chuckled a little upon realizing that Neba was watching him from the corner of his eye, trying to figure out what to do next. "Never mind, never mind," he waved away Neba's chagrin at getting caught. "Put that down before you catch your finger on a pin."

"I guess I'm not a fur trapper." Neba managed a small smile. The closer they got to leaving, the tighter the knot in his stomach became. "Did you know I thought I was a Dragon Soldier?" Jartz silently raised his eyebrows and Neba kept talking. "Jerl Barruan, Dragon Soldier of the first order."

"Sounds mighty convincing to me." Jartz reached for another pelt.

"It did to me, too." Neba's shoulders slumped. "I'd still believe it if Leuna hadn't known better."

Jartz shook his head. "She don't talk about her patients." Deftly, he secured the pelt and set the frame aside. "I guarantee she had good reason, though, if she told you that you wasn't this Jerl somebody-er-other."

"She did." Neba nodded. He'd collapsed under the strain of a mind fever when confronted with the truth that what he'd 'remembered' was false. He still sometimes had to use the words she'd taught him—*I control my mind. No one else*—to ward off a relapse. "She sure did."

"Well, then." Jartz set another pelt aside and stretched as he rose, popping his back. "Why don't you tell me what's really botherin' you whilst we get the supplies packed and ready to go?"

Neba rose and walked over to the small pile of supplies stacked by one wall. They would each carry their own personal items, extra clothing, blankets, that sort of thing, and divide the food stuffs between them. Shaking out a bag made from the waterproof lehorra cloth, he loaded it with half of the flour, dried beans, and other dense items.

"What if we figure out who manipulated my mind, get my memories back, and it turns out that I'm a poacher?" Neba asked, his back still to Jartz.

Jartz studied him a moment. "Might be." He held steady when Neba swung around to look at him, his brown face contorted with anger and fear. "And might not."

Neba swallowed hard. "Every minute that I spend wondering is like a starving eltxo fly whining in the dark, taking bites out of my peace of mind."

Jartz scratched his chin and shoved a strand of brown and white hair back out of his face. "The longer you sit in one spot, the more eltxo flies gather, the worse it gets."

Tying off the second heavy bag, Neba considered the statement.

"I can't say as I know what you're goin' through," Jartz admitted, arranging the cook pot and pan for easy transport. "But I reckon the only way to kill this fly is with the truth."

Neba almost laughed at the simplicity of it. He'd always intended to follow-through, to find the 'doctor' who'd deprived him of his memories. However…

"It's…hard." Neba fought for the words to express what he was feeling.

"Bein' around Leuna?" Jartz winked knowingly at him. "I'm right proud of you two. It's a tough situation, no two ways about it. Handsome young man, purty young woman." He shrugged and reached for the fishing poles. Carrying smoked fish would lighten their packs as well as simplifying mealtime on the trail, so he figured to use what daylight there was to lay in a supply.

The packing done, Neba squared his shoulders. "I care too much to offer what may not be mine to give."

"I know that already." Jartz nodded approvingly. "Reckon you'll be glad to learn the truth of whether or not you're bound to another." Handing Neba a rod, he headed towards the stream.

"If I'm not…" Neba hesitated. Leuna's parents were both long dead, yet he knew Leuna planned for them all to stay at her grandparents' home while they were in Ibilia. Jartz seemed the closest thing Leuna had to family in Herrixka. Or should he wait and speak to her grandfather? He shook his head ruefully. How could he possibly explain his situation to a stranger?

I don't know who I am, but your granddaughter calls me Neba. We're going to get my memories back and if I'm not already bound to someone else, I'd like your permission to seek her favor.

Jartz chuckled. "How about we take things one at a time, huh?"

Neba grinned sheepishly. "Sounds like good advice." After a clean bait and cast, he asked, "Who'll take care of your trap line while we're gone?"

"Zoli has agreed to keep an eye on things for me, but there ain't much to be done this time of year," Jartz shrugged. "Kastore have already started moving towards their bruma home near the sunbelt. Too soon for the fancy furs, like bisoi or azeri. They won't be ready till after the snow falls."

Neba nodded, feeling better about having Jartz

along now that he understood he wouldn't be interfering with the man's livelihood.

They took turns cleaning the fish they caught and keeping a small smoke fire going until the light began to fade. Two of Jatorri's three moons were full that night, but they packed it in anyway, knowing that it would be an early morning for them all.

www.ingramcontent.com/pod-product-compliance
Lightning Source LLC
Chambersburg PA
CBHW070513170726
48291CB00008B/2734

* 9 7 8 1 9 5 1 2 4 8 0 1 7 *